THE LION AND THE FIVE DEADLY SERPENTS

A *Just Cause Universe* Novel

Ian Thomas Healy

Local Hero Press Edition

The Lion and the Five Deadly Serpents
A *Just Cause Universe* Novel
Published by Local Hero Press, LLC

1st Printing
Local Hero Press: trade paperback, October 1, 2015
Printed in the United States of America

ISBN-13: 9781971445083

Cover art by Jeff Hebert
Book design by Local Hero Press, LLC

Books by Local Hero Press

The *Just Cause Universe*

Just Cause
The Archmage
Day of the Destroyer
Deep Six
Jackrabbit
Champion
Castles
The Lion and the Five Deadly Serpents
Tusks
The Neighborhood Watch
Jackrabbit: Big In Japan
Arena
Hero Academy
The Path
Cinco de Mayo
Search and Rescue
Rooftops
Plague
Soldiers of Fortune
Just Cause Universe Compendium
Destroyer of Earth
Flint and Steel
The Club
Jackrabbit: Rinse and Repeat
Posse
Extinction Event
Rain Must Fall

Pariah of Verigo

Pariah's Moon
Pariah's War

Three Flavors of Tacos

The Guitarist
Making the Cut
The Scene Stealers

Collections

Airship Lies
High Contrast
The Good Fight
The Good Fight 3: Sidekicks
The Good Fight 4: Homefront
The Good Fight 5: The Golden Age
Muddy Creek Tales
Caped

Other Novels

Assassin
Blood on the Ice
Funeral Games
Hope and Undead Elvis
Horde
The Murder Squad (2026)
Roast Wyvern (and Other Recipes)
Starf*cker
Strings
The Oilman's Daughter
Troubleshooters

Nonfiction

Action! Writing Better Action Using Cinematic Techniques

The Legends of Lines and Language

It seems like I'm always writing these little blurbs about people I want to thank for their help in writing, editing, and producing books so I can deliver them to you. Luckily, it's a part of my job I don't mind at all, because if I took the time to tell you how grateful I am for everyone's assistance and support, I'd never get around to writing any more books, and nobody wants that! I am deeply grateful to Jenn Zukowski for her introduction and her wide-ranging knowledge of martial arts; to Michelle Brown for jumping into edits with the skill and alacrity of a ninja (even though we all know ninjas aren't Chinese, right?); and once again to Allison M. Dickson, who probably knows more about the Just Cause Universe than any person alive besides me. I'm thrilled to have another superb cover from Jeff Hebert. I'm thankful to the Colorado Chapter of Modern Arnis for giving me a good grounding in several martial arts styles back when I was young and less fat than I am now. As always, I'm grateful to my family for their continuing love and support of this habit of mine. And last but not least, thanks to you, the fans of the *Just Cause Universe*, for buying my books and writing your reviews and even taking the time to send me occasional emails. I appreciate each and every one of you.

—*Ian Thomas Healy*
September, 2015

Introduction

Ian Thomas Healy and I go way back. Far back into the realm of The Nerd—like, junior high Creative Writing Club territory. That far. Way back when being a nerd was not cool, but would attract the bullies from every school corridor. We both cut our teeth on the same fabulous literature, and the generous teachers who spent extra time with our special brand of creativity. I may have a club picture somewhere I can use for blackmail purposes . . .

Suffice to say that I know very well that worlds of wonder are second nature to Ian, and also that he has had a stellar education in the creation thereof. What I have found in the *Just Cause Universe* books I have been honored to have read, is that vitality of the kid coming of age into a superpower, now tempered with real writing skill. The fearless details of worldbuilding now made by a man who has created children, a family, and who knows the tough real world well. So what we get in the Just Cause Universe is an alternative, parahuman-full world that feels so much like our own, whether the protagonist is a teenaged superhuman or a middle-aged woman just trying to be a good security guard. Either way, we can feel for and identify with our heroes, whoever they may be.

In *The Lion and the Five Deadly Serpents,* we are transported into a real-life *wu xia* film: the questions of honor, the romance, and of course the spectacular action all intact. What the Just Cause books consistently do well is present us with realistic characters we can relate to, and this book is no different. Except there's a lot of kick-ass martial arts.

I hope you enjoy this action-packed ride as much as I did. Now excuse me: I've got to go dig up that old typewritten magazine from junior high . . .

—*Jenn Zukowski*
May, 2015

Chapter One

"The journey of a thousand miles begins with one step."
—*Lao Tzu*

March, 1980
New York City, New York

The form was everything.

Lionheart pivoted smoothly on the ball of one foot and lashed out with the other, catching a sand-filled training dummy up high, where its chin would have been were it alive. He followed through with the blow in a full spin, dropping into a crouch with one arm raised above his head as if he wore a shield across it. His hips twisted like a spring and uncoiled with tremendous power as he delivered a double palm strike to the midsection of the dummy, sending ripples of sand through the reinforced bag to shatter imaginary ribs and explode theoretical organs like water balloons. He slapped aside one of the dummy's flailing wooden arms and caught the other on the outside of his arm, thrilling to the solid impact. His knee came up into the dummy's side, brutalizing it once more, and he raked his claws across the hapless bag's leathery face, which bore the scars of numerous previous attacks from the leonine man. Sweat matted his mane as he delivered

1

blows with his palms, with his fingers, with his elbows. The dummy shuddered almost like a living thing, doing its best to recoil on its heavy spring base as Lionheart worked over it.

At last, the form came to its end with a pair of devastating strikes. His double footed lunging kick tore the dummy from its mounting hardware, followed by Lionheart twisting around to rip out a piece of the leather bag that would have been the throat of his opponent.

Sardonic applause filtered in past the pounding of blood in his ears and he looked up to see Javier leaning against the *dojo* door, his face twisted into half a grin beneath his thick Puerto Rican mustache. "I'd say we're safe from any further problems with that dummy." He raised his hands to his mouth to light a cigarette.

Lionheart glanced down at the sand leaking out from a half dozen spots on the bag and the splintered wooden base. "Yeah, I'd say so. Hey, you mind not smoking in here?"

Javier shrugged and blew a lungful of smoke out into the hall. "I gave up almost all my other vices. Let me have this one."

Lionheart picked up a towel from a nearby rack and wrapped it across his shoulders, which were covered with short, golden fur like everywhere else on his body except on his head, where it spread into a magnificent mane any male lion would have been proud to wear. Even though Javier was trying to be polite and not breathe smoke near him, Lionheart could still smell the tobacco, and it made him wrinkle his broad nose in disgust. "Don't usually see you up so early in the morning, Javi."

Javier shrugged. "When the tinkering muse comes, you have to appease it." Javier was known as the flying armor-suited superhero Javelin outside of Just Cause.

He was constantly trying to upgrade and improve his suit as technology advanced around the world. His latest project involved networking his suit to the two Cray supercomputers in the center of Just Cause headquarters, high up in World Trade Center Two. It was all well beyond Lionheart, who found his patience with technology ran out with telephones and walkie-talkies. "Actually, there's some body here to see you."

"Somebody?"

"Some *body*. I mean it. She's a foxy Asian chick I wouldn't mind getting to know better if I weren't already attached to Irlene." Irlene was another hero of Just Cause, with the ability to shrink objects and people down to fractions of their original size. She and Javier had connected after the events involving her brother, the Destroyer. It was more a lapse in taste than anything else, Lionheart thought at the time. Somehow, though, she'd managed to keep her patience with the inventor's plethora of bad habits and even cured him of some of them. It had been a long time since anyone had found Javi sprawled on his floor, unconscious after too much booze or too many pills.

Lionheart wrinkled his nose again as another breath of smoke crossed it. "She asked for me?"

"She did. Has your side thing got another side thing going on?" Javi smiled his insufferable, knowing grin that always made Lionheart want to hit him. He was referring to Lionheart's complicated relationship with his teammate Pony Girl, which was further complicated by the fact she was married.

"I don't have a side thing going on," Lionheart lied as he tried to dry his mane. When he sweated, he took on the scent of a wet dog—or a wet cat, which was closer to the truth.

"Of course not. Anyway, she's in Devereaux's office. I'll let you tell him you need more victims for your chop socky gym." Javi nodded toward the ruined training dummy and then sauntered away.

Lionheart sighed. He knew his training was hard on the equipment, but it came with the territory when one was stronger, faster, and tougher than normal humans. He had wicked sets of finger and toe claws, and fangs to chomp through bones if he were so inclined. When in public, he was careful to keep himself composed and smiling as much as possible so people tended to associate him more with a character like the Cowardly Lion from *The Wizard of Oz* or King Richard from the Disney film *Robin Hood* instead of a vicious beast belonging in a zoo. It was the cross he had to bear, looking like an anthropomorphic lion, gifted with parahuman abilities, cursed with the appearance of a monster.

He pulled on a New York Mets t-shirt so he'd look a little less threatening, and tried to smooth down his mane some as he padded through the halls of Just Cause. He nodded at John Stone, who was hunched over a desk doing paperwork, an oversized elementary-school pencil clutched carefully in his thick granite fingers. He wondered where Pony Girl was, and then quashed that thought. The two of them had only acted on their desperate attraction to one another a half dozen times over the past few years, and even though they'd only been caught once, it had caused some rifts among the team that might never heal properly. Once or twice a year, it seemed, the simmering attraction boiled over and the two of them would find someplace to be alone, something which was surprisingly difficult even in a city as cosmopolitan and blasé as New York.

It was one of the reasons Lionheart had thrown himself into his training. When he was busy punching training dummies—or less frequently, bad guys—he wasn't thinking unproductive and dangerous thoughts about the woman who'd stolen his heart years before.

Lane Devereaux had a large corner office of the Trade Center, and the tableau of the New York skyline sparkled in the early morning sunshine, promising a beautiful spring day. The man himself was perched with one hip resting on his desk, his salt-and-pepper hair gleaming with overuse of styling cream. He looked as dapper as ever in his gray suit as he gestured with his pipe and smiled at the young woman sitting in the chair before him. The office smelled of the cherry-flavored tobacco he preferred and Aqua Velva aftershave. The Asian woman had a strangely familiar scent to Lionheart, a mixture of Far Eastern spices with floral overtones in her clothes, and skin reminding him of someone he'd known long ago. "Ah, Richard, please come in," said Devereaux, his voice carrying only the slightest hint of the French accent he'd grown up with. "This is Chou Lihua. Ms. Lihua came here asking to speak to you."

"Ms. Chou, actually," said the young woman. "In China, we give family names first, Mr. Devereaux."

Lionheart stiffened. He knew the family name *Chou*. It could only mean . . . "You are related to Master Chou." He didn't make it a question. Huizhong Chou was the man who'd taught him *Shizi Hou,* Lionheart's trademark fighting style, the man who'd seen the hero hiding beneath the fur, the man who'd saved his life.

"He is my father," said Lihua. As soon as she said it, Lionheart wondered how he could have not seen it before. She had the same defiant cast to her jaw as her father, which spoke of a willingness to buck authority and to question the status quo. Her eyes were the same as his, although her nose turned up at the end whereas his had been broken so many times to be almost unidentifiable as a proboscis. Even pulled back into a ponytail, her dark hair still cascaded halfway down her back. She wore a sky blue and white tunic over flared white trousers and sandals making her look like a stewardess.

Lionheart bowed, falling into the old formalities as easily as if he'd never left them. "My apologies. How is your father? I haven't spoken with him in many years."

Lihua bowed her head. "He is dying, Mr. Lyons. He has asked to see you."

Lionheart nodded. "Of course." He looked at Devereaux. "I'm going to need to take some time off."

Devereaux touched a match to the bowl of his pipe, drawing air through the stem. "Of course, Richard. Take all the time you need. God knows you've earned it."

"Where is he?" Lionheart asked.

"Hong Kong," said Lihua.

Lionheart grimaced. "I don't have a passport. And people get a little freaked out when I get on a plane. Last time I flew, they treated me like I was a hijacker."

Devereaux shook his head and blew out a puff of smoke. "That's ridiculous. Let me put my people to work, Richard. I'll have a passport for you in six hours. And as far as planes go, take my Learjet."

"Oh, I couldn't—"

"Nonsense, I insist," said Devereaux. "Flying to Paris on an airliner is bad enough. At the very least you'll be comfortable and be served decent meals. What's the point of being wealthy if I can't lavish it upon my friends in their time of need?" He drew another lungful of the fragrant cherry smoke. "Besides, my accountant is quite creative. I'm sure he'll figure out a way to deduct the entire expense." He smiled at Lionheart. "Pack your bags, my friend."

Lionheart bowed to Devereaux, the gesture the best way he knew how to show respect and gratitude to the man who'd given him a job and a purpose and a place to utilize the parahuman abilities he'd been granted.

狮 和 五 致 死 蛇

The suitcase seemed almost too small for a voyage of several thousand miles. Lionheart sat on the edge of his bed, regarding the single bag holding all his worldly possessions. Even after years of being part of the greatest superhero team in the world, everything he owned fit into a single suitcase. It was as if his entire life had been defined by impermanence. It was very much a Taoist type of philosophy, one which Master Chou would have appreciated.

When Master Chou had first come into Lionheart's life, it was to intervene in a would-be fatal beating about to be administered upon him by a fellow parahuman. It had been in a small and remote Midwest town, and Lionheart had been living the lifestyle of a wanderer, never staying in one town for long, working enough odd jobs to stay fed. Being of such an inhuman appearance in Middle America was even worse than being a black man in the South. He was as unwelcome as hippies in a conservative town or women in a gentleman's club, even with his exceptional physical abilities.

He'd run afoul of a gang of biker punks, like Hell's Angels, except they were led by someone like him—a man with parahuman powers and a demonic, inhuman visage. They took offense at some imagined slight, looking for a reason to start trouble, and Lionheart intervened before really thinking about it. He made a reasonably good accounting of himself at first, but then the parahuman leader entered the fray, and Lionheart had his first true taste of parapowered combat. The gang leader beat him up and down the street, and was about to murder him when Master Chou stepped up and immobilized the thug with a couple of pressure point strikes. The first word he spoke to Lionheart was "Coming?" and Lionheart realized he'd been given a powerful invitation that might never be repeated.

The two men began traveling together. Master Chou was wandering, like Lionheart, across America for no specific reason other than it was another leg of his lifelong journey. In time, Chou taught Lionheart some basics of Wing Chun and found the leonine young man a willing and capable student. Eventually, Chou developed a style ideal for someone of Lionheart's build and abilities, basing it upon the Tibetan Lion's Roar style of *Shizi Hou.*

Eventually, the two men parted ways. Lionheart went to New York to join Just Cause and become a well-known and respected superhero, while Master Huizhong Chou disappeared, and Lionheart hadn't been able to track him down again. At some point the man returned to China, and apparently he at least had a daughter. Lionheart would have to ask Lihua more about what happened with her father and why he'd gone on his journey, leaving his family behind. They'd have time; it was a long flight to China, with several stops for fuel along the way.

The suitcase seemed to beckon to Lionheart, as if chastising him for sitting around when there was traveling to be done.

"How long you going to sit there staring at that thing?" asked an all-too-familiar voice. Lionheart looked up and smiled at Faith, who called herself Pony Girl. She was in her costume and smelled of exhaust and popcorn, having likely just returned from patrol in Central Park.

Her hair was piled up in a stylish teased tower atop her head, held in place by spray and laughing at gravity's attempts to pull it back downward.

She looked beautiful.

"Not much longer," said Lionheart. "Devereaux should have my papers done shortly, and then I'll be off."

"All the way to China. I heard," said Faith. "That's a long way."

"It's a call I can't ignore."

"I'll miss you, Rick." Faith was fast, and suddenly she was standing right before him, holding out her hands to him.

He stood and embraced her. "I'll miss you too, but maybe it's for the best."

Her lips brushed his, lingering, so slow compared to the speed at which she did everything else. "God, I wish you weren't going. But you're right. It's for the best. We can't keep doing this forever."

Lionheart nodded. "No, no more."

Faith stepped back. Her eyes were bright with tears, but she smiled at him. "Don't stay away for too long. Just Cause needs you. We need you. I . . ." She didn't say she needed him, but it could remain unsaid and both would know it was there regardless.

"I'll come back when it's time."

Faith leaned into him, whispered "I love you," into his ear, and then ran from the room.

"I love you too," said Lionheart into the quiet of his solitude.

狮和五致死蛇

Most of Just Cause had turned out to see Lionheart off. A van with its suspension heavily-modified in order to transport John Stone's massive bulk had joined a pair of black Lincolns on the tarmac of JFK, outside Lane Devereaux's private hangar. Stormcloud, Javelin, Imp, and Imp's younger sister Reggie had ridden in the first car. Lihua and Lionheart had ridden with Lane Devereaux in the other. John Stone and the Steel Soldier had been joined by Sundancer and her younger sister Sunstorm, the newest member of Just Cause. The only ones who hadn't come out were Pony Girl and her husband Audio, and nobody was particularly surprised.

"I can't believe Devereaux is putting me in charge," said Javi, shaking Lionheart's hand as the stewards loaded his and Lihua's bags on board the Learjet. "That's like giving a sixteen-year-old the keys to a Ferrari and telling him to keep it under fifty."

"You'll do fine," said Lionheart. "You've come a long way the past few years."

"And if he has any problems, I'll shrink him down to the size of a cockroach and stick him in Reggie's terrarium," said Imp, grinning like her namesake.

Reggie, only eight years old, threw her arms around Lionheart and let him pick her up and swing her around. "Imma miss you, Lionheart," she whined. "When you comin' back?"

"I'll be back just as soon as I can," he told her, ruffling her braids. "I don't want to miss you growing up."

She stuck out her lower lip. "Who wants to grow up? Not me."

Stormcloud pushed his hood back, exposing his leading-man good looks. "You be careful."

Lionheart shook his hand. "You too." And he meant it. Since the Blackout of '77, the hero formerly known as Tornado had become a grim, dark shadow of his former self. His lifestyle had likewise changed, with him turning up in seedier parts of Greenwich Village, involved with seedy young men with seedy habits.

The Steel Soldier was a futuristic combat android, and yet over the years, it had become as much a friend to Lionheart as anyone else on the team had. The machine had some almost human characteristics to its behavior, and it shook Lionheart's hand with solemnity. "I WISH YOU THE BEST OF LUCK IN YOUR TRAVELS, LIONHEART," it said, its vocoder crackling through the speaker in its chin.

"Thanks, Steel."

Sundancer hugged him. In public, she wore a full-face mask to cover the burn scars she'd received when her own powers had been reflected into her face by Destroyer. It had taken her a long time to accept they would be permanent, and it had been an emotional nightmare for the former *Playboy* model. "I'll miss you too, you big dope," she said. "Bring back souvenirs, okay?"

"I will."

Sunstorm wasn't nearly as demonstrative as her sister. She'd only been with the team a few months and in a lot of ways still seemed like an outsider. She nodded at Lionheart and he nodded back and it was good enough for the both of them.

John Stone was careful not to squeeze Lionheart's hand when he shook it; his granite fingers could have pulped Lionheart's. "It will be quiet in headquarters without you around, my friend," he said. "Do come back as soon as you can. We're hearing some rumors the Weathermen are reforming under new leadership."

Lionheart grimaced. "You guys be careful. Take them down as soon as you can. I'll read the reports when I come back." He turned to Lane Devereax. "Thanks again for letting me use your plane, sir, and for letting me take the time off. I'll be back as soon as I'm able."

Lane Devereaux nodded. "Of course, Richard. Clear skies to you."

Lionheart looked at Lihua, who'd stood quietly off to one side while he said his goodbyes to his friends. "You ready?"

She nodded. "Yes."

Lionheart took one last look at his friends and teammates, wishing one more had been there, but glad she wasn't. He gestured to the door of the Learjet and smiled at Lihua. "Let's go to China."

Chapter Two

*"Life and death are one thread, the same line
viewed from different sides."*

—*Lao Tzu*

March, 1980
Hong Kong

By the fourth leg of the flight to Hong Kong, Lionheart could barely tell which way was up. The only reason he hadn't torn the side of the plane open to throw himself out to a merciful death was Lane Devereaux's jet was the most comfortable way he'd ever traveled. Plush seats with padding in all the right places, room to stretch one's legs, and a selection of interesting wines and meals ameliorated a lot of the misery of air travel. But after stopping for fuel in Seattle, and then again in Anchorage, Lionheart wondered if maybe his old master could have had the good graces to just send a goodbye letter.

The stopover in the unpronounceable Siberian town of Omsk took much longer than anticipated, thanks to the curious and suspicious Soviet officials who boarded the jet and searched it from top to bottom, removing numerous items of "contraband" that the stewardess plied them with using blatant bribery. She apparently spoke flawless Russian and translated their questions to

Lionheart and Lihua. They seemed to be on the verge of grounding the jet and hauling off all the occupants as capitalist spies, which was an outcome that made Lionheart's knees quake. Not many things scared him, but the idea of rotting away in a Soviet labor camp in Siberia made suicide sound like an attractive option. The stewardess kept up her nonstop chatter with the officials, pushing bottles of wine and delicacies like caviar and American candy bars at them until at last they relented, signed off on all their papers, and permitted the jet to complete its refueling and depart upon the final leg of the journey.

"Tell me about yourself, Lihua," said Lionheart as the stars swirled above them. He had no idea what time it actually was, but it felt to him like late afternoon. "Your father never spoke of his family to me when we traveled together."

Lihua shrugged, her feet drawn up beside her on one of the plush chairs. "There is not much to tell. He departed when I was only seven and my brother seventeen. Our mother had just died from . . . I do not know the English word. *Liugan.* The sickness that burns and fills the lungs."

"Pneumonia? Or the flu?"

"Perhaps. Father chose to deal with his grief by taking a lengthy journey. We did not know he went to America until after he returned last year."

"Wait, how long was he gone?" Lionheart blinked in surprise.

"Nine years." A muscle twitched in Lihua's jaw.

Lionheart shook his head. "Unbelievable. I never would have thought him the sort of man to run away from his family."

"He did not run from us!" Lihua sat up, sparks flashing in her eyes. "He was honoring our mother. She dreamed of traveling around the world, and read to us from pamphlets she got from British travel agencies. Father chose to honor her by taking the voyage she never could."

"For nine years. That's far out."

"Things are different in China, *Shi Xin*."

"What is that? *Shi Xin*?"

"That is how you say *Lionheart* in Cantonese."

"*Shi Xin*. I like it."

"You will be a curiosity in Hong Kong. There are no superheroes in China."

"I find it hard to believe. I've seen the numbers on how frequent abilities appear in a given population, and China's got one of the biggest populations in the world. There must be dozens, or hundreds of parahumans."

"There may be, but they are not superheroes. They do not wear costumes and live in great towers as you do."

"I don't . . . well, I guess maybe I do live in a tower. But that's just out of convenience. So you've never even seen another parahuman?"

Lihua shrugged again. "I do not know. Perhaps the government keeps them locked up."

"Are they going to try to lock me up? Here we just got out of Russia with no worse than an empty cupboard. I'm not sure we have anything left to bribe Chinese officials with."

"We will not have to bribe Chinese officials. Hong Kong is a British colony. You will find many people who speak English there, although perhaps not as well as I." Lihua's face brightened into a smile. "Our mother read to us every night. She spoke lovely English. She learned in a British school."

"So who cared for you and your brother after she died and your father left?"

"Zheng Yaoting. Our *nan pu*. Like a servant. He cares for the house and the school."

"You have a school?"

"*Yingtao Mu.* It is the Cherrywood Academy, where my father once taught his arts and now my brother Qiao does."

"You have a Kung Fu school. Fantastic," said Lionheart. "I wonder how different it is from the ones in the movies."

"It is very different. Much smaller. Few people even notice it, tucked away against the Aberdeen docks like it is." Lihua's face crumpled into a frown. "It has been in my family for generations, but perhaps not for much longer."

Lionheart leaned forward. Whatever was upsetting her, this seemed to be the root cause of it. "Why? What's going on?"

Lihua turned to stare out the window at the night, unrelenting but for the faint glow to the left side of the plane of the approaching sun. "There is . . . a Triad."

Lionheart had heard of Triads before. They were Chinese organized crime clans, like the Mafia. If his old master's family was mixed up with that, it could lead to all kinds of trouble. "Who are they? What are they doing?"

Lihua didn't look back at him. "They are *Wu Zhiming She*. The Five Deadly Serpents. They are a heroin cartel smuggling into and out of Hong Kong."

"Sounds like bad people."

"They are the very worst sort of people." At last, Lihua looked back at Lionheart. Her eyes were bright with concern. "They want our school."

"Why would they want an old martial arts school? Wait . . ." An idea occurred to Lionheart just as he'd started to speak. "You said your school was against the docks. It could be turned into a covert front for smuggling."

"Qiao believes the same as well. They own the slip adjacent to the school. It would not be difficult to bring heroin into the school and then have the 'students' distribute it out into the city."

"And nobody would be the wiser," said Lionheart. "Unless they knew why the Five Deadly Serpents had acquired the school in the first place."

"There are dangerous fighters among the Triad. *Dashe Yongshi*. Serpent Warriors. A school would be a logical place for them to train."

"They don't have a school now?"

Lihua's laugh was bitter. "They probably have a dozen. Training the fighters they have takes time and resources. The only reason they would have to want Cherrywood is because of its location."

"I've got a real problem with that." Lionheart squeezed his hands into fists. "I've dealt with a lot of Mafia and Westie gang issues back home. Nothing good can come from organized crime, no matter where they are."

"My father also had a problem with it," said Lihua. "Which is why they have poisoned him."

狮 和 五 致 死 蛇

Yingtao Mu, the Cherrywood Academy, was a traditional Chinese *siheyuan* residence in the town of Aberdeen on Hong Kong Island. Ten-foot-high gray walls surrounded the enclosure, decorated with a repeating geometric design in red. Entering through the tall red gates felt more to Lionheart like he was walking into a fortress than into someone's domicile. The gates opened into a large open courtyard with a garden shrine against one wall and the entrance to the private courtyard opposite it. The courtyard itself was formed from stones worn smooth by thousands of footsteps brushing across them in training, for it was where first Master Chou had held his classes and now his son Qiao taught. A rack against one wall held a selection of training weapons like wooden swords, staves of varying length, and blunt spears. A small gong hung beneath a sharply-angled roof in a small overhang. Papers with *hanzi* characters inked upon them were pasted beside all the doors. Lionheart asked what they were and Lihua answered they were wards against evil spirits. Lionheart made sure not to snort in derision; he knew how important magic was in Chinese culture.

They passed through the second gate into the interior courtyard, surrounded by four houses facing inward. The quadrangle had cherry blossom trees growing in each corner, and each one sported a thick mass of pink and white blossoms. The high walls deflected the sea breeze, allowing only a gentle swirl to circle the yard, ruffling Lionheart's mane with the scent of salt water and the harbor. The walls likewise blocked much of the sound of the docks beyond, making the area seem like a peaceful island amid the chaos of industry. Each house facing the courtyard had bright red doors and pillars supporting the overhanging roofs, while the walls were a brilliant white.

To avoid undue attention as they crossed town, Lionheart had drawn the hood of his sweatshirt up over his head, but once they were beyond the walls of the *siheyuan*, Lihua told him he could uncover. "There are no unfriendly faces here," she said. "Yaoting? Qiao?" She called something out in Cantonese.

A man who might have been anywhere from forty to ninety years old came out from the house across the courtyard. He wore baggy pants that flapped around his knees, slippers over his socks, and a shapeless tunic. His face lit up in a gap-toothed grin, developing crags and wrinkles all over. "*Qingfu Lihua!*" he cried, and uttered in sing-song rapid-fire Cantonese. Lihua replied to him, and Lionheart felt thoroughly lost at sea.

"I'm sorry, Shi Xin. This is Zheng Yaoting, the housekeeper and caretaker of my father. He has been filling me in on my father's condition and asking if you are the one I sought. He speaks very little English. "

Yaoting bowed to Lionheart. "Please meet you. Please welcome."

Lionheart bowed back and then looked at Lihua. "He's not freaking about my looks?"

"He had some idea what to expect," said Lihua. "Come, I am sure father will want to see you while . . ." She swallowed and grimaced, as if she'd just tasted something terrible. "While he still lives."

"Where's your brother?" asked Lionheart.

Lihua shrugged. "Yaoting said he is not here. He does not know where Qiao went. Qiao is not dealing well with father's illness."

"How are you holding up?"

Lihua bowed her head. "I am coping."

Lionheart reached out and took her hand. "You don't have to do it alone."

She shook her head. "I must. Qiao has the school to look after, and prepare for father's funeral. Yaoting has to care for the house and watch over my father when he can. I will grieve when the time comes, but until then, I must be strong." She pulled her hand away from Lionheart and glanced down toward his feet. "Please take off your shoes."

He nodded. "Of course." And he reached down to untie his black Chuck Taylors.

"Your feet . . ." Lihua stared at them.

Lionheart looked down at his hybrid human-lion feet, with the thick rounded toes and claw nubs poking out from them, all covered in the tawny fur spreading across his body. He wiggled his toes, honestly glad to be out of the shoes. The soles of his feet were tough enough to go without shoes pretty much anywhere it was permissible. Converse were the only shoes he could buy off the rack to fit his unusual feet, so when occasions required it, those were his footwear of choice. "They get me from place to place," he said with a laugh. "My mother used to say when I told her I didn't like them and I wished they were like other kids' feet. She'd say *they get you from place to place just like everyone else's feet*, and that was the end of it."

"Hush, here we are." Lihua's voice dropped to a whisper. "He may be asleep." She slid a panel door aside and looked into the room beyond.

"Lihua . . ." said the weak voice of Master Chou Huizhong.

"*Fuqin*," she said in a soft voice. "I have brought Shi Xin, as you asked."

"Richard," said Master Chou. "Come in, my young friend. My time is not long."

Lihua stepped aside to allow Lionheart to enter Master Chou's room. Despite the bright morning sunshine, the room was kept dimmed by silk curtains over the high windows, but they were open to allow a hint of breeze. Papers with columns of hanzi characters sat beside every window and were even on the door. Candles burned on a rack off to one side, along with a smoking brazier of some mild floral incense. A woven reed mat hung on the wall behind Master Chou, whose head was propped up on a European-style bed. A small table beside him held a clay pot of what smelled like strong green tea.

Lionheart was appalled at how much his master had wasted away. Chou Huizhong had never been a fleshy man, even despite his years spent in America where food was hardly dear. But to see him now, he looked like one of those devastating starvation victims on late-night UNICEF commercials. His skin was stretched taught across his bones, and yet despite being paper-thin, it had collapsed into his cheeks, giving him the appearance of a recently-exhumed mummy. His eyes were rimmed with red and his skin had taken on an unhealthy jaundiced appearance except in the places it had become blackened with incipient gangrene. Despite the candles and incense burning, and the breeze carrying hints of cherry blossom and the sea with it, there was an underlying odor of decay making Lionheart's stomach twist.

"My God," Lionheart whispered. "What happened?"

"It is some kind of poison," said Lihua. "We have had the best British doctors we could afford here, as well as Chinese physicians. They all agree on poison or venom, but they cannot identify the source, and cannot treat it effectively." Tears streamed down her face. "I feared he would be gone before I returned with you. It will not be long now."

The way Master Chou's eyes looked right at him without seeing made Lionheart wonder if his master was already dead despite the slow, irregular rise and fall of his chest. "He's in pain?"

"We have been giving him morphine, but his blood does not flow right. It is very thick, like mud. A side effect of the poison." Lihua dabbed at her eyes with a silken cloth.

"Richard . . ." Master Chou's voice was weak, the whisper barely carrying over the gentle hiss of the breeze.

Lionheart made himself overcome the distaste at the odor to come to his side and take his hand. "I'm here, Master."

"You were . . . a good student."

"I'm still a student. I never stopped studying, even after we parted ways."

"Yes. Good student."

"You asked me to come. What do you need to tell me?"

A slight spark came into Master Chou's eyes. He coughed and thick blood splattered across his lips, like

21

someone had spilled black currant jelly upon his face. "The day we met . . . you fought a man. Not like you, but like you."

"He was a parahuman."

"Yes. Not like you, but like you."

Lionheart glanced up at Lihua, but her eyes were affixed upon her father, not even seeming to notice him. "Go on, Master, I'm listening."

"I do not . . . have long left. Wu Zhiming She . . . Not like you . . . but like you."

A new voice interrupted. "So . . . this is the *gweilo* who stole from us." Lionheart looked up to see a solid young Chinese man wrapped up in a long gray robe under which his shoulders bulged like cantaloupes. The corners of his mouth turned down in distaste as he glared at Lionheart.

"Qiao!" hissed Lihua. "How dare you?"

"How dare *I*? How dare *he*." Qiao set a parcel on the small table beside his father's bed. "More morphine, for all the good it does. Perhaps we should go to Wu Zhiming She and see what they have that is stronger. I am certain they would be glad to help us. They have already helped Father into an early grave."

Lionheart stood and stepped back from Master Chou's side. It had been a great many years since he'd felt like someone was offended at his mere presence. A lot had changed in America in the years since he'd been born, and people had not only grown more accepting of parahumans, but they treated them like movie stars or sports heroes. Being instantly disliked was something Lionheart didn't miss, and he felt his hackles rising. "I'm sorry. I'm not sure what I did to offend you, Chou Qiao, but I apologize." He bowed, hoping to forestall any further arguments in front of the ailing Master Chou. He was still trying to wrap his mind around what Master Chou had told him. The nearest he could figure was there were parahumans in the Five Deadly Serpents Triad, and that was why Chou had called for Lionheart.

"You are not welcome here, *gweilo*," said Qiao.

"Stop it, Qiao. You are being very impolite." Lihua's tears subsided in favor of righteous rage on Lionheart's behalf. "Shi Xin is our guest."

"Qiao." Master Chou's voice crackled with fluid in his lungs. "Shi Xin . . . honored guest. You will . . . treat him as such." He closed his eyes and breathed out.

He did not breathe in again.

Chapter Three

"Man's enemies are not demons, but human beings like himself."
—Lao Tzu

The last funeral Lionheart had attended had been for a young woman named Gretchen who'd been killed during the New York City Blackout of '77 as she helped Just Cause save the city from burning to the ground. She had been buried with full honors and given a plaque on the Wall of Fallen Heroes at the entrance of the World Trade Center, even though she'd only been barely inducted onto the team at the time of her death. Funerals were supposed to be somber occasions, but hers had hit a lot of people particularly hard because of her selfless sacrifice. The mayor and governor had both spoken at her service, and it had been attended by thousands of people wishing to give their gratitude for her heroism.

But when it came to funerals, he figured maybe nobody went all out more than the Chinese.

Qiao hired an undertaker who came in and ran the funeral much in the same way some people back in the States hired wedding planners. Instead of Master Chou's body being taken to a funeral home, the coffin was set up right in the main house. The undertaker's assistants carefully cleaned and dressed the body and set it up in the coffin, but that was only the beginning. They covered all of the statues around the house with red paper and took all the mirrors out of the buildings and moved them into storage. They also hung a white cloth and a gong by the main entrance to the *siheyuan*.

There was a wake, but instead of drinking and storytelling like Lionheart had heard the Irish did, there was a solemn procession. Neighbors and students came to the house, lit candles and incense, offered donations of money and food. Many of them stared in open-mouthed wonder at Lionheart, until he felt like he should just go hide in the guest room until afterward. Lihua wouldn't hear of it and broke protocol once to whisper to him she was glad he'd come and spoken to her father before his death.

It still seemed odd to him that a group of attendees were gambling out in the courtyard, playing something like dominoes called *pai gow*, but he gathered it had something to do with managing the grief of the visitors and what Yaoting called *guarding the dead*. Whatever else it was, the death of Master Chou was a highly spiritual experience for all involved. The undertaker brought a Buddhist monk in to chant prayers as the mourners gathered before the coffin. Lionheart felt like more of an outsider than ever before. He watched the rites and stayed as far out of the way as he could without being insulting to his hosts.

Lihua openly cried, sniffling and sobbing as the rites continued. Qiao stood beside his father's coffin, his face impassive as he stared out across the mourners, listening to the funeral chant. He stiffened suddenly and clenched his fists, shooting a look of naked hatred toward someone in the back of the group of mourners. His vicious gaze made Lionheart's hackles rise, and he followed Qiao's eyes until he spotted the targets of the man's anger: two Chinese men who could have been the personifications of *yin* and *yang*. One was slender and packed full of muscles under his somber black suit. His nose was flattened like a hockey player's, perhaps from being repeatedly punched, and his teeth seemed too large for his mouth. The other man was tall, even for a Chinese man, with a barrel chest and a neck threatening to burst the seams of his robe. His head was shaved, the expanse of skin making his already wide face seem even broader.

Qiao shouted something at them, making the mourners gasp at his sudden fury. His face turned thunderous and he started toward the two men, pushing aside mourners. Lihua grabbed at him, tears streaming down her face as she pleaded with him, but he pushed her aside. She stumbled and would have fallen had Lionheart not stepped over to support her. "What's going on?" he asked, sensing it was all right to speak as conversation had arisen among the mourners like wind rippling through the trees.

"Wu Zhiming She," said Lihua. "Five Deadly Serpents. Those are two of their elite warriors. Their leaders. Lang She and Wang Wen Mang."

One of them, the man with the shaved head, called something back to Qiao that incensed him even further.

"They came to pay their respects to the dead," said Lihua. "Even though they may have killed him. That is why Qiao is upset."

"Should I stop him?" Lionheart gauged the distance between Qiao and the two Serpents, and considered whether he could intervene before things got out of hand.

"No. And even if I said yes, I do not believe you can stop Qiao. He is highly trained."

"I'm not exactly small potatoes myself, you know."

Lihua managed a smile. "You are not a potato of any kind."

Qiao bellowed a challenge, and the surrounding funeral mourners fell all over themselves to get out of his way as he dropped into a low cat stance, his weight upon his flexed back leg with his front foot just brushing the courtyard floor. His right hand came up in front of his chest while he extended his left, edge on, ready to attack or defend as needed. Lang She and Wang Wen Mang both took on their own ready stances; Lang She dropped down into a low crouch with one leg extended, his torso bent nearly horizontal while Wang Wen Mang moved into a more traditional front stance, forward palm up with all his fingers curled inward but for his index.

"Come for the funeral, stay for the show," murmured Lionheart, who was fascinated with the developments. In spite of his years of training under Master Chou, he knew he'd barely scratched the surface of world of martial arts, and there would be styles and moves he'd never learned, never seen, perhaps never even imagined.

Qiao attacked Wang Wen Mang, rolling the larger man's punch off like a duck shedding water from its back. He sidestepped, moving in a circular path around Wang. Wang lashed out in a flurry of short, powerful strikes Qiao redirected past him. Qiao responded with blows that seemed to come from all directions, circling Wang all the while. Lionheart was sure Qiao was using Pa Kua Chang from the way he kept circling his opponent. The soft, deceptive style seemed a good match against the Choy Li Fut that Wang used.

Lang She hung back, waiting for his chance in his fighting crouch. It only took a few seconds before his moment came. Qiao's circle tightened around Wang just as Wang attempted a rapid leg sweep. A double palm strike from Qiao sent Wang staggering back across the courtyard. Wang winced, rubbing his chest.

Lang She sprang at Qiao in a leaping attack resembling one Master Chou had taught Lionheart, at least at a superficial level. Qiao sidestepped the charge with ease, but when he turned his circle in the Pa Kua Chang style, Lang She was no longer there. The wiry man's fighting style was, if possible, even more circular than Qiao's, and it was compounded in difficulty by the way the man kept low, actually fighting while on his side upon the ground. As Qiao stomped downward, Lang She wrapped himself around Qiao's leg and drove a hard kick upward into Qiao's groin.

Now it was Qiao's turn to stagger back in pain. Lang She rolled onto his back and flipped himself up onto his feet.

Wang Wen Ming closed in on Qiao in a flurry of whirling kicks and punches, a brutal assault putting Qiao on full defense. He backed across the yard, deflecting some blows, dodging others, and meeting still others head-on. Then just as Lionheart was about to intervene despite Lihua's warning, Wang Wen Ming made a misstep and Qiao flowed behind him like smoke on the breeze. All of Wang Wen Ming's aggressive force was turned against him and Qiao threw him to the courtyard floor.

Lang She growled like a dog as he came in low at Qiao, lunging and twisting as he tried to pull Qiao down to the ground with him.

Qiao leaped over Lang She, dodging the ground-fighter. When he came down, he stomped so hard onto the spot where Lang She's ankle had been that he cracked the tile beneath his foot. The smaller man wriggled out of the way and somehow got his own legs snaked in between Qiao's, locking his knees. Before

Qiao could try to counter the lock, Wang Wen Ming jumped him from behind and wrapped his arms around Qiao's throat. Qiao slumped almost immediately.

Lionheart roared.

It was something he'd practiced, but didn't do very often, because it was a painful exercise in voice strain. He'd started with a close approximation of a lion's roar in the wild, a booming, grating howl sounding enough like one of the tawny beasts to give anyone pause. Then he amped it up, using his greater-than-human strength to force the sound out harder, making it loud enough that nearby folks would wince and belatedly cover their ears.

The mourners shrieked in fear and surprise, and Lang She and Wang Wen Ming dropped the unconscious Qiao, taken aback by the sight of Lionheart leaping over the railing of the courtyard.

"Go." Lionheart pointed toward the gate. He guessed they probably didn't speak English, but whether or not they did, he figured he could make himself very clear. The language of warriors transcended mere dialogue. The two Wu Zhiming She fighters would be able to see Lionheart had been trained by the way he moved, and he would be no pushover. He popped out his claws to further strengthen the idea he was trying to convey. "You are not welcome here."

Lang She and Wang Wen Ming glanced at each other and apparently decided they were done disrupting Master Chou's funeral ceremony. Wang Wen Ming reached into his pocket and dug out a sheaf of bills which he threw onto the courtyard floor. "*Wu Zhiming She gei zhege qian duixian Chou Huizhong.*" Both men bowed at the astonished mourners. "*Wo men shen de bu dang xingwei.*" They departed untouched, for nobody dared to pursue them after they'd dropped Chou Qiao with such apparent ease.

狮 和 五 致 死 蛇

Chou Qiao spent the rest of the evening as what Javier would have defined *drunk off his ass*. After his sound beating by the two Serpent Warriors, he'd been so badly embarrassed. Lionheart worried he might harm himself somehow, but instead Qiao had apologized profusely to the mourners and asked them all to leave so he could spend the time praying to his father's spirit for forgiveness. Then, once they'd all left, murmuring amongst themselves about what was sure to be the talk of Aberdeen in the morning, Qiao ordered Yaoting to bring him plum wine, and to keep it coming. He wouldn't let Lihua look at the bruising to his face and groin, and shot venomous looks at Lionheart until his eyes weren't focusing so well any longer.

"What should I do?" Lionheart asked Lihua as they stood off to one side of the courtyard, near the shrine, and watched Qiao take a long pull at another bottle. "He hates me. He blames me because your father spent time training me instead of him. Honestly, Lihua, I didn't even know Master Chou had any children at all."

"It is not your fault, Shi Xin," said Lihua. She'd changed from her expensive mourning clothes to a simple pair of calf-length trousers and a tunic with a sash tying it shut around her waist. She smelled freshly-bathed, with a hint of citrus about her skin and hair, which she'd braided into a pair of plaits hanging over her shoulders to frame her face. "My father . . . He cared for us, despite what Qiao may think." She sighed, putting her knuckles to her lips for a moment in a forlorn gesture reminding Lionheart of a lost child.

"What is it?" asked Lionheart.

"In America, you tell your parents you love them. Here in China, we do not. We respect and honor them, and honor their memories when they have passed. We do not tell our children we love them. We provide for them," said Lihua in a soft voice. "Father kept this *siheyuan* for us. He kept Yaoting for us. Neither Qiao nor I have ever wanted for anything in our lives. This is how I know my father cared for us."

"You never told him you loved him?"

"It would have been . . . uncomfortable for both of us."

"I never knew my father, but he didn't provide for me or anything. I guess I can safely say he didn't love me." Lionheart felt like his smile was hollow. Not even knowing half of his own parentage had bothered him as he grew up. Had his father been a parahuman? If so, was it someone Lionheart might have ever met in his life without realizing it?

"Yaoting . . ." slurred Qiao. "*Dai lai geng duo de jiu!*" To illustrate his request, he hurled the empty bottle against the high wall surrounding the courtyard where it shattered into a thousand pieces. A dog barked somewhere nearby in response, and a cat yowled back.

Yaoting padded into the courtyard, saying, "*Bu! Qing sifu Qiao . . .*" and waving his hands in a placatory way.

"I said bring me more wine, you damn old fool!" roared Qiao in English.

Lihua gasped and turned away from her brother, her fists clenched at her sides, unable even to speak her mind.

Lionheart touched her shoulder, the lightest brush with his velvet paw, and then stepped into the courtyard. "Qiao, in my country it's rude to let someone drink alone. May I join you?"

Qiao glared at him, or near him, as his eyes were slowly spinning around in their sockets. The paper lanterns around the courtyard reflected in the black pools of his irises. "Why?" he said at last.

Lionheart sat on one of the low benches beside the painted wooden table where Qiao was drowning his sorrows. "Because you don't have to drink alone."

"No. Why . . . why are you still here? *Gweilo.*"

"You keep calling me that. What does it mean?" Lionheart saw Yaoting standing at the edge of the courtyard, a bottle in his hand, uncertain whether or not to proceed. He waved the old man to approach.

"It . . . means . . ." Qiao screwed up his face in thought, making the swelling around his eye bulge out in the lantern light. "Ghost man. It means you are foreign devil. White man. *Gweilo.*" He rolled the word around as if savoring every syllable.

Lionheart blinked. He knew he was white—of course he was, his mother had been—but it was something he'd never thought about. He certainly didn't look like any other white man out there. He'd suffered discrimination for his appearance in ways far more in line with what black folks had to deal with than whites. "Your sister calls me Shi Xin. She tells me it means Lionheart. I kind of like that."

Yaoting set down the bottle upon the table and a clay mug beside it, then bowed and made a rapid exit before any more bottles were flung around.

"Shi Xin." Qiao snorted. "Shi *Lian* is better." He pulled the cork out of the bottle with his teeth and spat it across the courtyard.

"Shi Lian," repeated Lionheart. "It sounds more like *Lion*. What does it mean?"

"Lion *face*." Qiao burst into giggles. "Shi *Lo*. Lion Guy. *Sei Shi Lo*. Bad Lion Guy." He splashed some wine into Lionheart's cup and raised the bottle in a sardonic, blurry salute. "*Kong bei, niang yang.*"

An audible gasp emerged from the shadows in the direction of where Yaoting had gone.

"What's that?"

"Bottoms up, motherfucker." Qiao upended the bottle, drinking hard so very little spillage splashed down his cheeks. The wine sluiced down his throat and Lionheart winced, knowing it would likely find its way back out shortly. He wasn't a heavy drinker, preferring to keep his wits about him at all times, but he'd had to babysit Javelin plenty of times when the Puerto Rican had fallen off the wagon, and it never ended in anything except ugliness.

"Yao . . . *Dai lai* . . ." Qiao's slurred sentence devolved into an incomprehensible babble and he rolled off his low bench, sprawling on the courtyard tiles. After a few seconds, his juicy snores seemed like they would shake the cherry blossoms off the nearby tree.

"Lihua," called Lionheart softly.

"Shi Xin." Lihua stepped up from the shadows. Her dark eyes showed love and concern for her brother. "Is he all right?"

"He's done for the night, that's for sure. He'll wake up with one hell of a headache. Do you want to leave him out here? If he pukes, it'll be easier to clean up."

"No. He should sleep in his bed. I would not dishonor him by leaving him outside."

"Show me where to put him." Lionheart reached down and tried to get Qiao on his feet, but the man was well and truly unconscious, and Lionheart decided honor was less of a factor than simplicity, and he swung Qiao up into his arms like he was carrying a bride across the threshold.

Lihua slid open a panel in the house directly opposite the courtyard from the one where Lionheart was quartered. She turned a dial and a couple of dim lights ensconced inside paper globes hummed to life, showing an austere room that, in Lionheart's opinion, fit Qiao's personality perfectly.

The bed was low to the ground but sat upon a raised *kang* with heat flues beneath it. A bench sat at the foot of the bed and a chair off to one side. A small table sat near the cylindrical pillow beneath the headboard with nothing sitting upon it. The only decoration in the room at all was a large fan hung on the wall above the bed and some filigree on a folding privacy screen in the corner. Lionheart carried Qiao into the room and laid him on the bed, wishing he had a big plastic sheet to put over it first. He started stripping off Qiao's funeral clothes so the man wouldn't ruin them should he be sick in his sleep.

"What can I do to help?" asked Lihua from the door.

"See if Yaoting has a bucket Qiao can keep by his side. And a big pitcher of water."

"Of course." Lihua passed along those requests in rapid Cantonese to Yaoting, who bowed and rushed away.

Lionheart finished pulling Qiao's clothes off. Lihua took the discarded clothing, carefully folded it, and set it on the bench at the foot of the bed. All the while, Qiao's snores rattled the fan on the wall over his head.

At first, Lihua suggested they should leave the dimmer lights turned down low but Lionheart overruled her. "He'll be hurting when he wakes up. Better to reduce the light as much as possible."

"You are being very kind to him, Shi Xin, and he was so rude to you."

Lionheart shrugged. "Life's too short to be an asshole. I learned that lesson a long time ago." He looked down at the unconscious Qiao. "I hope your brother learns it too."

Lihua touched Lionheart's hand for a moment, a tender and unexpected contact he found himself wishing was repeated. "Thank you. I am in your debt."

Lionheart smiled down at her. "Just another day in the life of a superhero."

Chapter Four

*"If you know the enemy and know yourself you
need not fear the results of a hundred battles."*
—Sun Tzu

Lionheart awakened before the dawn, as had been his habit for many years. He'd slept poorly despite the comfortable bed in the guest house. His biological clock was still on New York time, and he wasn't even sure what time it really was in Hong Kong. Regardless, as the shadows turned to gray light in his room, his eyes opened and he realized he'd gotten some sleep after all. He yawned and stretched out his back, rump raised in the air and arms forward just like a cat. Somewhere beyond the walls of the *siheyuan*, he could hear the faint sounds of the docks as the early morning stevedores loaded and unloaded cargoes, and beneath it the whisper and hum of the ocean as it lapped against the island. The air carried with it a hint of floral blossoms from the trees in the courtyard that had closed up their buds against the night air, the tang of coal smoke, and a pungent grassy jab in the nostrils of green tea with toasted rice.

Lionheart knew there wouldn't be coffee, or if there was, he'd probably have to head into the main part of town to try to find some. Between the British occupying the island and the native Chinese, though, he'd have all the tea he could ever want. He smiled to himself. When in Rome—or in this case, Hong Kong—do as the natives do. He pulled on his jeans and his Mets t-shirt and padded out of the small house into the courtyard. The tile path was cool beneath his bare feet. A gentle breeze made tiny wind chimes in the trees tinkle like singing crickets. He shook out his mane and let the dawn air rejuvenate him, at least as much as it could without the infusion of caffeine. Tea had caffeine in it, didn't it? He wondered if Yaoting was awake yet. The old housekeeper seemed like someone who knew his way around a kettle, and if anybody could get the lion to forsake his coffee for something native, it would be Yaoting.

As he passed by the room where he'd laid Qiao, Lionheart heard thick snoring and smiled. Qiao had drunk a tremendous amount of wine, and he might sleep the entire day. If he didn't, Lionheart reflected, he'd probably wish he had. Would the classes be suspended during the mourning period for Master Chou? Qiao was in no condition to teach. Perhaps Lihua was an instructor, although she hadn't said anything about her role in the school. It would be something to check out later, though, because Lionheart had awakened with an idea in his mind that had only grown in resolve as he left his room. Perhaps it was the superhero in him, seeking a means to justice, to protect those who needed it. Perhaps it was his own personal sense of honor and duty.

Or perhaps he was just looking to beat up a bunch of gangsters.

Either way, Lionheart had decided he would go pay a visit to the Five Deadly Serpents on his own and suggest to them—with respectful politeness, of course—

they might leave the Cherrywood Academy alone and find some other means to smuggle their drugs in and out of the country.

Yaoting was awake, and he stood at a small cast iron stove, stirring something in a pot when Lionheart poked his head into the kitchen. The old man had a long black robe on with a cloth tied around his forehead. Lionheart didn't want to startle him; he knew his fearsome appearance could be a lot more challenging for someone who wasn't used to it or expecting to see it. He cleared his throat. "Uh, good morning, Yaoting."

"Oh!" Yaoting gasped as he saw Lionheart's mane and broad nose and clutched at his chest. For a moment, Lionheart was terrified the man was going to have a heart attack right there on the spot, but then the Yaoting's expression softened. "Hello! Yes. Shi Xin. Yes."

"Yaoting, you don't have any coffee around here, do you? Coffee? I don't know the word for it in Cantonese." Lionheart paused. "Actually, I don't really know any Cantonese at all." He looked around the kitchen, spotted a fine china teacup, and picked it up, pantomiming blowing on a hot drink. "Coffee?"

"*Kafei*? No. No *kafei*. We no *kafei*. *Cha*. Tea." Yaoting nodded his head toward a copper kettle. "You like?"

"Sure, why not? Anything to get me a bit more awake."

Yaoting shrugged and smiled. "I don't know." He went back to stirring his pot of whatever-it-was. It smelled like rice and fish and ginger and garlic and something else Lionheart couldn't identify. Whatever it was smelled pretty good. He watched as Yaoting prepared him a steaming mug of a rich, dark, smoky tea reminding Lionheart of camping with his mother in Nevada when he was barely a cub. If someone had handed him a marshmallow at that moment, he would have died a happy man. He found himself sniffing the delicate steam rising from the cup with a broad smile.

"*Lapsang souchong*. Good tea. *Sifu* Chou like. You like?" asked Yaoting.

"Yes, very much." Although he was seated, Lionheart inclined his head in a bow.

Yaoting smiled and returned the bow. "You eat? *Zhou*? You like?"

"Yes, please," said Lionheart. He didn't know what he was being offered, but Yaoting seemed to be warming up to him, and he knew the housekeeper would likely be a valuable fountain of information if he could just bridge the language barrier. Lionheart frowned. He'd never considered learning a second language in his life, but it seemed studying of Cantonese would be necessary if he was going to stay in Hong Kong for any amount of time.

With yet another bow, Yaoting placed a wooden bowl before Lionheart. It was a lumpy white porridge of some kind he guessed was rice. Mixed into it were small pieces of grilled fish, chunks of something green and black with a strong briny odor, and slices of green onion and ginger root. The whole thing was topped by what he could only characterize as shredded jerky. Despite the disparate ingredients, it did smell good, and he ate it all, even the stuff he didn't know what it was. Being picky was for people who'd never been hungry, and when he'd been traveling and working odd jobs before he'd met Master Chou, Lionheart had gone through some lean times where he wouldn't have turned his nose up at any kind of food at all.

Lionheart finished his bowl of *zhou* and drank the rest of his tea. It hadn't been anything like the Chinese food the team sometimes ordered for all-nighters when they were working on a case back home in New York. He felt like he could get used to it. "Yaoting, that was very good. Thank you."

Yaoting beamed. "*Xiexie, Shi Xin.*"

"*Xiexie?*"

"You thank. *Xiexie.*"

Lionheart filed it for future reference. Anything he could learn about Cantonese would be useful in his forthcoming investigation. "Does Qiao have a car? An automobile?" Yaoting smiled and said nothing, putting the burden of translation in Lionheart's lap. "Um . . . You know, a car?" He held up his hands like they were clamped upon a steering wheel and made a rumbling sound like an engine.

"Ah! *Qiche.* No," said Yaoting. "*Motuo che.*" He made a popping sound with his lips and held his hands out in front of him like they were clamped upon . . .

"*Motuo* . . . A motorcycle?" Lionheart grinned. He knew bikes. "Show me."

狮 和 五 致 死 蛇

Yaoting hadn't wanted to tell Lionheart where to find the Five Deadly Serpents. He pretended not to understand what Lionheart was asking, and then he begged not to answer, but in the end he really had no choice. Lionheart was a guest of the household; Yaoting was bound to do his best to accommodate the guest's needs, and at last he relented.

Lionheart hadn't enjoyed pulling rank with the old man the way he had, but sometimes the results were more important than the means by which one acquired them. It was something he'd learned during his time with Just Cause, and he made a point never to forget the lessons he learned in the School of Hard Knocks.

If it had been back home in New York, he'd have ridden with only a pair of goggles over his eyes, letting his mane flow free. For one thing, he liked the way it looked, and when he rode somewhere, he wanted people to know who he was. He represented Just Cause, and was proud enough not to hide his face behind a helmet and visor.

In Hong Kong, though, nobody really knew who he was, and the sight of a lion-faced man riding through the streets of Aberdeen would surprise even the most jaded citizens. Qiao had a scuffed black helmet with a fixed visor brim. It was a tight fit over Lionheart's massive mane, but he squeezed it into place and strapped on a pair of aviator goggles. It didn't completely hide his face, but by the time anyone took a second look at him while in transit, he'd already have passed them by.

The Five Deadly Serpents Triad was based in a large mansion in the hills above Aberdeen. It looked like solid European construction, with the local influences evident in the upslope of the corners of the roof and the Chinese-style lion statues on either side of the front door. At first, Lionheart was surprised the mansion didn't even have so much as a wrought-iron fence around it, but then he considered the possibility that the Wu Zhiming She were so fearsome, so powerful, nobody but a fool would dare to approach them with intent to do anything untoward.

Then, he supposed, that made him a fool as he rode up the cobblestone drive and stopped the motorcycle in the circle before the house. The red brick walls loomed three stories tall, with windows framed in brilliant white arches. A large carriage house sat off to one side, the doors gaping wide to display a couple of large black Mercedes sedans, a couple of nondescript Datsuns, several motorcycles, and a gorgeous cherry-red Pontiac Firebird that must have cost a fortune to import from the United States. The grounds were lush with early spring flowers and the cottony cherry blossoms. Birds sang in the trees and the breeze carried with it only the scent of the sea and none of the stink of the harbor. It wasn't quite enough to hide the hint of gun oil on the two men in jeans and sunglasses and lightweight leather jackets standing by the front door, leaning casually against the lion statues. They made no aggressive moves as Lionheart put down the kickstand and swung his leg over the saddle. He pulled off the goggles and helmet, tucked the former inside the latter, and set it upon the bike. He didn't think anyone would take it; he suspected the Triad would consider stealing from a guest rude, and if they were confident enough in their own security to not bother with any passive protection like a fence, the bike would probably be just fine.

The two guards rose to a heightened state of alertness as Lionheart approached the front of the house. "Either of you fellas speak English?" he asked.

They glanced at each other. "Yes," said one. "What you want?"

"I'm Lionheart. Shi Xin. From America. I'd like to speak to whoever's in charge."

"Shi Xin?" said the other man, wrinkling his forehead behind his sunglasses as he considered what the words meant.

"*Ta shi yige meiguo de chaoji yingxiong,*" said the first one.

Understanding spread across the other man's face. "*Chaoji yingxiong!*" he breathed in wonder. "*Weida de zhengyi de shiye.*"

"Yes. Just Cause," said the English-speaker.

"Justa Causa," repeated the other man with a snaggletoothed grin.

"We know you, *gweilo*. Why you want speak boss?"

"I'm trying to clear up a misunderstanding without any unpleasantness," said Lionheart, but he could see he'd exceeded the man's reach of the English language. "Say it's for business."

"Business. Yes. Wait here." The English-speaker said something to the other man in Cantonese and then knocked upon the front door. A small window opened and he said something to whoever was behind the door. Then he was admitted, leaving Lionheart alone with the man who didn't speak English. It might have made for an awkward and uncomfortable silence, the way the man stared wide-eyed at Lionheart's mane, feline nose, and jowls, if Lionheart hadn't decided to amuse himself by counting how many armed guards were watching him from hidden locations. He lowered his eyes to only half-open so he could focus more upon the scents of the area, and by the time the first guard returned from inside the mansion, Lionheart had located four additional guards by their body odor, tobacco, gun oil, and a sweet smoky smell he suspected might be opium residue.

Lang She, the ground-fighter that had crashed Master Chou's funeral along with Wang Wen Ming, stepped out from behind the door with the first guard. He was dressed far less formally than he had been at the funeral, in wide-legged trousers, slippers, and a short-sleeved tunic. The slabs of tight muscle laid over his narrow frame gave him a distinctive bowlegged appearance, like an English bulldog. He looked up and down Lionheart, putting on a show of being unimpressed by the leonine face and sweeping mane. "What do you want, *gweilo*? Jingguo can barely speak Cantonese, much less English. He makes no sense to me."

"I'm here to speak to the head of your Triad."

Lang She's face broke into a sardonic grin. "You are mistaken. There is no Triad here."

Lionheart matched Lang She's grin with a toothy smile of his own. "Perhaps I've received some incorrect information then. Somehow, though, I doubt it. You have four men with guns trained on me right now. I didn't think it was possible for anyone to stink worse than you, but they do. They stink. And you stink. And this whole country stinks." He dropped his voice to a dangerous growl. "And I don't like being lied to."

Lang She hunched down a bit, settling into what some might see as a more defensive stance but Lionheart identified it as a prelude to an attack. "You have come a long way to deliver insults, *xiao mao*."

"I have come a long way to honor *sifu* Chou. The insults are incidental."

Lang She tensed and Lionheart pushed his claws out, planning how he would jump *that* way and rebound off *that* wall to avoid the initial burst of gunfire, but a strong British-accented voice called, "Lang She, stand down and don't be rude."

A momentary snarl of displeasure crossed the dog-warrior's face but he straightened up and bowed a precise, insulting millimeter to Lionheart. "A thousand pardons."

Lionheart's bow was no deeper. "I apologize as well."

Lang She melted aside as an older Chinese gentleman stepped through the door. Although his face was mostly unlined, a few wrinkles around the corners of his eyes suggested he laughed often. His graying hair was cut short and neat, and his suit was of traditional Chinese cut, unadorned and plain brown. His feet and hands were small enough to seem delicate, but somehow he carried with him a sense of quiet lethality. The way the guards around him straightened up and became more alert and professional, as well as how Lang She was practically fawning over him, told Lionheart that this was a man much higher up in the Triad.

The man bowed. "I apologize for the exuberance of my fellows. There have been some troublesome elements around our home recently. Undoubtedly they have mistaken you for an unwelcome guest. Allow me to be the first to welcome you to Wu Zhiming She. I am Lian Kui."

"Lionheart. You're in charge here?" Lionheart tried not to be rude, but the fact was he'd very nearly been attacked by armed guards, and it was painting the Triad in a negative light.

"Let us say I am first among equals. Will you join me for some refreshments? I have tea, of course, some American Coca-Cola, and a delicious plum wine."

Lionheart made himself swallow his anger. He reminded himself the reason he'd come was to try to broker some kind of peaceful arrangement so the Triad would leave the Chous alone. "A Coke sounds great. It must cost you quite a bit to import it."

Lian Kui stepped aside to allow Lionheart to enter the Triad's house. "We are in the business of importing and exporting. It costs very little more to bring a case of American soda along with regular freight from Guam or Hawaii. And several of us here have acquired a taste for it."

"As well as some other American things, I saw." Lionheart stepped through the door into a wide foyer with two separate staircases that curved up and around to meet on a second-floor landing. "That car."

Lian Kui smiled. "You must be referring to Lang She's fire-breathing dragon out in the carriage house."

"It's a real beauty." Lionheart thought how much he'd enjoy dragging his claws across the Firebird's pristine finish. He could sign it when he was done. It would be like writing his name in the snow, only more permanent and far more offensive to Lang She.

"Yes, but quite impractical for the narrow streets of Aberdeen. He spends far more time admiring it than he can manage to drive it."

"You disapprove?"

Lian Kui opened a door at the far side of the foyer that led into a wood-paneled library filled not just with books, but rolled scrolls and folding codices. Overstuffed chairs with velvet covers sat at angles to a stone fireplace, which glowed with dying embers. The room smelled of old paper and fresh tea as Lian Kui slid open the curtains to let in the cold gray light of the harbor far below. "Let us say that there are many of us in Wu Zhiming She, and at times we do not see eye-to-eye."

"But you're first among equals?"

Lian Kui went to a sidebar and took a bottle of Coke from an ice bucket. He popped the top and poured the contents into a tall glass tumbler. "That is a reasonable assessment of my duties." Hi indicated one of the two overstuffed chairs by the fire. "Please, sit with me awhile." He pursed his lips and emitted a soft whistle.

A door that Lionheart hadn't noticed before opened and a young woman poked her head into the room. "*Wo keyi bang ni ma?*" Lian Kui said something to her. She bowed and replied, "*Shi de, xiansheng.*"

Lian Kui turned to Lionheart. "I have requested some light refreshments. Now, we shall talk. I understand you have come to speak with me. What is on your mind?"

"It's about the Cherrywood School." Lionheart sniffed at the Coke in his tumbler, making sure that it didn't smell of anything unusual. As far as he could tell, it seemed to be safe enough. Just the same, he politely wet his lips but only took the smallest of sips.

"*Yingtao Mu*. Yes, it is a most desirable facility, one which I hope to purchase." Lian Kui held up a glass of sweet plum wine to the light, swirling it around in a gentle circle before he, too, sipped at it.

"It's not for sale."

Lian Kui turned to smile at Lionheart. "Everything is for sale, my American friend. It is only a question of price."

"Not everything." Lionheart bristled at the implication. "The Chous don't want to sell their school. Their father left it to them."

"I was saddened to hear of Master Chou's untimely death. Such a tragedy for an honorable man. I sent two of my associates to pay respects to him."

"They weren't very respectful."

Lian Kui sipped his wine. "As I understand it, Chou Qiao was the instigator of the unpleasantness. Is that an unfair representation of the events?"

"Yes. Kind of. Look, you just need to lay off of them, all right?" Lionheart was in the unfamiliar position of being on the defensive in a conversation, and his martial training hadn't extended to that type of battle. Lian Kui seemed like he was a master conversationalist. Lionheart wished he had any of his allies from Just Cause beside him. Nearly all of them were far better at diplomacy than he.

"Did they send you?"

"No, I came of my own accord."

Lian Kui regarded him for a moment. The older man's piercing eyes felt like they were seeing right through Lionheart, trying to tease out his deepest, darkest secrets. "Shi Xin, I would be greatly honored if I might show you the rest of the grounds."

The young woman who'd gone to fetch refreshments started to enter the room but stopped at the door as she saw Lian Kui stand. She held a tray loaded with a selection of *dim sum* in baskets. "*Xiansheng*?" She looked back and forth between Lian Kui and Lionheart, indecision spreading across her face.

Lian Kui raised a hand and waved toward a side table. "*Houmian women hui chi.*" He looked at Lionheart. "I told her we will eat later. I sincerely hope you will join me."

"We'll see." At first, Lionheart had thought to reject Lian Kui's invitiation, but then he considered that he was in the camp of the enemy, as it were, and any intelligence he could gather could only benefit him in the future. "But yes, I'd love a tour."

Lian Kui bowed. "Very good."

Chapter Five

*"He who learns but does not think, is lost! He who
thinks but does not learn is in great danger."*
—Confucius

The mansion of the Five Deadly Serpents was a curious dichotomy in architectural styles. The original design was clearly European in origin—probably British, Lionheart thought as he accompanied Lian Kui through the wainscoted halls and the parquet-floored chambers. And yet, everywhere he looked, he saw traditional Chinese statuary, art, and decorations. The art of *feng shui* was well-evidenced, the way certain chambers drew the eye toward potted plants isolated in spots of daylight or miniature stone fountains.

The mansion was well-cared for, with numerous staffers working everywhere Lionheart went. They polished, wiped, dusted, cleaned, and otherwise made themselves look very busy even though they were clearly there to watch him. Despite the pervasive stink of their unwashed bodies, Lionheart caught numerous whiffs of gun oil and mineral solvents, which he presumed were used in the care of bladed weapons. Beneath it all, there was a sharp, sour smell like vinegar.

Lionheart knew that scent from his days babysitting Javier at his worst. Somewhere in the mansion, probably in the basement, heroin was being made.

The initial part of the tour seemed like it was designed to impress Lionheart with the Triad's wealth. Lavish furnishings competed for space with expensive and showy items like jewel-encrusted breastplates, polished jade statues, and murals dating back centuries. The amount of detail Lian Kui had retained about each piece was remarkable. Lionheart didn't think he could have kept it all straight himself, but then, he wouldn't have known if Lian Kui was feeding him a big heap of bullshit either. The so-called servants were in every room and hall ahead of Lionheart and Lian Kui, their diligence plain to see. Nevertheless, he was starting to recognize a few of them and wondered how they were moving through the mansion without being seen. There must have been a network of secret passages throughout the building. Lionheart was feeling that which had killed the cat, but managed to keep it in check. Instead, he gave polite nods of encouragement and asked brief questions of his host.

There was an old Mafia saying Lionheart had heard once and never forgot: *Let the man talk; when he is finished, let him talk some more.* Lian Kui was talking a lot, and Lionheart was listening not just to what he said, but to what was going unsaid. *Look at all this wealth* was the subtext of Lian Kui's tour. *You can't compete against this.*

We can buy and sell you as we wish.

Lionheart was about to apologize and make an excuse to leave when the tour took an interesting turn.

"I believe you witnessed a small demonstration of martial skills at Master Chou's funeral," said Lian Kui as he led Lionheart out of the mansion into a large, high-walled courtyard behind the building. In it, some two dozen men and a couple of women as well were hard at work, training in various fighting styles. Lionheart recognized several of them as the "cleaning crew" that had been working so diligently inside the mansion. The difference was that there, they seemed out of place and barely competent at such simple tasks as sweeping or polishing. In the training courtyard, they were true Serpent Warriors.

One group focused on shifting between painfully low stances, compressing power into their legs until they quivered with the effort. The instructor was none other than the broad-faced Wang Wen Mang who had joined Lang She at Master Chou's funeral. He shouted out a specific cadence of commands, and the group following his lead changed their position with each shout. They dropped down to a low dragon stance, crouching on one leg with the other extended straight to the side, then shifted across to the opposite side. Another shout and they pushed upward into a cat stance, all the weight on their bent rear legs with their front feet barely touching the tiles. Wang Wen Mang shouted once more and the entire group leaped into the air, spinning around with a rapid roundhouse kick. One student stumbled on his landing and fell.

The others froze as Wang Wen Mang interrupted his commands to scream at the one who'd fallen. The hapless young man scrambled back to his feet, bowed and pled forgiveness. Wang Wen Mang shouted, "*Zuo yibian!*" and the man jumped up, nailing his roundhouse kick and landing. "*Zuo yibian!*" Wang Wen Mang repeated, and the man jumped again.

"Do you speak much Cantonese, Shi Xin?" asked Lian Kui.

"Not a word of it." Lionheart figured it was better to come across as stupider, even though the number of

Cantonese words he did know could probably be written across the back of a postage stamp.

"Some schools use corporal punishment to great effect to instruct their students why failure is wrong," said Lian Kui. "I do not ascribe to that philosophy. The student who is beaten merely for failing a training task learns nothing but to fear his instructor." He nodded toward the student, now repeating the same kick over and over again, sweat flying off his hair and his legs shaking with the repeated effort. "This Serpent Warrior will instead learn how to perform a *huixuan ti*, and afterward, he will be a better warrior."

"I see." Lionheart only had to look at the young man to see Wang Wen Mang had instilled fear in him instead of desire to succeed. Several of the other students had apprehensive expressions as Wang Wen Mang returned to the training regimen. They were afraid of him, and since Lian Kui had already suggested the school was his, that meant they were afraid of Lian Kui too. Lionheart couldn't blame them; despite his soft-spoken words and gentle demeanor, there was an iron core to the man, which Lionheart knew would neither break nor bend under the strongest assault.

Another group nearby worked with paired sticks, the bamboo shafts clacking off each other in a rapid staccato rhythm. The instructor goading them was a slender woman dressed all in black. Her hair was pulled up in a ponytail and a golden sweatband kept her bangs out of her eyes. She had four sheaths on a belt at her waist, but only two showed the angular tops of sais. The lithe movements of her arms and legs as she demonstrated techniques were the smoothest Lionheart had ever seen. Her voice was rough and harsh and when she turned, Lionheart saw the reason why: she had an ugly, ragged scar across her throat. Lionheart couldn't imagine how a wound creating that scar hadn't been fatal, but she was living proof it hadn't.

Lian Kui saw his guest observing the stick fighting teacher. "Kobura came to us from Okinawa. She brings her native *kobudo* and *karate* to us. My Serpent Warriors are well-rounded."

Again, Lionheart read the subtext clearly. *We have an army. We are many, while you are few. You cannot stand against us. To fight us is to die.*

"Perhaps you would enjoy a sparring session with one of my *dashe yongshi*. Any of the Serpent Warriors would be honored to test himself against a great American superhero."

Lionheart bowed. "Although I would enjoy nothing more, I'm afraid I have other pressing engagements that will prevent it. Perhaps another time." He smiled, showing his sharp feline teeth, conveying his own subtext. *Bring it on.*

"Then I must not keep you. Please allow me to escort you out, Shi Xin."

"Of course." Lionheart took one last look at the training warriors. He had to admit they were a formidable force, and he didn't like the idea of having to battle more than one or two of them. Enough termites could bring down a mighty oak tree, and the Serpent Warriors were far more dangerous to him than termites to a tree.

They walked back through the house. It was devoid of the retinue of housekeepers. Of course it was, thought Lionheart. They were all out back in the courtyard, learning how to kill. "Shi Xin . . . Lionheart . . . I must ask you. Will you speak to Chou Qiao for me? You know I wish to purchase the Cherrywood School. I will give him far more than a fair price for his property. He and his sister will be wealthy from it, enough for them to purchase a large dwelling in Hong Kong or even to emigrate to the United States, should they wish it. All I ask is for you to lend your weight to mine in convincing the Chous to sell."

"I doubt even John Stone's weight would be enough to sway Qiao's mind," said Lionheart. "And even if it was, he would refuse on the grounds that the decision would be the Chous', and theirs alone. I must refuse as well."

Lian Kui bowed. "Of course, I understand, my American friend." He opened the door to the front of the mansion and held it open for Lionheart. "I am honored that you have visited me. It would honor me further should you choose to do so again in the future."

Lionheart nodded. "You have been a gracious host, Lian Kui. Thank you for your hospitality." He descended the steps to where Qiao's motorbike was parked.

"Shi Xin," said Lian Kui after him.

Lionheart turned.

"Unlike in America, there are no superheroes in China. There are only two kinds of parahumans here—those who are dead, and those who are very, very powerful. The Five Deadly Serpents are not without resources in that area. It would be a great tragedy were I to have to bring any of those resources to bear to get what I want. And I always get what I want."

"I'll keep that in mind." Lionheart pulled his helmet back on. "Best of luck with that."

狮 和 五 致 死 蛇

A scooter pulled out in front of Lionheart only a minute after he'd departed the grounds of the Five Deadly Serpents. He had to maneuver the frail motorbike into a powerslide, leaning it down and swinging it to the side to avoid rear-ending the dirty red Japanese bike that stopped right in front of him. He threw aside his helmet and was about to give the other rider a roaring tongue-lashing that would cause nightmares for many months, except she pulled off her own helmet and cried, "Shi Xin!"

"Lihua?" Lionheart's fury evaporated like clouds in a summer breeze. "You almost killed me. What are you doing here?"

"I came to find you." Sparks flashed in her eyes and Lionheart realized even though his own anger was gone, hers was winding up to full force. "Yaoting said you borrowed Qiao's motorbike. I figured you might have come up here. I hate that I was right."

Lionheart shrugged. "I was investigating. That's what superheroes do when we're trying to solve crimes."

"Why would you risk yourself in that . . . that terrible place? The Wu Zhiming She are killers. They have more weapons than the Hong Kong Police. You could have been . . ."

"I wasn't. See? I'm right here, Lihua." Lionheart reached out one of his paws to touch her hand, which was shaking in fury as it clenched around the scooter's handlebar. "I'm not afraid of killers. When you've faced some of the supervillains I have, a few gangsters *kung fu fighting* aren't enough to even raise my blood pressure." He stopped as he saw she was on the verge of tears. "Hey, don't cry. I'm all right. I'm sorry I worried you."

"Qiao would never forgive himself if you got yourself killed."

"Oh, I think he'd find a way to. He doesn't like me."

Lihua looked away from Lionheart. "No, he does not like you, but he respects you. And you are a guest in his house, which means you are under his protection. If you are killed, it is his dishonor for failing to protect you."

"I don't need his protection."

"Yes, you do!" Lihua raised her voice enough that a couple of pushcart vendors down the road looked up from their wares, curious about the carryings-on. "This is not America. The rules you know do not apply."

Lionheart clamped his teeth down on his tongue and counted to five. It was one of the best ways he knew to keep from losing his temper. Being screamed at was one of his triggers, and the burst of pain and swirl of blood on his tongue distracted him enough to keep from lashing out. "So teach me," he said at last. "Show me how to live here. Can I buy you lunch?"

Lihua looked like she was going to unload on him for a moment, but then her face softened. "I am sorry. I did not mean to be angry. I was worried for you." A flush crept up her cheeks and Lionheart realized the truth with sudden clarity.

Lihua *liked* him.

And on the heels of that revelation came another. He liked her too. *Liked* her.

He was grateful that his facial fur hid his own blush response. He shouldn't feel that way. His heart was still with Faith.

But Faith was a very long way away.

He licked his lips with a tongue that had suddenly become far too dry. "Thank you for caring. Listen, uh, I'm really thirsty. Can we go get lunch and some tea or something?"

Lihua nodded and pulled her helmet back on. "I know a place that has delicious noodles. Follow me. My treat." An impish grin crossed her face as she buckled the helmet beneath her chin. "Try to keep up."

The red scooter was pokey enough Lionheart thought he could have kept up with it using no more than a brisk jog. Following it on the motorbike presented no challenge at all as they rode down the twisting road from the hills back toward the harbor. Traffic picked up the further away from Five Deadly Serpents' estate they got, requiring them to weave around rickshaws and other carts laden with everything from fresh fish to bags of rice to bamboo cages filled with squawking chickens. Lionheart nearly ran down a bicyclist holding his handlebars with one hand while carrying a tall rack from which a dozen smoked ducks hung. The smell made his stomach clench, reminding him that his congee breakfast hadn't been particularly satisfying.

As they found their way through Aberdeen, more than once Lionheart had to keep his feet down on the filthy cobbles as he barely stroked the throttle enough to creep the bike forward through the crowds. He was glad he wasn't carrying any money with him, for pedestrians sometimes pressed close enough that he might not have noticed anyone picking his pocket even from the back of a moving motorcycle.

At last, Lihua bullied her way through a group of men gambling in the street, resting in crouches and shouting over the dice they threw back and forth. They yelled insults at her but she waved them off. Their angry words died upon their lips when Lionheart removed his helmet and gave them all a snarl. They all remembered pressing business elsewhere and vanished down the road, only pausing long enough to retrieve their dice.

Lionheart looked up at the hanzi characters on the tall sign hanging from the awning of the sidewalk cafe they'd found. They still looked like so many hen tracks to him, but a rich smell redolent of meat broth and herbs was coming from the large cast iron pot hanging over the open flame of burning cherrywood. Although the proprietor appeared to have room in the building behind him, he'd brought his entire kitchen out to the street where he could more effectively market his foodstuffs by letting the smells do the work for him. His counter was crowded and diners slurped up noodle soup and drank tea. A young boy ran back and forth from inside the building behind the kitchen, carrying clean bowls and clearing the dirty ones just as fast as he could. As they took notice of Lionheart, diners set down their bowls, left coins on the counter, and shrank away into the street. Lionheart, used to people freaking out when they saw him, ignored the rudeness and sniffed at the air. "What is this? It smells amazing."

"The stand is called *chuse di hailuo tang*," said Lihua. "It means *excellent conch soup*."

"What's conch? I thought that was those big shells on the beach that you can hear the ocean inside of."

"Yes. Conch is sea snail."

"Whoa, whoa . . . You want me to eat snail soup?"

"It *is* excellent soup." Lihua turned to the proprietor, who looked both aghast at the lion-faced man standing at his counter and the sudden loss of his customers. Lihua spoke to him in rapid Cantonese, gesturing at Lionheart all the while.

Experience had taught Lionheart a friendly smile looked to everyone else like he was about to rip out their throats with his razor-sharp fangs. Instead, he was careful to keep his lips closed about them and stood in as neutral and non-threatening a pose as he could manage.

At last, the proprietor gave a stiff bow and inquired something of Lionheart in Cantonese.

"He begs your pardon and asks if he might prepare you some of his finest shrimp noodles," said Lihua. "You should say yes."

"*Shi, xiexie*," said Lionheart, bowing back to the man, whose eyes widened as the monstrous American spoke to him in passable Cantonese. "That pretty much exhausts my Cantonese for today."

"He is honored to serve you," said Lihua. She pushed a handful of *xianjin* at the man, who tucked it beneath his apron and bowed again.

"But not *that* honored," Lionheart muttered.

If nothing else, the proprietor was a quick and efficient chef, placing two steaming bowls of spiced noodles with grilled shrimp before them, packed with sliced vegetables of some kind and coated in a thick, sweet brown sauce. Lionheart took a pair of chopsticks from a cup on the countertop, struggling to use those with his thick fingers. The noodles were firm and spicy in a way that warmed Lionheart all the way to his toes. The shrimp were the most delicious he'd ever had, and he thanked the proprietor again.

Lihua poured out some toasted rice green tea into a clay cup for Lionheart. He'd picked up enough of local customs to remember to tap the counter with his fingertip as a way to thank her. "What possessed you to visit the Wu Zhiming She? They are killers, Shi Xin."

"I'm a killer too, Lihua. I figured the best way to get to know what we're up against at the school would be to check out the opposition."

Lihua sipped her own tea. "I do not know whether to think of you as brave or foolish."

"Sometimes when you're faced with a, uh, a lion's den, you have to go inside to find out if the lion is a worn-out, toothless beast or not." He smiled. "So I marched right into the lion's den. Felt right at home."

"And what did you discover?"

"They're pretty well-organized. They have a heroin lab in the basement of that mansion somewhere. I'd bet a year's salary." Lionheart tapped the side of his nose. "I might not be a bloodhound, but I've got a better sense of smell than any normal human. I've smelled enough drugs in New York to know when there's a manufacturing facility nearby. You were right before when you said they have a lot of weapons. Lots of guns, especially for a place that is training its warriors martially."

"They are warriors. Why would they not fight with guns when they can? A gun is a very useful weapon and one easily respected by those who see them. Most people who have not ever trained in *kung fu* cannot recognize the weapons of the empty hands and feet of a trained warrior."

"But everyone understands a gun." Lionheart abandoned his attempts to retrieve a particularly difficult shrimp with his chopsticks and speared it with one of his claws instead. "Lian Kui seemed very intent upon showing me how I was wasting my time siding with you and Qiao. He wanted me to go talk to your brother, to convince him to sell."

"You will not?"

"No. Lian Kui is a slimy son of a bitch, and he's so cool that butter wouldn't melt in his mouth. I can't stand people like that, who think they're above everything. Whatever you and Qiao need, I'm taking your side on it. It was your father's final request of me, and I can't help but honor that to the fullest of my abilities."

Tears sparkled in the corners of Lihua's eyes. "*Xiexie, Shi Xin.*"

"Tell me more about the Wu Zhiming She."

"They are the most powerful in the area. Perhaps fifty *dashe yongshi*, plus the lieutenants and Lian Kui himself. You have already seen Wang Wen Mang and Lang She, who came to father's funeral."

"And Kobura, from Okinawa."

Lihua grimaced. "She is a stone killer. It is said that she wears four sheaths for her sais, two lined with poison."

"Poison . . . Like how your father was killed? Could she have delivered the fatal dose?"

"I do not know. Perhaps. Without knowing what poison she uses—if that is true about her—we would have no way to know." Lihua poured out some more tea for Lionheart and herself. "There is one more. The dwarf, Ai Haishe. He is the lieutenant in charge of the dock."

"A dwarf?"

Lihua held her hand at waist height. "No taller than this, but he has great fighting skill in *taijiquan* and there is more. They say he moves through water like it is air."

"Moves through water like it is air," Lionheart repeated. "That sounds like a parahuman ability. Lian Kui said he had *resources* when it came to Chinese parahumans. You think he meant this Ai Haishe guy?"

"There are rumors. It may not just be him, but perhaps all of them."

Lionheart finished his bowl of noodles and bowed to the proprietor, who was watching with apprehension. "Rumors usually have some kind of basis in fact."

"This is true."

"Well then . . ." Lionheart smiled at Lihua. "Tell me more."

Chapter Six

*"The good fighters of old first put themselves
beyond the possibility of defeat, and then waited
for an opportunity of defeating the enemy."*
—Sun Tzu

Lionheart parked Qiao's motorbike and left the helmet hanging from one of the handlebars. He had a lot of information about the Five Deadly Serpents to digest, and thinking wasn't really his strong suit. Even back home, he'd left a lot of the more difficult brainwork to Faith, who could think a lot quicker than most people, or her husband Bobby, who was just plain smart. Even Javier could be surprisingly insightful when he was lucid.

Lionheart was better at hitting people until they stopped moving.

He found Qiao sitting at the table in the private courtyard, shading his eyes from the afternoon sun with one hand and nursing a large cup of tea with the other. The sour smell of the previous evening's alcohol still wafted around him as it worked its way out through his sweat glands. "Good afternoon, Qiao. I didn't think I'd see you at all today."

Qiao grunted without saying anything specific and took another drink of the sharp-smelling tea. Its medicinal odor made Lionheart's nostrils wrinkle in sympathy. If it tasted half as bad as it smelled . . . he was frankly amazed that Qiao could stomach it.

"May I join you?" Lionheart didn't wait for Qiao to answer and instead sat down at the table. Now down at Qiao's level, he could see the young man's eyes were bloodshot and sunken and he winced. "Wow. You really tied one on last night. I've got a friend who starts a lot of his mornings this way. He swears by greasy cheeseburgers and Bloody Marys, but I'm guessing neither of those are your thing."

"I do not know what those things are." Qiao grimaced at the sound of his own voice. "You are loud."

"Sorry." Lionheart saw Yaoting across the courtyard, sweeping outside of the kitchen. He waved to get the man's attention and once he had it, pointed at Qiao's mug and then at himself. Maybe Qiao would brighten up a bit if he wasn't the only one suffering. Yaoting bowed and went into the kitchen.

Qiao sipped at his tea and said nothing.

Lionheart obliged the other man's silence by maintaining his own. Instead, he shut his eyes and let the ocean breeze over the walls tickle his nose with the tantalizing scents from the docks beyond the school. Qiao's stomach rumbled dangerously and Lionheart opened one eye to check in case the other man was about to be ill, but he drank more tea and grimaced as it settled down.

Yaoting came over to the table, bearing a tray laden with another pitcher of tea and a large steaming bowl of *mi zhou* like he'd served Lionheart for breakfast that morning. It had strips of cabbage or lettuce sliced into it, and some wrinkled objects that looked kind of like prunes but had a salty, bitter smell that made Lionheart's own stomach rumble unexpectedly. "What are those?"

"*Xian meigan.*" Yaoting bowed.

"Salted dry plums." Qiao glared at the offending bulbs in his own congee. "Kobura would call them *umeboshi.* They are supposed to be good for *su zui.*"

"That must mean hangover." Lionheart nerved up and nibbled at one. It tasted about like it smelled. He wasn't sure he could choke one down, but Qiao was soldiering through his congee, salted dried plums and all. Lionheart wasn't going to let Qiao one-up him that way. "I met Kobura this morning. Well, I didn't meet her, but I saw her training Serpent Warriors."

Qiao spat to the side. "Japanese trash."

"She seemed like a competent fighter to me."

"She is very good. Very dangerous." Qiao looked at Lionheart for the first time since he'd sat down. "She could be who killed my father."

"But you don't know for sure."

"No. Unless she confesses, I will never know for sure."

"I'm sorry. That must be tearing you up inside."

"What do you know about it . . . *Shi Lian?*" Qiao's glare was more effective than before when amplified by his hangover face.

"He was my friend and my teacher, and I miss him too."

Qiao glared at him, chewing and swallowing an *umeboshi.* "I suppose."

Lionheart set down his chopsticks. "Listen, Qiao, I am not your enemy. Your enemies are up there in that mansion up in the hills. Wu Zhiming She. I went up there this morning, because one should study one's enemy given the chance. *If you know the enemy and know yourself you need not fear the result of a hundred battles.*"

Qiao snorted. "My father told you that?"

"Yes, but Sun Tzu wrote it first. Wise man. Maybe you've heard of him."

Qiao finished his tea. Before he could reach for the pot, Lionheart grabbed it and refilled Qiao's cup. Qiao paused and then reached out to tap his finger on the table. "I . . . am sorry. You are trying. You dropped everything to come to Hong Kong when my father called for you. I do not even know what you left behind. And you came anyway, and you have been a far better guest than I have been a host. I ask your pardon."

"You have it. You've been through a very trying time. I want to help. I can help. Tell me what I can do."

"You are the legacy of my father's teaching." Qiao poured Lionheart some tea without being asked. "What he taught you is the last thing he taught any student in this world. I would be honored if you would show it to me."

Lionheart blinked in surprise. "You want me to show you *shizi hou*? The Tibetan Lion's Roar?"

"I would be greatly honored to test myself against it."

Realization dawned upon Lionheart. "You want to spar."

Qiao stood and undid the sash of his tunic, letting the shirt fall to the ground. He was tightly-muscled like a middleweight boxer. "It would be an honor."

Lionheart removed his own tunic. "Likewise."

狮 和 五 致 死 蛇

The two men retired to the main courtyard where they wouldn't disturb the tranquility of the family's private courtyard.

They squared off a half dozen paces apart and bowed to each other in the manner most appropriate for each style. Qiao sank back into an oblique pose, one hand raised high over his head while extending the other toward Lionheart, palm up. Lionheart curled his fingers into fists with his thumb curled beside the fingers instead of clenched over them and extended his right fist forward while keeping the left centered over his heart. Without a referee to signal them to begin, they nodded to each other and commenced their battle.

Qiao immediately began circling around Lionheart, following the approach of *pakua chang* like a moon orbiting its planet. Lionheart grimaced; he hated circular fighting styles because his own *shizi hou* was much more direct in its combat style. Nevertheless, Qiao had asked to spar and Lionheart couldn't well deny the request of his host. He lunged forward, attacking with a low kick to knock Qiao off balance.

Qiao sidestepped past the kick and he was past Lionheart's guard almost before Lionheart could react. Qiao's elbow looped around and Lionheart deflected it aside and followed up with a straight punch up the gut, but once again, Qiao wasn't where the blow landed. As Qiao's arm snaked underneath Lionheart's, going for a grapple in advance of a throw, Lionheart threw himself sideways in a one-handed cartwheel. His feet came up in a blur and whiffed right past Qiao's face as he leaned back beneath the double strike.

Lionheart came back up to his feet and took a ready position. Qiao likewise assumed a new stance and the two men nodded, each accepting that the first bout had been a draw. Lionheart pulled his punches, not wanting to risk injuring Qiao with his greater than human level of strength, but Qiao had the fastest, most deft hands of anyone he'd ever battled, and he knew he'd have his hands full regardless of the other man's lack of powers.

The second bout began, lasting much longer than the first. The two men circled each other, trading blows and parries in a blur that made Lionheart feel like he was fighting against Pony Girl instead of Qiao. The man's circular style was highly effective and he avoided nearly all of Lionheart's blows whether from foot or fist. On the other hand, when Qiao successfully connected, Lionheart took the blow, trusting to his innate parahuman strength and toughness to absorb the blow and instead counterattack.

Master Chou had showed Lionheart a weapon called a tiger spear, which looked more like a pitchfork or a trident than a spear. When Lionheart asked about the construction, Master Chou explained that a tiger is a powerful, vicious attacker that will leap onto a spear even as it slays the wielder. The tiger spear was designed to keep the tiger at bay for that extra moment, perhaps long enough to kill the creature before it could land a lethal swipe or bite upon the spearman.

"You are much like a tiger in your body." Master Chou curled his fingers into the *hei hu quan* style fist. "You will absorb an attack to deliver your own. See that you do not become careless in your strength, for it will be your undoing."

"But how will I know when to absorb and when to defend?" Lionheart took on the combat stance Master Chou had taught him.

"Experience."

Master Chou had well and truly thrashed him that day. Lionheart's toughness had served him well enough to keep him out of the hospital, but little beyond that.

Qiao displayed few of the techniques that Master Chou had taught to Lionheart, and it was frustrating to face a truly skilled martial artist with an unfamiliar style that was little like anything else he'd encountered previously in his training.

Those damned circles were proving Lionheart's undoing. One moment he had Qiao squarely in his sights and the next, Qiao was nearly behind him. Lionheart was spending more time on defense and repositioning himself than on attacking. After several minutes, his sides were heaving and he knew his American diet and lifestyle was starting to catch up to him.

Qiao's leg blurred around and as Lionheart ducked beneath it, Qiao's second leg caught him squarely across the face and he tumbled across the tiles.

Lionheart tasted blood in his mouth and got back to his feet, his features twisting into a snarl.

Qiao stood in a combat stance, elbow presented forward while his other hand rose above his folded arm like a cobra raising its head. His lips curved into a slight smile; he knew he'd drawn first blood.

Lionheart leaped across the open space, covering the distance between him and Qiao in a flash. A handless cartwheel made Qiao move aside right into Lionheart's sweet spot for a roundhouse kick. He whipped it around in a continuation of his cartwheel. Qiao wasn't the only one who could use a circular attack pattern.

Qiao caught his foot and stepped around Lionheart, driving his elbow around to connect with the back of Lionheart's head. Lionheart dropped his weight, legs spreading in a wide split, pulling Qiao down to the tiles.

Ground-fighting was one of Lionheart's specialties, and he twisted around Qiao, working his legs into a superior position. Qiao was difficult to pin down, never seeming to be quite where Lionheart expected him with every move, but at last Lionheart got him into a lock. He bent Qiao's wrist inward as he extended the man's arm, pressing a foot against his neck. With only a little more effort, he could easily dislocate Qiao's shoulder. With a lot more, he could have torn the man's arm off or snapped his neck.

Qiao slapped at the tiles with his unencumbered hand to indicate his surrender and Lionheart released him. The two combatants returned to their feet and bowed to one another.

"Impressive." Qiao wiped sweat from his brow. "I did not expect you to be as fast as you are."

"You're a slippery bastard. There were a couple of times I think you could have had me." Lionheart checked his teeth to make sure they were all where he'd left them before the sparring match.

Qiao smiled. "I may have held back. It would not do for me to cause permanent harm to my house guest."

Lionheart felt a twinge of anger, but suppressed it, reminding himself that Qiao was not his enemy. "Yeah, and I could have torn off your arm and fed it to you."

Musical laughter made both men turn toward the edge of the courtyard, where Lihua stood beneath the pavilion at one corner, leaning against one of the red posts and watching. Beside her, Zheng Yaoting beamed at the two men before he commenced sweeping up the courtyard.

"*Da nanzi zhuyi.*" Lihua smiled. "Such machismo. You look like you should both be eating raw meat and drinking blood from the heart of your kill."

Qiao's expression turned sour. "Your teasing is rude."

"Lighten up, Qiao. Listen, you're very good, and I can't say honestly that you're not better than me. Your *pakua chang* makes you a tough opponent. I'd be honored if you would let me train with you."

Qiao bowed. "The honor would be mine, Shi Xin."

Lihua laughed again. "Oh, Qiao. You are almost drooling you want to work with him so badly."

"Lihua . . . you be still."

"Hey, be nice to the lady." Lionheart stepped forward, ready to battle for Lihua's honor.

"She is no lady. She is my sister. And she is a . . . a *bingchonghai.*"

Lihua stepped out from beneath the pavilion. "You call me a pest?"

"Want me to beat him up for you?" Lionheart grinned. Although he had no siblings of his own, he recognized the kind of verbal sparring that so often went on among the members of Just Cause.

Lihua snorted. "I can handle myself, thank you."

"You're trained?"

She sank into a low stance, balanced on one foot with her hands curved downward at the wrists, fingers pressed tight together into a beak shape. "Fujian White Crane. Care to try me, Shi Xin?"

Lionheart felt unsure whether such a thing was permitted. He looked at Qiao, trying to determine whether the insult would be a polite refusal or an eager acceptance of Lihua's offer. Qiao gave no indication. His face settled into a stoic, unreadable mask. He could have been made of granite, like Lionheart's friend John Stone, except for the raised welt high on his cheekbone where Lionheart had caught him with a glancing knuckle.

Lihua stepped out of her slippers and walked out onto the tiles of the courtyard. "Are you afraid to face me, Shi Xin?"

"No . . . I—I don't want to offend . . ." Lionheart felt the words backing up in his mouth. He hated sounding so unsure of himself. It reminded him of when he was younger, still in school, being bullied daily because of his inhuman appearance. The other children shunned him, spat at him, threw rocks at him. He knew it had toughened his skin below the surface, but deep down he had always longed for the acceptance that had evaded him all through his youth. When the gangs of students descended upon him, he'd never known whether it was worse to flee or to ignore or to stand his ground. Most days, it seemed that whatever path he chose, it was the wrong one. Now that he was faced with another difficult decision, his uncertainty was as fresh as it had been when he was in grade school.

Lihua put her hands on her hips and sniffed at him with exaggerated disdain. "*Zhen kexi ni fumu qin dangshi mei neng chuqu sanbu.*"

With a gasp, Zheng Yaoting dropped his broom. He looked scandalized. "Chou Lihua!"

Qiao's face broke apart as he burst into laughter. Lionheart felt his face growing hot as Lihua tittered while Qiao guffawed, eventually wiping tears away and collapsing onto a bench. "Oh, Shi Lian . . ."

Lionheart folded his arms. "I remember what that means. Lion Face. What did she say, Qiao?"

Qiao took a deep breath, struggling to keep his amusement in check. "She said *what a pity your parents didn't go for a walk instead.*" He lost it again.

Despite the clever insult, Lionheart found the humor in it, and soon he, too, was chuckling. "That may be one of the most subtle insults I've ever heard." He turned to Lihua. "In America, you could have just called me a pussy and left it at that."

"Does that not mean cat? Why would I call you a cat?" Lihua scrunched up her face in confusion, but Lionheart couldn't tell if she was still making fun of him or not.

"Believe me, it's more trouble to explain than it's worth." He velveted his paws, pulling the claws back inside his fingers so he wouldn't risk harming Lihua, and took a fighting stance. "Now, I believe you wanted to spar with me?"

If sparring with Qiao had been a difficult but enjoyable engagement, working against Lihua was an exercise in frustration. Her Fujian White Crane style proved to be Lionheart's undoing. In only a few seconds, she avoided his initial attack, returned with a flurry of counterstrikes that threw him off-balance, and finished him with a combination of a backhanded punch across the back of his neck and a leg sweep. He was on the tiles so fast that his head was still spinning as she lunged downward, her beaked hand halting right above his eye. She could have plucked it out with only the slightest additional effort.

Shocked and embarrassed at such a complete failure, Lionheart barely remembered to slap the floor in surrender. Lihua smiled down at him, her head framed by a swirl of cherry blossom petals caught on the breeze. She smelled of jasmine, and tea, and sweat, and Lionheart found it an intoxicating combination. "I'm impressed." He kept his voice to a throaty growl, barely above a whisper. He didn't want to desecrate the moment with anything more. "I've never been beaten so soundly or quickly."

Lihua nodded, still leaning over him. "There is much we can learn from each other . . . Shi Xin." Her voice was soft and melodic, a counterpoint to the tinkling of wind chimes around the courtyard.

Behind them, Qiao cleared his throat. "Yes. Lihua is skilled in Fujian White Crane. I do not think it would be sensible for one such as you to study it. It is not . . . appropriate for your fighting style and abilities."

Lihua stepped back, allowing Lionheart to regain his feet. "Wouldn't it be good for me to learn how to fight against it? I mean, she beat me in just a few seconds. What if I meet someone else in the future who fights like Lihua? Like she said, pal, there's much we can learn from each other. I can teach you *shizi hou*, as your father trained me. And you can teach me *pakua chang*, and Lihua Fujian White Crane. Between us, we should all become better warriors."

"Shi Xin is right, brother." Lihua clasped her hands before her and bowed her head. "I would be most honored to share my knowledge, and I would be grateful were he to teach you his."

Qiao rubbed his jaw. "It would make the school more attractive to students. We struggle to find those willing to come to our classes."

"It's only a school if there are students." Lionheart brushed dust off his furry chest. "Otherwise it's just an old building with a pleasant courtyard. More students mean it's harder for Wu Zhiming She to buy you out."

Qiao glanced at his sister. She smiled and nodded, encouraging him to make the right decision. "Very well. We shall work together. Perhaps we may yet keep Yingtao Mu the way our father would have wished."

Lihua stepped over to Lionheart and raised her hand, not to strike but to pluck away a piece of bark lodged in his mane. She showed it to him. "You could use a good bath and a combing."

"Thank you, I believe I'll do just that." Lionheart smiled down at her. "Perhaps you would help me comb out my mane? It's a hell of a chore and I never could reach all of it."

She lowered her eyes, not meeting his gaze, but she smiled. "I would be honored, Shi Xin."

Over her head, Lionheart caught Qiao's glare. It was clear Lihua's brother disapproved of the spark between her and Lionheart. Lionheart told himself to behave, that he was a guest and it would be inappropriate for him to act in any other fashion.

And despite that, when he looked down at Lihua, his blood raced.

Chapter Seven

*"Secret operations are essential in war; upon them
the army relies to make its every move."*
—*Sun Tzu*

Only seven students showed up for the evening class.

Lihua whispered to Lionheart it was fewer than they'd ever had before.

"Do you think the Five Deadly Serpents are scaring them off?"

"Yes." Lihua clenched an angry fist. "If we lose all our students, we cannot afford to keep the school open, to pay for expenses, or even to buy food. We will have to sell the school."

"And the Serpents will be only too happy to oblige." Lionheart grimaced. "Clever bastards."

Qiao spent a lot of time with the seven who came, giving each of them far more personalized instruction than they might have received in a class of a dozen or more. Most of them were young men, full of fire and eager to learn and display what they'd learned. One young woman came as well, and she had Qiao's eye as she walked the edge of the training circle, her hands following the prescribed forms.

"Your brother has an admirer." Lionheart didn't want to distract the students from their class and so he stayed to the shadows, watching from afar. He and Qiao would do their own training session later.

"Her name is Jinjing. She is the daughter of a fisherman." Lihua sniffed in ill-hidden disdain. "I do not think she is good enough for him."

"He seems to think otherwise." Lionheart watched as Qiao corrected a misplaced hand in Jinjing's form, gentle and attentive as a lover. "And you can't judge someone by their parentage. I'm a bastard, you know. I never knew my own father, and my parents were never married. For that matter, my mom is a waitress. Does that make me not good enough? Good enough for . . ." He stopped himself. He was going to say *good enough for you* and almost did before he realized where he'd been going. He couldn't allow himself to continue down that path. Qiao would be furious, and Lionheart knew that his presence might be the one thing stopping the Five Deadly Serpents from moving on Yingtao Mu. His reputation as an American superhero preceded him, and doubtless stories of his bigger-than-life escapades had traveled to China. He didn't know how long he could stay in Hong Kong, but he owed his old master a lifetime of service, and if that meant spending many years defending the school from would-be villains, so be it.

Fighting evil was already his stock in trade.

"Shi Xin . . ." Lihua stepped inside his guard with her quick, well-trained steps before he could respond. She glanced over toward where her brother was teaching a leg-sweeping technique to the students. His back was turned to them. She reached up to touch her hand to Lionheart's furry cheek.

"Lihua?" Lionheart's voice was barely audible, but it sounded like cannon fire in his ears.

She whispered to him, "You are good enough." Her palm traced down the side of his face and neck, brushing his chest for a moment before it was withdrawn. She shrank back further into the shadows. Lionheart could smell the desire wafting off her body. He wanted to take her in his arms, carry her back to his room, taste her skin with his rough cat's tongue. Instead, he made himself turn away and lock his fingers around the railing, anchoring himself in place.

Qiao would kill him. Of that he was certain. And in all fairness, were he in the same position, he'd have no problem murdering the would-be suitor of his sister if he'd had one to defend. Except *suitor* was an archaic term. Lionheart's desires were far baser than that. Surely, all he wanted was some rough-and-tumble with Lihua's exotic beauty. He was confusing lust for something deeper, wasn't he? His heart belonged to Faith.

But Faith was half a world away, and it might be years before he saw her again. Or it might never again come to pass. How long would he carry a torch for a woman he had no right to love? She was married, to a man Lionheart had dared to call his friend. The continuing consummation of their attraction would eventually be their undoing. He didn't have the right to tear apart the marriage between his friends. Perhaps he would be better served looking elsewhere to fill the void in his heart. But when he turned to look in Lihua's direction, he saw she was gone. He hadn't even heard her slip away. He filled his lungs with air and blew it out in a long, tension-draining sigh. He'd scared her away, of course. Most women found his leonine features too much to bear, and even though they desired to be with him on an objective level, his inhumanity intimidated them.

It was probably for the best.

He watched as Qiao wrapped up the lesson and instructed the students to spar in pairs for several minutes to finish their practice for the evening. The men paired off with each other while he and Jinjing circled each other, her graceful but amateurish techniques slow and awkward compared to Qiao's fluid movements. Lionheart studied the movements of the students, watching how they used the circular patterns as Qiao had taught them, how effective they could be when done correctly—or how ineffective when incorrect, he saw when one man mistimed a step and wound up getting his nose broken by his sparring partner. The crunching snap that came when knuckles intersected with bone made Lionheart cringe. His bones were made of stronger stuff than a normal human's, and he'd only suffered serious injuries when facing other parahuman foes.

Would Qiao, as well-trained as he was in the internal arts, be able to focus his *chi* effectively enough to hurt Lionheart? Could another highly-trained martial artist? Lionheart didn't want to find out the wrong way, but in the controlled environment of a training session, it would be useful information to have. He promised himself to speak to Qiao about it later.

At last, Qiao brought the class to a close and bowed to his students, thanking them for giving him the opportunity to teach them. They bowed back, honoring their instructor, and then filed out of the courtyard, laughing and slapping the back of the one whose tunic was bloodied and still held a sodden rag to his face.

Zheng Yaoting stepped out of the main house. "*Qiao sifu, yu yi zhunbei.*"

Qiao nodded. "*Xiexie.*" He saw Lionheart watching him. "I will bathe and then we will dine."

Lionheart bowed. Qiao walked past him into his own house at the side of the courtyard, opposite where Lionheart was staying. Lionheart sniffed at his own fur, wondering if he ought to bathe before dinner as well. For him, bathing was a fairly major operation thanks to all his fur, and he had to be cautious about what types of shampoo and conditioner to use. Fortunately, the fur itself exuded an odor that wasn't unpleasant for most people unless they found the smell of pets disgusting.

Since there would be some time before dinner while Qiao bathed, Lionheart wandered out into the courtyard and began trying to recreate some of the forms he'd watched Qiao instruct the students in during his class. He understood the basic idea of *walking the circle*, which formed the root of *pakua chang*, even if he didn't get a lot of the hand and arm motions correct. He found a worn circle painted upon the tiles, almost completely faded by years of feet tracking around it, and chose it as his starting point. He twisted his hips and shoulders to face inward, raised one hand high and kept one low, and started to walk around the circle. A younger Lionheart might have grown impatient with such training, not seeing the benefits to learning something that wasn't readily obvious as being useful in combat. But that was before his years of experience, and even in the few minutes he'd spent sparring against Qiao, he had to admit there was something to *pakua chang* after all, and he would be a better warrior and hence, a better person—by taking the time to learn it.

"You are doing it wrong."

Lionheart looked up to see Lihua watching him from the covered porch of the main house. He stopped his circle walk and smiled. "So show me."

She moved down to join him, stepping out of her slippers and positioning herself opposite him on the circle. "Your feet should move like you are stepping through mud, always turning inward, always stepping the same distance. Do as I do." She turned her hips forty-five degrees in and raised her inner hand up to shoulder height, palm facing the center of the circle. Her outer hand she placed several inches below the inner.

"Like this?" Lionheart struggled to match her posture. It was difficult with his barrel chest and broad shoulders, when she was as slender and flexible as the crane from which she took her fighting style.

"Relax everything. You are so tense I can see it from here." Lihua smiled. "Soften your shoulders. Let the small muscles hold up your arms, not the large ones. Your large muscles are tired and overworked. They will welcome the rest. Hollow your chest, as if you were embracing a ball. And . . . do not forget to breathe, Shi Xin. Center yourself, let your *chi* flow."

Lionheart tried to settle into his own body, to become one with the flow of life energy that he'd heard was supposed to suffuse him. Master Chou had talked about *chi* at length with him over their years of training, but it had all sounded pretty outlandish to Lionheart. He never really understood the idea of *chi*. Still, it was such an important part of Chinese martial arts, and he made an honest effort to try to get it.

Lihua took a step forward, sliding one foot along the circle just barely above the tile, and then put it down. Her hands stayed locked in place as if they were gliding along shelves at two different heights. Lionheart tried to match her step, finding the right angle and distance between his feet. "How was that?"

"Shhh." Lihua took another step, so Lionheart did the same. Then another. Then another.

The world seemed to grow smaller as they walked the circle. The small muscles in Lionheart's arms cried out at the task of holding his arms in place, but he worked through the pain and kept his shoulders relaxed. He became aware of the pattern of his own breathing, inhaling with one step and exhaling with the next. His heartbeat slowed into a rhythm, four beats for every step. The blood drummed in his ears as he walked. At first his eyes focused on his hands in front of him, but then that seemed too close. He imagined a pole at the center of the circle and focused his eyes upon that spot, even though there wasn't anything between him and Lihua. Then that spot became too close as well, and he looked past it until he fell into Lihua's eyes.

They were pools of obsidian, smooth as glass, soft as a baby doe, reflecting the starlight from above as well as the paper lanterns that hung around the courtyard. They entrapped him the way a moth circled in toward a light bulb until it died in a glorious combustion against the hot glass. He wanted to step into the circle, to cross it, to meet her in the middle. Instead his feet continued their slow, steady trudge around the circumference, his hands locked into place as he mirrored every move of Lihua's.

The sound of someone clearing his throat made Lionheart start in surprise. Lihua stepped back from the circle, surprise mixing with embarrassment on her face. She bowed her head, letting her hair flop forward to hide her expression. Lionheart blinked, feeling like he'd just been awakened from a deep sleep. He almost didn't have to look; he could feel Qiao's disapproval on his back. It was the same feeling that came from Faith's husband back home.

"Dinner is ready." Qiao's voice grated into the awkward silence. "If you are hungry, you may eat."

Lihua wouldn't meet Lionheart's questioning gaze. She fled the courtyard, mumbling something about needing to freshen up. Lionheart felt like he should say something to Qiao, but his host had already turned his back and went back into the main house. Left alone in the courtyard, Lionheart looked up into the starry night and wondered if he would ever figure out his personal life. He sighed and returned to his room to wash his hands and splash some cold water on his face. "What are you doing?" He regarded his reflection in the mirror. "You are here for Master Chou, nothing else." He almost felt like his reflection was going to chastise him in return, but the leonine face in the mirror said nothing unexpected.

Zheng Yaoting made a comforting, satisfying repast of sweet and sour pork and shrimp chow mein, served with a large bowl of fluffy rice and several pots of hot green tea. The four diners sat around a table of polished cherry wood. An ornate mahogany Lazy Susan held the platters of food and rice, and the others waited while Lionheart served himself first. He made a point of serving tea to the others, knowing it was a proper and polite thing to do.

They ate in frosty silence. Qiao studied his plate, never once looking up either at Lionheart or Lihua. His anger was palpable and Lionheart wondered if perhaps he ought to just let the man beat him to a pulp. He discounted the idea as impractical; if Qiao could really hurt him, it would make it that much harder for Lionheart to help defend the school. If Qiao couldn't beat him down, it would only strengthen the man's anger. Lionheart knew the best thing would be for him to stay quiet and as far away from Lihua as possible. Every time he arrived at that conclusion, he glanced up from his own plate toward the slender young woman and found her eyes meeting his. Her gaze carried the weight of worry, the sadness of disappointment, and the hunger of a would-be lover all at the same time.

It was driving Lionheart crazy.

After three of the diners had pushed the food around on their plates sufficiently to call the meal finished—Zheng Yaoting ate heartily, seemingly unaware of the stresses between the others—the housekeeper stood and bowed. "Would any of you care for wine?"

"*Wu.*" Qiao pushed away from the table. "Forgive me. I must record finances for the school. Lihua, you will help me."

Lihua shot an apologetic look in Lionheart's direction and then bowed. "Of course, brother." From the cast of her jaw, Lionheart could tell that a storm was brewing, and it would probably blow into full force as soon as the two of them were out of reasonable earshot of their guest.

Lionheart forced himself to look away from her, not to watch her as she departed in her brother's wake. He cleared his throat. "Actually, Yaoting, I'd love a glass of wine. Dinner was delicious."

Yaoting beamed at him. "Sir too kind."

Lionheart shook his head. "No, it really was good."

Yaoting brought over a dark bottle and filled Lionheart's cup. His hand shook the tiniest bit as he poured.

Lionheart didn't miss the shudder. "Are you all right?"

"Yes. Too kind, sir."

"Perhaps you'd like to join me in the courtyard? Have a glass with me? Tell me some stories about Master Chou before he left Hong Kong."

Yaoting smiled and his eyes fogged over with memories, but then he bowed and held up his hands. "Much cleaning to do. Thousand pardons."

Lionheart sighed. "Then I guess I'll enjoy this wine myself. Thank you, Yaoting."

Yaoting bowed again. "Mistress Lihua, good girl. Master Qiao, much anger."

"Yeah, I see that. Poor guy." Lionheart paused to take a sip of his wine. It was tart and crisp like a cinnamon apple. "Yaoting?"

The housekeeper looked up from where he was wiping the tabletop.

"She is pretty great, isn't she?"

"*Shi.*"

Lionheart knew that meant *yes.*

狮 和 五 致 死 蛇

A storm was brewing over the harbor. Heavy, dark clouds hung low, the speckle of lightning dancing across them in a constant flickering like flashbulbs at a press conference. The growl of thunder competed with the whistle of wind and the unsettled sea crashing against the docks. Even in New York, spring storms were the worst, thought Lionheart as he sat on the steps to his guest house, watching chilly rain pelt down into the courtyard. He'd much rather have been at the stone table in the courtyard's center, or even beneath the cherry tree at one end. The wind and rain were knocking down the brilliant blossoms like snowfall, and for some reason it made him feel sad. It didn't help that the wine was potent and it was unlocking a storm in Lionheart's heart that dwarfed the cloudburst overhead.

He could only tolerate the never ending spiral of thoughts for so long before the need to pummel something would become too great for him to withstand. Javier, who had an ear for offensive stereotypical jokes, had once related to him a chestnut about leaving an Irishman alone in a room long enough without anyone else to fight and he'd eventually beat himself to a pulp. Lionheart understood how that mythical Irishman felt. He could have punched his own face. Why was he fawning after Lihua like some pathetic teenager suffering from puppy love? He was twenty-seven years old; he should have been long past that clutching-at-daisies kind of behavior.

He finished his wine and thought about calling to Yaoting for more, but no, the old man had done so much for him already. Let him enjoy the rest of his evening without being disturbed by the loud and annoying American guest. Thunder banged overhead like someone pounding upon metal sheets with mallets. Maybe Yaoting wouldn't get the restful evening Lionheart wished upon him. It seemed the Chinese Rain God was well against anyone passing a peaceful night.

Light streamed out from the main house to Lionheart's left for a moment. He looked over, expecting to see Yaoting, off on one of his puttering errands around the *siheyuan*. Instead, his heart skipped a beat as he saw Lihua standing at the edge of the porch. She had changed her day clothes for a sky blue silken robe, printed with a floral pattern and tied shut with a black sash around her waist. Her hair was pinned up in preparation for sleeping. She looked at once vulnerable and desirable to Lionheart, and he thought maybe he should turn around and retreat inside his guest house for the remainder of the evening. A good thousand pushups might be enough to drive thoughts of Lihua from his mind.

It took him almost a full minute of staring at her while trying not to be obvious about it before he realized she was doing the same thing. They locked eyes and he knew he'd fallen into a snare. Almost without realizing he'd moved, he was halfway across the courtyard. It wasn't until the rain soaked through his fur to touch his skin that he noticed he was no longer sitting on the steps of his house. And Lihua was standing before him, rain dampening her hair as she gazed up into his eyes. The look on her face was one of longing.

"Lihua . . ." He didn't know what to say, but her name was like the scent of fresh-cut flowers and grilled steak and fresh coffee all at the same time.

"Shi Xin." She reached out to take his hand. It was warm like a fresh steel ingot in the cold rain. "This way. Quickly, before Qiao sees." She tugged at him and he let himself be led across the courtyard to a corner between the other guest house and the dividing wall between the family courtyard and the training courtyard. Right away, Lionheart saw it was hidden from view of the main house. Qiao would have to step out of the door and come all the way to the end of the porch before he spotted either of them.

Lightning flashed constantly overhead, and peals of thunder would have made conversation impossible, had that been the goal. As soon as Lionheart had stepped into the isolated corner Lihua had led him to, she spun around and melted into his arms. He knew he shouldn't, couldn't dare to, but his arms encircled her and his lips found hers. Some women were repulsed by his feline features; they saw his bifurcated upper lip, his squashed but broad nose, and the fur covering his entire face, and they ran the other way. Lihua didn't show the least bit of reticence as she dug her fingers into his mane, kissing him like she was possessed.

Lionheart's head spun like crazy as Lihua drove away the memories of Faith with her lips and teeth and tongue. Faith was a world away, but Lihua was right there with him, desiring him. She braced her arms around his shoulders and raised her legs to grasp his waist. She wore nothing under her robe and Lionheart felt the heat of her bare skin as he reached beneath her to support her. As he nuzzled her neck, she made a soft moaning sound, quieter than the thunder and more felt than heard.

He stepped back, still holding her clasped against him, until he had his back against the courtyard wall. He could have pressed her up against the wall, held her there, loved her until they were both satiated, but he didn't want to be the aggressor. Walking the circle with her earlier in the evening had a profound effect upon him, and he knew he didn't always have to charge in and throw himself into everything. She ground her hips against him, moaning again with greater urgency.

The hint of a new, unfamiliar odor crossed his nostrils. The stink of sweat almost vanished beneath the driving rain, the ozone from lightning, and the musky scent of Lihua's desire. Still holding her, he leaned his head back from her mouth for a moment. "Did you—"

Something dark and supple looped around his neck from above and tightened.

狮 和 五 致 死 蛇

Whatever it was, a leather strap or a silken rope, it squeezed Lionheart's throat shut in the blink of an eye. It jerked him upward, yanking hard enough to break the neck of a normal human but not to kill the leonine parahuman. Even so, his vision blurred out as blood flow to his brain cut off. He flailed at the noose with arms weighing a thousand pounds apiece.

Lihua's scream echoed in his ears like it came down a subway tunnel, but even as he was fading into unconsciousness, Lionheart realized it wasn't a cry of terror, but one of challenge and rage. Just as his eyes shut, the pressure on his neck released and he crumpled to the courtyard floor. His parahuman recovery kicked into high gear, blood rushing back into his head and air into his lungs. He raised his head just in time to see a half dozen black-garbed warriors boil over the courtyard wall like cockroaches in a New York apartment. Lihua stood over him, rain soaking her silk robe and her hair, which flopped loose, for she held a long, steel hairpin in each hand like a stiletto.

Six to one odds. Lionheart would die before he left someone he cared about to face that uneven of a battle. As the first warrior charged Lihua, she engaged him, her hairpins whirling in a blur as she sidestepped and stabbed him. Lionheart pushed off from the wall and bowled the second man over, using the expeditious method of ripping the man's face half off with one swipe of his claws.

More attackers came over the wall, their battle cries counterpoint to the thunder overhead, and instead of four, they had eight invaders coming at them.

Lihua fought another well-trained warrior, embedding one hairpin all the way to the handle in one of his arms but losing the other when he delivered a solid blow to her wrist from a tough angle. Lionheart leaped to her defense, grabbing the man and twisting his head until his neck popped.

Someone delivered a devastating blow to his kidneys and he roared in agony. He knew that later he'd suffer for that strike, but it wouldn't matter if the attackers succeeded in killing him and Lihua. As Lionheart staggered from the pain, Lihua stepped around him, spun around his attacker, and wrenched one elbow over the other, breaking it. Before she could follow up with a killing blow, another fighter kicked her ankles out from under her.

The attackers were everywhere, striking out from every direction. For every blow that Lionheart deflected or dodged, two more connected. Lihua wasn't a good ground-fighter, and he struggled to defend her as stomps and axe kicks hailed down toward her. The rain made footing treacherous as the battle raged across the courtyard. A hard kick to the side of Lionheart's thigh made his entire leg go numb and he folded. Then Lihua was the one standing over him, her soaking robe torn off one shoulder. She used the silken sleeve as a weapon, flicking it at the eyes of the attackers or looping it around careless limbs to trap for a moment.

Lionheart snagged one warrior's leg, hooking it with his claws and raking the black trousers to shreds. Dark blood mixed into the puddles of rainwater, streaming toward the gutters at the courtyard's edge. The man's acute screams of agony gave the others pause for a moment, long enough for Lionheart to regain his feet, although he couldn't put his full weight onto his damaged leg. He and Lihua backed against each other, meeting at a diagonal angle to their attackers, bracing one another up with their shoulders. They raised their fists, showing their readiness to engage the remaining six fighters.

"You're going to need a hell of a lot more men than you brought." Lionheart didn't care if any of them spoke English. Despite the pain in his leg, his kidneys, his swollen forearms, and what might have been two broken fingers on his left hand, he would remain defiant to the end.

"If you wanted to study kung fu, you should have come to our class today." Lihua spat blood into a puddle and squinted through a blackened eye. "But we will give you a free lesson tonight."

One of the black-garbed warriors spoke in a rough voice. "*Ni dai gei shuang quan jian zhandou.*" The others laughed. "You bring fists to a sword fight, *gweilo.*"

The attackers produced short swords from scabbards strapped to their backs.

Unarmed, wounded, and faced with six blades, Lionheart knew their moment was upon them. Tigers in the wild were known for jumping onto a spear to slay the man wielding it, hence the invention of the tiger fork weapon. The warriors' swords weren't tiger forks by a long shot, and Lionheart figured he'd take a sword in the guts if it meant one fewer fighter to threaten Lihua.

Qiao leaped out of the main house, leading with a spear twice as long as he was tall. He landed on the wet tiles, his weapon at the ready. "And you bring your little *jian* to a spearfight."

The invaders whirled to face the new threat. Qiao lunged at them, deflecting their swords aside as he advanced. The spear tip flashed in the lightning like a bird, its tassel the wings. Three of the combatants moved to flank him, leaving Lihua and Lionheart the remaining three. Qiao swung the spear around like ten-foot sword, making it whistle and hum even louder than the thunder. The blade cut through raindrops as they fell, making a fine mist spray in all directions.

Lihua stepped inside one fighter's guard, wrapping her tattered robe sleeve around his throat and snapping it tight. He fell without a sound, and she caught his sword before it could hit the tiles.

Lionheart dodged back as the remaining two warriors pressed him, flicking their sword tips at him, nicking bits of his fur away. He still had to favor his leg as it was unwilling to take his full weight. The warriors realized it and redoubled their efforts until his back was against the courtyard wall. As one swung at throat level for a decapitating blow, the other lunged in straight, leaving Lionheart only one possible defense. He twisted himself sideways into a one-handed cartwheel, diving over the straight-line attack while letting the swing whistle just behind his head and ahead of his legs.

The lunging attacker's sword went point-first into the wall behind Lionheart and stuck for an instant. As he came around in the cartwheel, he punched upward with his free hand in an open palm strike against the flat of the warrior's blade. It snapped in half, the handle flying free from the surprised man's hand. He fled, running for the far wall and the docks beyond.

The man who'd tried to take off Lionheart's head continued his swing around in a circle and brought it in at waist-height just as Lionheart's feet returned to the ground, catching him flat-footed.

Lihua leaped into the fray, deflecting the blow with the sword she'd taken from her last opponent. Lionheart was treated to an impressive display of swordsmanship as she battled the warrior across the puddles. The blades sang and shrieked as they whistled through the air and the rain against each other. Lihua danced back in a straight line, drawing her opponent away from Lionheart and giving him a chance to catch his breath. Blood ran down his arm, mixing with rainwater in his fur. He hadn't realized he'd been cut but one look told him it was pretty bad and would need stitching.

Lihua's robe gave up its last tatters and the sodden silk tore away, leaving her completely naked but for her sword. It caused a final, fatal distraction to one of the fighters facing Qiao, enough that he got the end of the spear across his throat. Lihua was nonplussed and transformed her straight-line battle into a circle. Her spinning dance around the side of the warrior was faster than he could shift his own strategy, and a moment later she sliced off his sword hand at the wrist. He screamed and fled.

Lionheart shook himself, realizing he was staring at Lihua. The way the rain pelted off her ivory skin while she ran to her brother's aid was enough to make him forget momentarily that they were all embattled in a fight for their lives. He gritted his teeth against the pain in his leg—and his arm, and his kidney—and charged into the fray.

Qiao lunged forward at one of his two remaining opponents and then drove the butt end of the spear back in a surprise punch to the other fighter, whose nose shattered in a spectacular spray of blood and gristle. He fell, making a blubbering sound.

The remaining man reached inside the back of his trousers and pulled out a short, ugly pistol. Before he could squeeze off a shot, Lionheart grabbed him from behind, yanked his head back, and tore out his throat.

Chapter Eight

*"He who knows when he can fight and when he
cannot, will be victorious."*
—*Sun Tzu*

With the survivors fled, Lionheart and the Chous had
two dead bodies and two wounded unconscious fighters
to deal with. They also had their own injuries, and none
of them had come through the combat unscathed
except Yaoting, who'd been smart enough to cower
under a table while the men in black had swarmed the
Cherrywood School. Qiao shouted rapid orders in
Cantonese to Yaoting while Lionheart and Lihua
staggered over to the two wounded and unconscious
attackers. Yaoting bustled over bearing a fresh robe for
Lihua to cover her nakedness.

When Lionheart yanked off the first man's mask,
the bloody ruin of his face made it unrecognizable, but
when Lihua removed the second man's mask, Lionheart
recognized the man's high cheekbones and pencil-thin
mustache. "The gloves. Pull them off."

They removed the men's gloves and discovered a
tattoo on the back of each man's left hand. It was a *hanzi*
character surrounded by a pentagon. Lionheart didn't
have to ask what the character meant; he'd seen it often
enough recently. "Serpent Warriors." Lihua rolled her

tongue around her mouth and spat blood into a puddle. "This attack was from the Five Deadly Serpents."

"Of course it was." Qiao hurried over with Yaoting in tow. The old housekeeper had his arms full of bottles and jars and scrolls. "Get these men out of my home and then I will treat your injuries."

"What about you? Aren't you hurt?" Lionheart nodded toward a bloodstain on Qiao's shoulder.

He looked down and sniffed in disdain. "It is not mine. The fighters I faced were rank amateurs."

Lionheart felt his mane bristle. "Yeah, we took care of the professionals before you showed up."

Lihua touched Lionheart's hand and it doused his surge of anger like water upon a candle flame. "We will remove these men. What of the dead?"

"They will not trouble us for the moment." Qiao glanced up at the clouds. Lightning reflected off his face. "The storm will wash away the blood. We will deal with the bodies soon." He turned to Yaoting. "Hot water. Apple-garlic tea. Cold compresses. Prepare a table in the main room and bring my *zhenjiu zhen*."

Lihua opened the courtyard gate and Lionheart threw both unconscious men out onto the street. He was neither gentle about his throw nor concerned about the force or destination of their landing. If they were further injured by his actions, so be it. He hurt all over now that combat had ended, and all he wanted to do was drink a fifth of scotch and pass out on his cot. Lihua shut and barred the gate and the two of them looked at one another with the exhaustion and camaraderie that could only come from fighting for their lives side by side.

They were careful not to touch each other by unspoken agreement as they entered the front room of the main house where Qiao and Yaoting had set up their trauma station. Yaoting had laid blankets and towels for the two to walk upon so as not to stain the floor or rugs with their blood.

Lionheart spotted a European-style chair with arms and a back. It beckoned to him as if to say it was the most comfortable resting place ever, although to be fair, he would have collapsed upon the hard wooden floor if it was all he had. Yaoting snapped a blanket over the chair and bowed to Lionheart. Lionheart was too exhausted to bow more than an inch as he collapsed into the seat. "Treat Lihua first."

"Shi Xin, you are our guest." Nevertheless, Lihua let Qiao move her onto the table, too tired to resist his goading.

"And you are family, and that is more important. I'm a superhero. I'll heal right up from this. I've had much worse." It wasn't entirely untrue of him to say that, but it had been years since he'd received such a thorough beating.

Despite her appearance to the contrary, Lihua's injuries were neither serious nor difficult to treat. By and large, she'd mostly suffered bruising from the stomping and kicking upon her when she had fallen. One of her eyes was swollen all the way shut. The most worrisome of her injuries was a deep cut to her tongue. Qiao used his *zhenjiu zhen*, acupuncture needles, to block the pain to her tongue while he cleaned the wound.

Lionheart struggled to keep his eyes open. He was pretty sure he was going into shock from the injuries he'd sustained. Yaoting held a bandage tight against the deep wound in his forearm, but Lionheart was only dimly aware of the housekeeper's presence beside him. He started when he realized Qiao was inserting needles into his arm.

"You have lost much blood. You should have told me of this wound." Qiao clucked his tongue in irritation.

"Hold still. I must assume your body has the same acupuncture lines as a normal human. Otherwise I cannot treat you."

"Do . . . what you have to." Lionheart's voice sounded hollow in his own ears, as if it was coming from a mouth much further away than his own.

"Yaoting, *ca die da jiu, datui he shoubi.*"

Yaoting opened a wide-mouthed bottle that looked like swamp water but smelled of powerful herbs in rice wine. Lionheart recognized the scent as the *iron hit wine* that Master Chou had used as a liniment for the portion of their training that required heavy impacts. Lionheart had often gone to bed smelling like he'd bathed in the stuff, but it kept him moving the next day and his bruises disappeared overnight. Yaoting bathed his injured thigh and forearm liberally in the mixture while Qiao spun the needles he'd placed along Lionheart's arm.

Lionheart went lightheaded, and barely noticed while Qiao stitched up the deep cut in his arm, slathered another liniment over the injury, and wrapped the whole thing up in a bandage. When his head cleared next, he discovered he was lying on the cot in the guest house. Qiao sat on a low stool beside him. "How long?" Lionheart grimaced at the unpleasant taste in his mouth, like he'd been sucking on a handful of rusty nails.

"Not long. You recover quickly. It is still raining." Qiao stood and walked over to stare out the window at the droplets as they tracked down the glass. "I . . . must say something."

Lionheart swung his legs off the cot. His thigh hurt, but he could move it, and felt like he might try standing up in a moment. His bandaged arm hurt as well. The more he moved, he realized, he hurt pretty much all over. Chinese medicine was all well and good, but he could have put some aspirin to good use. "I'm listening."

"I . . . am grateful that you are here. If you had not come, the Serpent Warriors might have killed Lihua. Perhaps all of us. You changed the balance of power. For that, I am grateful. For the rest . . ." He turned to look back at Lionheart. "I am . . . working on it."

Lionheart stood, testing his thigh. He could put most of his weight upon it. It might not be combat-ready, but at least he wouldn't be a complete invalid. Qiao's admission must have been extremely difficult for the pent-up young man to make, and Lionheart's respect for him grew. "You're very observant. It's hard to keep anything from you, Qiao."

"I see how she looks at you. As a brother, it is difficult. You are a *gweilo*. A ghost man. And you are Shi Xin. Lionheart. And you are a great warrior." He held up a hand to forestall any protest. "To fight beside you is an honor. You carry in your movements the spirit of my father. That is a marvel to me, that I should see him in so much of you. It is . . . difficult."

"I understand, Qiao." Lionheart clenched his fingers, feeling the stitches pull in his forearm.

"You will of course not mention this conversation to Lihua. It is best if she does not get her hopes up, for you will eventually leave."

"Oh, I don't know. I kind of like it here. The food is . . . I don't know, soulful. And it might be awhile before the Five Deadly Serpents finally leave you alone. I wouldn't leave before that happened. I swore an oath to your father."

"If I were to release you from it?"

"Then I'd camp outside your gate and still protect you from outside the walls."

A wry smile crossed Qiao's lips. "I believe you would, Shi Xin."

"How is Lihua?"

"She was less injured than you. Perhaps you should defend yourself better."

Lionheart snorted. "Yeah, that's good advice. Next time, don't get hit."

"Precisely."

"What are you doing about the bodies? The longer they stay here, the more likely it is that someone will discover them. I'm assuming you can't just ring up the Hong Kong police about it."

Qiao's amused smile vanished. "No. Corruption in Aberdeen is still a great problem. Many of the police are paid by the Five Deadly Serpents. It would be unwise for the bodies to be associated with the school. Yaoting is wrapping them up in rugs with stones tied to them. We can dispose of them in the harbor. The sea life will make quick work of their flesh."

"That's your plan? You and me carry a couple of rugs to the docks and drop them in when nobody's looking?"

"It is the best plan I can think of. I am not experienced in the removal of dead bodies. Perhaps it is a more common incidence in your New York City."

"Yeah, well, we're working on it." Lionheart scratched at his chin, discovering that it, too, was sore. "It's probably the best plan in the short term. You need a professional Mob cleaner to really make a body disappear. It's how they got Hoffa." He stretched, trying to will away some of the pain that still rattled around his body. "I'm ready if you are."

Qiao frowned. "I do not wish to leave Lihua here to defend the school by herself should the Serpent Warriors return tonight."

"Oh, I think we gave them a pretty good ass-kicking. They'll be up the hill, licking their wounds."

"You do not know that any more than I do."

"I haven't been here long enough to know my way around the docks. Plus I'll be carrying a couple of dead guys in rugs. And I have a lion's head. I think I might stand out just a little."

"Yes." Qiao looked miserable. "Which is why I shall have Lihua accompany you and I will stay here to guard the school."

No wonder he looked so upset, Lionheart thought. Oh well. He was never one to look a gift horse in the mouth. "Good idea."

狮 和 五 致 死 蛇

It seemed like it had been raining for hours by the time Lionheart and Lihua slipped out of the gate from the school. Perhaps it had, thought Lionheart as he struggled with the large, unwieldy package of two dead bodies. They were wrapped in rugs, weighted down with rocks, and tied to a bundle of bamboo that kept them from flopping around in the way that dead bodies were prone to doing. It would have been difficult enough to transport them in full-on sunshine on dry cobblestones, but the rain was making it damn near impossible. The rugs tied around the bodies were soaking up rain water, and getting heavier with every step. Lionheart gave no consideration to shoes at all; his claws and bare feet would give him the best traction on uncertain terrain, especially once they reached the docks proper and had to travel across a network of gangplanks between junks and *sampan* out in the harbor.

"I thought Chinese people were supposed to be little. These guys feel like they all ate rocks for dinner." Lionheart blew rain water away from the edge of his poncho hood. He'd pulled it as far forward as he could to hide his features from anyone who happened to be braving the rain besides the two of them.

Lihua chuckled beside him. She'd dressed in practical clothes—loose-fitting trousers, a baggy tunic, and a broad reed hat shaped like an upside-down punch bowl. "You are a big, strong superhero, Shi Xin. Suck it up."

"Did you actually just say that?" He hefted the waterlogged parcel from one shoulder to the other. The exceptional weight wasn't helping his post-combat soreness at all. "You're welcome to carry this for awhile."

"No, it is better that anyone who sees us remembers me, not you."

"Let them recall the pretty face, right?"

Lihua bowed her head forward to hide her face from Lionheart, but he could tell she was smiling just the same.

"Lead on, Lihua. There aren't enough words in the English language for me to say how ready I am to crawl into my cot and sleep for a week."

Lihua led him up the road, past several more *siheyuan* until they reached a cross street that led directly toward the Aberdeen Floating Village. As they slogged down the wet cobbles toward the harbor, the rain began to let up as a breeze carried the storm clouds back out to sea. Lionheart sniffed at the moist air. The rain had rinsed away much of the accumulated filth that seemed to be common to all poor villages, but that meant that the harbor was awash in dusty mud, garbage, and waste. It made Lionheart's nostrils flare at the odor. He grimaced, wishing as he sometimes did that his nose wasn't quite so sensitive.

Lihua stopped before stepping from the cobbles onto the planks of the docks. She nodded her head to the left. "That way is the private dock of the Wu Zhiming She. Right behind our school."

Lionheart shifted his unwieldy parcel from one shoulder to the other. "No wonder they want your building. A couple of strategically-placed shipping containers and nobody would ever see what they were moving in or out of the school." He squinted beyond the edges of his hood. "Does it always rain like this?"

"Only in the spring." Lihua touched his arm with fingers that were warm despite the chill of the rain. "Come. From here we must cross the junks and *sampan.*"

"We just walk across other people's boats?" Lionheart looked out at the hodgepodge floating village. Some boats were tied together in rough rows, old tires lashed to their hulls to act as shock absorbers. Others seemed to be glommed together in amorphous blobs with no rhyme or reason. Many of the boats were dark because of the late hour, but others had the warm glow of paper lanterns hanging beneath their curved covers. A few early morning fishermen were already tightening their lines, preparing to head out beyond the harbor. Somewhere, a baby was crying and somewhere else, Lionheart could hear a couple making love with soft, rhythmic moans.

"Yes. Unless you can fly and have not told me."

"If I could fly . . . Man, I've always wished I could. Almost everyone else on Just Cause can. It's weird being stuck in traffic while everyone else is flying overhead."

"It must be amazing, being surrounded by such magical beings. Like spirits and gods."

"They're not gods. They're just regular people like you and me."

"You are not regular people." Lihua moved to stand right in front of him, looking up at his lion face beneath his hood.

"I'm not a spirit or a god."

"I would not care if you were." She reached her hand around the back of his neck and pulled his head down to her. Like her fingers, her lips were warm and when they touched his, it was like an electric shock running all the way through to the tips of his toes. He wouldn't have been surprised if his mane was standing on end. He growled, deep in the pit of his throat, not borne of anger, but of desire.

The unexpected sound made Lihua step back, alarm on her face. "I'm sorry!" Lionheart bowed his head forward, letting the hood obscure his face. "I didn't mean to scare you."

Lihua brushed wet hair off her forehead. "I was not scared, only surprised. As much as I . . . desire you, there are still things about you that I am discovering."

Lionheart managed a ghost of a smile. "Hell, lady, I'm still discovering things about me too."

"Come. Step quickly and lightly as you cross the decks. They may be slippery, and there may be clutter." Lihua trotted up a plank onto the deck of a darkened junk.

Lionheart shouldered his burden and followed her as best he could. Crossing the floating village was unlike anything else he had ever done in his life. The closest approximation he could think of was trying to run across a water bed. The boats shifted beneath his weight and the decks were slippery from the rain, as Lihua had warned. More than once he nearly lost his balance, which would have sent both him and the bodies careening into the water. Although the latter was the eventual goal of their journey across the floating village, Lionheart had to admit that he wasn't keen to get his fur any wetter than it already was from the unrelenting rain.

Most of the boats they crossed were silent, but as they stepped onto the decks of a couple, sleepy voices inquired after them in Cantonese. Lihua muttered something in reply that seemed to satisfy those who were mostly asleep. She led Lionheart across boat after boat until they were out near the middle of the waterway that allowed boats to travel out to sea. The rain was lessening and the clouds were growing lighter over the ocean. "Hurry. Do not let them splash, slide them instead."

"Anybody looking?"

"None that I can see, but we will not know unless someone questions us."

"Here goes nothing." Lionheart crouched down by the edge of the junk upon which they stood and slipped the bundle of dead men over the side. They sank right away, leaving behind only ripples and a small patch of bubbles to mark their watery graves. "Should we wait to see if they come back up?"

"No. Better we are long gone."

"You're the boss. Lead on, pretty lady."

They crossed the floating village again, taking a different route across the boats until they reached the land. The rain stopped during their return journey and a freshening breeze blew off the ocean, redolent with its clean, salty smell. They stopped once they reached the shore and paused to watch the sun peek over the edge of the water, lighting the clouds like fireworks.

Lihua took Lionheart's hand but said nothing as they drew in breaths of fresh air and let the early morning sun warm their faces.

At last, he yawned so hard he was afraid he might split his face open. "Let's go home. Back to Yingtao Mu."

Lihua smiled up at him.

狮 和 五 致 死 蛇

A pair of navy and white Ford Cortinas were parked out front of the school entrance, clearly marked with the Royal Hong Kong Police crest. Lihua gasped when she saw them and started to run toward the school, only to be brought up short when Lionheart grabbed her and pulled her back around the corner of a building.

"What are you doing? I must go see what has happened!" She struggled to pull away from him, forgetting her training in her concern.

"Lihua, stop and think for a second. You think those cops are there to take statements about what happened tonight?"

"What? No. How would they even know about it?" And then her eyes widened as she realized what must have happened. "No. How could they? They are the police. They are supposed to be guardians."

"Yeah, protect and serve. I get it. I've heard that the Hong Kong Police are corrupt. I mean, like, New York corrupt."

"Not so much recently. The new officials have been working hard to root it out." Lihua peeked around the corner of the building.

Lionheart leaned around as well, looking over Lihua's head while keeping his own well-covered with the hood. "You know damn well it was the Five Deadly Serpents who tipped them off. If we hadn't been disposing of the bodies, we'd be getting questioned too. They sent two cars."

"Four officers. Qiao could defeat them without trouble. They are poorly trained."

"Yeah, but he's smart enough to know not to do that. If he was to fight them, he'd be playing right into the Serpents' hands. All we can hope for is that he's keeping his cool and answering their questions without implicating himself."

"Keeping his cool?" Lihua snorted. "Have you met my brother?"

Lionheart chuckled. "Yes, I'm sure he's making friends left and right. Let's get a little closer, but you can be sure they'll want to talk to us if they find us."

Another car pulled up in front of the school, all black with small British flags fluttering from the quarter panels. "That is a government car. Why are they here?" Two white men in dark suits got out of the back seat of the car while the uniformed driver, also white, stood outside beside it.

"I don't know. Come on, keep close to the buildings, keep your head down. Don't look directly at them, but you can glance in their direction. That way you look like a typical curious pedestrian and they'll forget you as soon as they look away."

Lihua ignored his directive and walked straight toward the British car. Lionheart hissed through his teeth. "Lihua!" But he didn't dare follow her. He was in the country legally, at least, but it would be at the least awkward and at the worst an international incident if he was found out to be mixed up in some kind of legal trouble. He shrank back into the shadows as much as he could, given the sun was making its inexorable climb.

Lihua went right up to the driver of the government car and asked him in stilted English what was going on. He told her politely to mind her own business, it was an official police investigation. Lihua bowed, smiling through her bruises, and turned away. She came back to where Lionheart was doing his best impression of a wall. "We all look the same to the British. He would not recognize me even if he had been looking." She glanced back. "I think Qiao is in trouble."

"I know he is." Lionheart nodded toward the door of the school. Qiao came out, wearing handcuffs, flanked, preceded, and followed by police officers. The two British officials came out last. One of them took a sign and stapled it to the door, showing no regard for the honor of the building. Qiao's face was red with barely-suppressed fury as he climbed into the back of one of the police cars. Lihua took a step forward and Lionheart had to restrain her. "Don't, Lihua. You'll only get yourself arrested too."

"But . . . Qiao!" Tears ran unchecked down her cheeks.

"This is not the fight you want. It's not one you can win. As long as he's not there, the school is defenseless. It's up to us." He clasped her hands. "I'm sorry." He watched in impotent anger as the police car containing Qiao drove away into the dawn.

Chapter Nine

"Being deeply loved by someone gives you strength,
while loving someone deeply gives you courage."
—*Lao Tzu*

Once they were sure the police had left, Lionheart and Lihua hurried up the street to look at the sign the police had left upon the door. "*Closed by order of the Police.*" Lihua snarled like a tiger. "Who do they think they are? Dishonorable sons of whores."

"They're the pawns of the Five Deadly Serpents." Lionheart glanced around to see if anyone was watching, careful to keep his hood pulled forward. The fewer people who saw his unusual features, the better. Only a few pedestrians and bicyclists were out on the street, and all of them were hurrying to their various morning appointments and jobs. Nobody was giving the school the least bit of attention. More importantly, he didn't spot anyone observing the school nearby or making a careful effort not to be. If there were more cops in the area, they were very good at hiding themselves. He decided he should be the one to draw unwanted attention if it came, and he pulled down the sign himself. "And nobody closes this school unless it's you or your brother."

Lihua gave him a grateful smile, but then that smile vanished and her eyes widened. "Yaoting!"

Lionheart realized they hadn't seen the old housekeeper taken out with Qiao, and they hurried inside the *siheyuan*.

The door between the training courtyard and the family courtyard gaped open with a large crack running halfway down from the top of the door as if it had been kicked open. Lihua rushed through it and stopped so suddenly that Lionheart nearly bowled her over. Yaoting knelt in the middle of the family courtyard, his head bowed, dampening his lap with tears as he sobbed.

Lihua ran over to him. "Yaoting! Oh, Yaoting!"

She raised his chin and Lionheart saw that someone had slugged the poor fellow. One side of his face was swollen and a large, ugly bruise was forming around one eye. "Come on, let's get him indoors and put something on this bruise." Lionheart helped Yaoting to his feet. The housekeeper swayed, barely able to stand upright. Lionheart put his arm around Yaoting's shoulders and he and Lihua led the distraught man into the main house.

Yaoting babbled in broken Cantonese, stammering through sentences and blubbering. Snot mixed with blood from a bruised nose, making a pinkish froth on his cheek.

"He says the police came and accused Qiao of murder, but they were angry that they couldn't find any bodies. They saw his weapons rack and decided to charge him with assault. There is not a school in China that does not have the same rack. It is part of our heritage, Shi Xin!" Lihua snorted in disgust. "Yaoting argued with them and they hit him."

Lionheart shook his head. "It wasn't Yaoting's fault. There wasn't anything he could have done." He looked over the collection of salves and balms Qiao hadn't yet put away after treating his and Lihua's injuries. Half of them were marked with *hanzi* characters that meant nothing to him and the other half were unlabeled. He reached out, uncertain, and stopped with his hand halfway toward the tray. "What's the best one to use here?"

Lihua glanced over. "The brown jar with the red lid. Be careful you do not get any in his eye." She hugged Yaoting's head, gently stroking his hair as he sobbed. "*Wo hen baoqian, Yaoting.* He did not deserve this."

"None of you deserve this." Lionheart opened the jar and blinked as a strong menthol odor emerged from it, strong enough to make his nose run and his eyes itch.

"He is family in all but name. Many times when Qiao and I were younger, and the absence of our father weighed heavy upon us, Yaoting would comfort us with tea and sweets and funny stories." Lihua stood. "I am a poor storyteller, but I will make him some tea. He has made plenty for us over the years." She bowed to Yaoting and went back toward the kitchen.

Lionheart wasn't in the habit of comforting others. Doing so was more the kind of specialty of other, more feminine members of Just Cause. Nevertheless, Yaoting needed someone to take care of him, at least until he got himself under control. He sniffled as Lionheart spread salve across the swelling on his face. Whatever was in the mixture turned Yaoting's skin an angry red that generated unusual heat for a few minutes before fading. "I think you're going to be all right, Yaoting."

Yaoting put on a brave expression. "Y-yes."

"Don't worry. We'll get Qiao back, and get all this sorted out. I promise you that."

"Do not make promises lightly, Shi Xin." Lihua returned to the room, bearing a tray of tea leaves steeping in porcelain bowls and some sticky rice balls.

Lionheart stood and looked at her. "I don't. One way or another, I intend to save this school." He stalked back outside to the courtyard, needing the peaceful *feng shui* of the cherry blossom tree and the shrine after the exhausting night's events. Having faced so much discrimination over the course of his life because of his inhuman appearance, it had been remarkable to find himself so accepted by a stranger who had no business being that way. It was one thing to make an impassioned promise to the cheerful housekeeper who had been nothing but polite to Lionheart since his arrival, and quite another to defeat an entire Triad.

Lionheart didn't know how he was going to do it.

Time passed. The sounds of the docks carried over the courtyard walls. Fish, coal smoke, and Diesel fuel overpowered the scent of the sea. The sun wove behind high clouds shaped like fish scales. Shadows crept across the courtyard floor. He considered the possibility of contacting his friends in Just Cause. To help a teammate, he knew they would travel halfway around the world without a second thought. He would do the same if he was in the same position. The problem with that solution was they would leave New York—really, the entire East Coast—undefended were some new threat to arise. Destroyer's emergence during the Blackout of '77 had unleashed a wave of new parahuman criminals who had no compunctions about challenging Just Cause on their own terms. Just Cause had battled gangs like the Bowery Boys and the Warriors, who'd taken their name and schtick from the film of the same title. Individual parahumans rose to power like the Black Spade, Karate Charlie, Sista Sedgwick, and the Persuader. Gang members flocked to them, taking on their colors and fighting tooth and nail, block by block for territory until sooner or later they crossed paths with Just Cause. The new generation of gangsters were heavily armed, fearless, and felt they were owed the world and would do whatever they could to take it. After half a decade of quiet times in New York, the Blackout had unleashed a new crime wave like none the city had seen. Just Cause had its hands full trying to keep the peace, and Lionheart couldn't justify taking away the city's peacekeepers for something as small as a single Triad.

Lihua slipped out of the main house, carrying a pair of clay mugs. She had changed from the stained outfit she'd worn for their body-disposing adventures into another silken robe tied around her slender waist. It was a shimmering teal that shifted between sea green and indigo as clouds passed across the sun, and whispered as she set one mug beside Lionheart and then sat at the table. The scent of jasmine tea tickled Lionheart's nose, chasing away the memory of the menthol from Qiao's medicine jar. "Yaoting?"

"He is sleeping. I mixed his tea with rice wine."

"Good." Lionheart sniffed at his own tea and was a bit disappointed not to have his similarly doctored. He could have used a strong belt of something after the events of the previous night. The hours were catching up with him and he yawned, stretching a crick out of his neck.

"What are you thinking, Shi Xin?"

Lionheart turned to look at Lihua. Her eyes were wide and dark, one still ringed with a fading bruise. Qiao mixed good medicine. Back home, she'd be sporting the marks of her battle for a good week or more. Here, it might only be a couple of days. In spite of that, she still looked beautiful to him. Desirable. He needed a change of direction in his thoughts, to keep his focus better. "Do you know how I met your father?"

"Only vaguely."

Lionheart sipped his tea. It was sweetened with honey and left him licking the sweetness from his lips. "I was young. Younger than you are now. I'd been wandering across the country, working odd jobs, saving up until I had enough to eat and gas up and sleep a few nights somewhere and then I'd move on. I didn't know at the time what I was running from, or what I was looking for." He stared at the blossoms of the tree in the courtyard as they twisted in the breeze. "Anyway, I was in this little nowhere town outside of Chicago. It doesn't even matter what it was called. I was washing dishes. It was the kind of work someone who looked like me could get. It paid shit. Most jobs like that did, but when you're hungry and someone gives you a sponge and says they'll pay you to wash pans, you wash the damn pans."

"Wash the damn pans." Lihua smiled. "I will remember that."

"Your father was sitting in this diner I was in, eating some soup. I didn't know who he was. I barely even noticed him. Instead, I was watching this biker gang roll into town. You have biker gangs here?"

"I have not noticed if we do. Some of the Triads ride motorcycles, but then, many Chinese do."

"These guys were bad. I mean, they were real bad. Their leader was this big dude with actual horns. It was the first time I'd ever seen someone like me."

"You do not have horns." Lihua reached up, hesitated, and then stroked his mane.

It was distracting in the best sort of way, but Lionheart knew she would want him to finish the story. "No, but I could tell he was strong like me. Tough. A real bad mother, you know? He and his gang started, you know, causing trouble. Hassling people in the diner. Hassling the waitress. So I . . . got involved."

"You fought them?"

Lionheart drank some more tea, licked his lips, and smiled. "You could call it that. I got in a few good blows, and then they overwhelmed me. Like I said, they were real bad people. The leader, he was going to kill me, and there wasn't anybody who could stop him, except your father." He finished his tea. "He stepped in, did some kung fu to the leader. Knocked him out. Saved my life. Then he told me I was a great warrior and a great fool."

Lihua laughed. "That sounds so much like something he would say. He was . . . fond of calling others *fool.*" Her eyes sparkled.

"Nobody ever delivered that four-letter word like a *real* four-letter word the way he did." Lionheart grinned. "He asked if I was coming and stupid me, I almost said no. But then I realized what kind of opportunity was before me and I said yes. I traveled with him for a long time after that, and he taught me everything I know about fighting. He was a great warrior, but he was definitely no fool."

Lihua slipped into Lionheart's lap and brought her face close to his. "Neither are you, Shi Xin."

Her lips tasted of honey-sweet tea.

Lionheart didn't remember the two of them leaving the courtyard, because his reality had become a burning mixture of lust and exhaustion. They found themselves in his guest house, slipping each other out of their clothing as they kissed. The silk curtains across Lionheart's windows billowed as the breeze picked up, cooling the sweat that glistened on Lihua's skin and matted Lionheart's fur as they melded into one another.

Her fingers traced maps into the fur of his chest as she straddled him. Her hair, no longer pinned up, hung down like a raven-colored waterfall, sweeping back and forth across his muzzle as she ground her hips upon his. Each breath was punctuated by gasps of her pleasure and groans of his. He pushed himself up onto his knees, his hands beneath her as she continued her gyrations upon him. Their lips met again and again until her face was reddened by his whiskers and his fur was damp. Still they plied against each other, vying to reach every moment of pleasure, anxious to share it with the other.

Their lovemaking carried them from Lionheart's pallet to the mat beside it, across the floor, and at last to a support beam of dark wood between whitewashed walls. He pressed Lihua's back against it and her nails carved furrows through the fur of his back as he drove into her until she shuddered and clenched around him with her entire body. At last he could hold himself back no longer himself and he gritted his teeth in a practiced snarl as he spent himself, doing so to keep from accidentally biting her.

Satiated, satisfied, they both fell to his pallet, exhausted to the very core of their beings. For once, Lionheart wouldn't even have minded some pillow talk, as he was fast finding Lihua to be the most fascinating woman he'd ever met. His body had other ideas, and he fell asleep between heartbeats, one of his arms beneath her head, one of hers splayed across his chest.

Chapter Ten

"Never give a sword to a man who can't dance."
—*Confucius*

Lionheart awakened sometime after dark. The breeze blowing through his windows had turned cool and damp with the potential for more rain. It took his eyes a moment to adjust to the near-darkness. He and Lihua had lit a dozen candles at some point during a lull in their lovemaking, but only one was still burning, and its wick was short amid a puddle of wax. Gentle shadows flickered across the walls as the small flame danced in the light breeze from the open windows. Although he didn't have actual cat's eyes, his night vision was exceptional. He laid on his pallet, enjoying the warmth of Lihua's arm across his chest as she slept, her head tucked into the nest of his shoulder, her face like a pale moon amid the nighttime sky of her hair. Even having slept all day after a fight, disposing of bodies out in the floating village, and then a marathon lovemaking session, she still smelled delicious, like flowers and fresh-cut grass.

A soft footstep outside Lionheart's guest house informed him why he'd awakened. He sniffed the air but it gave no indications of anything amiss. Nevertheless, it required investigation, and he slipped out from beneath Lihua's arm with great reluctance. She stirred a bit and murmured something in Cantonese. He knelt down beside the pallet for a moment, drawing in the scent of her hair, of her skin, of their recent loving. It was as invigorating as a good strong cup of coffee. Or tea, he supposed, since that was more likely what he'd find in his cup in Hong Kong. He pulled on a pair of drawstring sweatpants from the pile of recently-laundered clothes that Yaoting had cleaned for him—one more reason he was beholden to the housekeeper.

He slid open the door of his guest house, moving it as slowly as he could to remain silent, and padded outside barefoot, stopping beneath the eaves to let his vision acclimate to the night sky and taking in the scents on the breeze. No sound nor odor arose to heighten his suspicion, and he began to think he'd imagined hearing the sound upon awakening.

Then he caught the quiet hiss of wood sliding upon wood and turned to look toward the bathroom, which was a building connected to one end of the main house but could only be accessed from outside. Yaoting stepped out of it, wrapped up in a thick robe and shuffling his slippered feet across the porch.

"Yaoting . . ." Lionheart spoke softly, not wanting to frighten the housekeeper.

Yaoting jumped at the sound, but then smiled as he saw Lionheart's mane. "Shi Xin."

"Are you well?"

"Yes. *Xiexie.* I sleep more. Make breakfast then."

Lionheart smiled. "Good idea. I'm glad you're feeling better. Rest well. I'm going back to bed myself." He hesitated, wondering if he ought to say something about his and Lihua's tryst. Yaoting gave the impression of a well-meaning bumbler, but Lionheart could see that the man's experienced eyes missed very little. He probably knew Lihua and Lionheart would wind up in bed together before the two of them had quite figured it out themselves. Since he had the good graces not to bring it up, Lionheart decided to hold his own tongue about it to preserve Lihua's dignity.

"*Shui de hao*, Shi Xin."

"Good night to you, Yaoting. Sleep well." Lionheart watched the housekeeper head back into his own private house. He yawned. A few more hours of dozing in Lihua's arms sounded like just what the doctor ordered to get him feeling back to his old self. He turned back to return to his room and froze.

Something was wrong.

His hackles rose, making his mane stand out even more than usual. He opened his senses wide, letting the odors of the air speak to him, listening for any variation in the sounds of the night. He wished he could pause his own heart so he could hear better. What had raised his sense of alarm?

The door. The door to his room. He slid it open to exit, and as he'd passed through it, by habit he slid it most of the way shut, leaving it unlatched so the sound wouldn't alert whoever had awakened him before he'd realized it was Yaoting. But perhaps it hadn't been the housekeeper after all, for the door was open to a width of several inches. It wasn't much—Lionheart couldn't have fit through that opening, but someone small and slender could have.

He took a deep breath, letting oxygen fill his system. His pulse pounded in his ears as he prepared his body for battle. If he was wrong, he'd burst in, terrify Lihua, and needlessly worry everyone. But if he was right . . . He went through the door—not sliding it aside, but shouldering it off its tracks as he rushed into the bedroom.

A figure wrapped in darkness crouched over Lihua, clutching a sai with a blade coated in a thick, pungent substance. His nostrils twitched even in the fraction of a second it took for him to catch a hint of the smell. There was no time to identify it as anything beyond poison.

The figure whirled as Lionheart crashed through the door. Something bright flashed toward him and he twisted aside, catching a good look at the four-pointed metal stars as they flashed within an inch of his face. *Shuriken* were Japanese, like the sai in the attacker's hand, and Lionheart had a very short list of Japanese people in Hong Kong who might wish harm upon Lihua.

Lihua rolled off the pallet and immediately moved into a fighting position. She was unharmed; Lionheart couldn't smell any fresh blood in the room, so he'd arrived just in time. He growled in the back of his throat and spread his claws. "Kobura!"

"*Rai on hato.*" Her voice was ragged as the first time he'd heard her, up in the Five Deadly Serpents' training center above Aberdeen. She was wrapped up in black like a stereotypical ninja, but when she melted back into the darkest part of the room, Lionheart lost her altogether.

"Where is she?" Lihua crouched in defense, walking a small circle, trying to watch in all directions at once despite the darkened room.

"I can't find her." Lionheart couldn't even smell her. How had she escaped? And then, as sudden as a bolt of lightning, she was behind him, her poisoned sais swinging around toward his throat. He thrust himself backward, bowling into her as he blocked her wrists with his forearms. He followed up with a vicious elbow strike but connected with nothing. It was as if she had vanished altogether.

A sai lunged at him from a different, unexpected direction and only by sheer luck did he manage to avoid it piercing his side. He twisted aside and struck at Kobura's wrist. She hissed at him and vanished into the darkness again. A cold shiver ran down Lionheart's spine as he realized the truth about Kobura. "Watch out, Lihua. She's a parahuman."

Kobura appeared from a shadow again, behind Lihua's graceful form, barely clothed in a thin silk nightshirt. Out of range, with no other options, Lionheart lunged downward, digging his claws into the carpet, and yanked upon it with all his might.

The jerking carpet spilled both Lihua and Kobura to the floor. Lihua lashed out with her feet, kicking at Kobura's face. The ninja grunted as one of Lihua's heels connected, and then Lionheart did smell fresh blood. He bared his teeth in a snarling grin. A bloodied nose or lip would make Kobura's ability to hide herself a lot tougher, because he didn't have to depend solely upon his eyes to fight an opponent.

He laid himself out in a lunging dive, slapping aside Kobura's sai like a cat batting at a moth. As one hand connected, tearing through the fabric over one shoulder, her knee came up into his abdomen in a blow that would have ruptured the organs of a normal human. They wrestled across the floor, her speed and agility making up for his strength and innate toughness, so that neither of them managed to gain the upper hand. He raked at her thigh with his claws and she jabbed at his eyes with stiffened fingers. He blocked her disabling blow and she brought her legs around him in an attempt to squeeze the life out of him.

"Not going . . . to happen . . . in this lifetime." Lionheart brought an elbow up into Kobura's side. He felt a rib creak and she rolled off him, hissing like the serpent for which she'd taken her name.

Lihua retrieved a bamboo curtain rod and went after Kobura with it. The slender pole whistled through the air as she lunged and swung, driving the ninja back across the room.

Kobura backed into a flickering shadow and vanished.

"No!" Lihua thrust the pole through the spot where Kobura had been but contacted nothing.

Lionheart sprang to his feet, keeping himself in a low fighting stance with his hands extended, ready to defend. She was still in the room; he could smell her blood, even if he couldn't see her. Another *shuriken* flashed out of the shadows at him, fast enough that he couldn't dodge. He got his hand up in front of his face just in time as a sharpened point went right into his palm. It burned, as if he'd dipped his hand in acid, and he roared in surprise and pain.

Poison was a coward's weapon. It had taken away Master Chou. Perhaps it had been delivered at the tip of one of Kobura's blades.

She would never poison another again.

Lionheart yanked the *shuriken* from his hand and threw it, not back where it came from, nor away to a safe place. Instead, he hurled it at the lone candle in the room. He didn't strike the flame itself—he wasn't an expert of thrown weapons by any means—but its passing extinguished the flame and plunged the room into darkness.

"You want to fight dirty? Fine, let's fight dirty." No longer distracted by his eyes, Lionheart used his ears and nose to find his opponent. Kobura could make herself invisible in the shadows, or travel through them, or some even more esoteric and exotic ability, but unless she could see in the dark, the odds were against her.

Blood and movement, there, to his left! He swept a foot low and connected with an ankle. It was yanked back out of his immediate reach, but now he knew exactly where she was. He lashed out, claws whistling through the air. One hand brushed against a piece of tattered fabric and he closed his fingers around it. Master Chou had taught him the most important trick about blind-fighting: once contact with one's opponent is achieved, vision—or the lack of it—becomes the least important of the senses.

Kobura knew this truism, and struggled to escape Lionheart's grasp, but he held on with dogged determination. She struck out, trying to stab him with her one remaining poisoned sai, but he smelled it coming and sidestepped. He knew her hand was *there*, because she couldn't have struck him any other way, and he smashed a fist down where her wrist ought to be. He was rewarded with the snapping of bone and the clatter of the sai as it struck the floor. He felt the handle of it against one of his heels and shifted his foot slightly to kick it well away. Stepping on it in the darkness would be as bad as if Kobura had stabbed him with it.

He pulled her into a joint lock, pressing one hand beneath her arm and pulling her hand back across his chest. If he flexed at all, either her shoulder would dislocate or her elbow would snap. "Who sent you? Was it Lian Kui?"

She cursed in Japanese and struggled to pull away.

He tugged on her hand, feeling her tendons stretched to their very limit. "Did you kill Master Chou?"

Something stabbed into his hip, hard enough to stagger him as it punched right into muscle. He roared and lost his grip on Kobura. The weapon was still embedded in his thigh and he reached down to feel a cold iron hilt. He yanked out what felt like a short shark-toothed knife. The wound was painful but didn't burn the way his hand had when the *shuriken* pierced it.

For a moment, Kobura's shadow was in the shattered doorway, and then she was out in the courtyard, racing for the wall.

"Lihua, are you all right?" Blood ran down his leg and Lionheart clenched his teeth against the pain. He would not be taken down so easily.

"Yes! Go after her!" Lihua was nearby him. He reached out for a moment, found her hand, squeezed it.

Then he roared his challenge and followed after the ninja, determined to exact payment on Master Chou's life from her before the night was through.

Chapter Eleven

"Victorious warriors win first and then go to war, while defeated warriors go to war first and then seek to win."
—*Sun Tzu*

Despite her parahuman ability involving shadows, Kobura remained visible to Lionheart as she sprinted across the courtyard. He didn't have time to wonder why as he scrambled after her. Maybe her powers were too taxing for her to use when fleeing. Or perhaps she'd worn them out and would need some time to recharge herself. Regardless, Lionheart wasn't going to let her get away.

Kobura leaped onto a railing, sprang toward a vertical support, and used it to catapult herself to the top of the Cherrywood School's courtyard walls. She was favoring her broken wrist, but kept it well out of the way as she dropped out of sight for a moment beyond the wall.

Lionheart forced himself to ignore the pain in his leg where she'd stabbed him. At least the burning sensation in his hand was growing fainter, so perhaps whatever had coated the *shuriken* tips that pierced him was wearing off. He jumped in mid-stride, hooked his hands over the top of the wall, and let his momentum carry him over the top. He hit the ground, rolled over his shoulder to absorb the impact of landing, and came back up on his feet without losing any speed.

They'd come over the wall by the docks. Early-morning fishermen and dockworkers gaped in awe as the ninja ran down the pier, pursued by an unholy mixture of man and lion.

Kobura vaulted a crate and flung another of her seemingly endless supply of *shuriken* at Lionheart as he followed her over it. He had to twist his body in midair like a cat to avoid the razor-sharp star.

A flatbed truck backed up, crossing Kobura's path. She didn't break stride, laid herself down, and slid beneath the driveshaft like a baserunner coming in to home plate. As she went under, Lionheart bounced over the top, scattering boxes like bowling pins in his wake. Angry Cantonese was shouted after them but they were already racing on down the docks.

Kobura seemed to have given up using her shadow abilities, focusing all her attention on escaping the pursuing American superhero. Lionheart pelted after her, his lungs burning and sweat flying from his mane. He wasn't built for long-distance running and he was already starting to tire. The surrounding docks transformed from small slips for individual fishing boats and junks into broad plains of concrete. Paper lanterns gave way to harsh yellow electric floodlights. Individual crates carried on bamboo poles or rickshaws became steel containers flung about by cranes. Far more traffic was in their way as Kobura and Lionheart weaved around forklifts, trucks, and longshoremen.

A crane hooked a cargo net full of burlap sacks and started to raise it off the pier. Kobura leaped onto it, grasping hold of the cable with her undamaged hand. She looked back toward Lionheart and threw another *shuriken* at him. He dove beneath the pile of bags and as it rose away from the ground, he wrapped his fingers around the cargo netting and felt himself lifted high into the air.

He pulled his knees up to his chest, arms aching with the strain, and then hooked his feet into the cargo net so he dangled below it like a spider. Then, like a spider, he began climbing around the underside of the net. His claws punctured bags, sending a steady stream of rice from every tear. It was like climbing the outside of a teardrop at first, but once he was no longer beneath the bundle and instead upon its side, he moved much faster.

Kobura saw him just as he spotted her, holding onto the cable for support. She hissed at him through her mask and pulled a knife from a sheath in one boot. As she cut through one of the ropes of the cargo net, Lionheart realized her intent and tried to climb faster. She cut more ropes and the net shifted, spilling several bags of rice into the harbor below. Lionheart flung himself upward and jumped just as she cut the last critical load-bearing section of rope. The cargo net tore away and the hook, relieved of its weight, flew upward toward the pulley at the top of the crane. Kobura hung from it, borne upward, but she had an unwelcome passenger.

Lionheart had snagged her ankle as the cargo net fell away beneath him, and she kicked at his face as they rose toward the gantry above. She couldn't stab at him; her broken wrist saw to that, and her good hand was clamped around the slip hook of the cable. He didn't know how strong she was but if her grip failed, they would both plunge to their deaths. He climbed up her body like it was a ladder, keeping his claws sheathed for the moment. She drove a knee into the side of his head but still he refrained from tearing her flesh open. An elbow followed, bloodying his lip, and still he held back. His hand closed around the cable, treacherous with grease and frayed steel, but he had his own hold and no longer needed to depend upon her for support. They hung, almost face to face, like lovers in the most dangerous embrace ever, and fought. She used knees and elbows; he used his free hand and his head.

The cable snapped to a halt at the top of the pulley, dislodging both of them upward like they'd been shot from a cannon. Kobura somersaulted and landed upon the maintenance walkway of the boom. Lionheart wasn't as agile, and only managed to catch a railing. Kobura lunged at his face, trying to force him to recoil and fall, but he took the blow like a tiger jumping upon a spear. He heaved himself onto the walkway and grinned as Kobura realized he was between her and the tower. "Give up, Kobura, there's no place for you to go."

She backed up, keeping him in sight, moving toward the very end of the boom. What was she doing? Surely she wasn't going to jump, was she? They were at least a hundred feet off the ground. Maybe an experienced cliff diver could survive such a plummet, but hitting the water even at a fraction off of the perfect angle would be like hitting a concrete slab. Lionheart approached her, cautious about the treacherous footing of the salt-corroded walkway.

"Surrender, Kobura."

Kobura reached the very edge of the walkway. There was no railing across the end, and she was framed only by the black square of sky.

She vanished.

"Shit!" Lionheart hurried toward the end of the walkway. Had she fallen?

He almost missed her lunging at him from the blackness of the night sky. Somehow she'd been able to use her shadow parapower to hide in plain sight against the darkness. Her rising fist glanced off Lionheart's chin just as he was jerking back. He stumbled on the uneven walkway and fell to a seated position. She leaped through the boom's framework and ran across the crisscrossing beams back toward the tower.

Lionheart scrambled after her, racing back down the walkway. He paced her, then passed her, and grabbed hold of a horizontal bar. He bent at the waist like an acrobat, letting his momentum carry him up and through the support beams of the boom. He twisted himself up and around and landed with his feet on two separate beams, balancing over the walkway, facing Kobura. He raised his fists in a ready position as she halted her own headlong rush. "You're not getting away."

"We see, *gaijin*." She put her damaged hand behind the small of her back and raised her other hand in challenge. "Come get me."

Lionheart danced across the beams, closing the distance with the Japanese warrior. If the footing had been dangerous before on the walkway, traversing the beams was a whole new level of crazy. He'd done a little training in gymnastics, but in the four standard events, he'd preferred vaulting and floor exercises, not balance beam. He gripped the beams with his bare feet, claws splayed in the hope that they might catch a little extra traction.

Kobura was at home fighting on the framework. She fended off Lionheart's off-balance blows easily with her one uninjured hand, and sidestepped around him with a seemingly innocuous stomp to his instep that nearly sent him pitching headfirst over the edge. He lost his balance and fell sprawling across a couple beams, which was fortunate because Kobura's back kick whistled over him instead of connecting and sealing the deal.

He skittered across the beams, grabbing for her ankle, and she feinted a dodge before aiming a stomp that would have broken his own wrist. He lashed out at her leg and raked across her shin with his claws. She hissed in pain, fumbled a step back, and went over the side.

Lionheart knew he should have let her fall, but he was still a hero, dammit, and it wasn't the way Master Chou would have wanted him to win. He dove through the framework of the boom, grabbing Kobura's arm with his hands and locking his legs over a steel beam like a trapeze artist.

Kobura cried out as the broken bones in her wrist twisted with Lionheart's hands wrapped around them. "Sorry." Lionheart was exhausted from the lengthy chase and fight, and it was all he could do to keep hold of Kobura as they both dangled high over the harbor. Blood rushed to his head, making his vision start to grow blurry. "Hold still or I'm going to drop you."

Kobura halted her struggles and went limp in his grasp. She looked up at him, her eyes black pools in the slit of her facewrap. "You should, *gaijin*."

"Nobody's committing *harakiri* tonight." Lionheart groaned as he flexed his arms, pulling the ninja warrior higher before reaching down to take a better grip on her arm above the elbow and taking pressure off her broken wrist. "Now start climbing or we're both going for a swim." He paused. "I'd take it as a kindness if you didn't try to kill me on the way."

Kobura reached up and pulled her facewrap down, exposing her whole face. "*Hai.*"

The symbology of her removing her mask wasn't lost upon Lionheart, and he felt like he'd done the right thing. Nevertheless, he remained vigilant as Kobura climbed up his body like a ladder. It wouldn't have surprised him if she'd made a move, perhaps with one of those *shuriken* she seemed to find at opportune moments, or even a barehanded strike to his throat, or his eyes, or his groin, unprotected as it was while he hung by his knees. But in the end, she didn't harm him as she reached the safety of the boom framework.

Instead of fleeing, like he would have expected her to, she crouched down and offered him her free hand, a shadow among shadows. "Take it. We will be even."

Lionheart could have pulled himself back up without help. At least, that's what he told himself, because sometimes one had to lie to oneself. His entire body was quivering with the tension of keeping his legs locked around the beam, and his abdomen threatened to cramp up and the resulting reflex would drop him. Kobura's hand was strong in his, and between them he pulled himself right side up once more and clambered onto the walkway.

They faced each other once more, Lionheart's back to the tower and Kobura's to the open sky at the end of the boom. "What happen now, *gaijin*?"

Lionheart found it hard to find more hate in his heart for the Japanese woman, despite her attempted assassination. Doubtless, she had acted under orders from Lian Kui. She had unmasked and in doing so confirmed her identity to Lionheart, giving him power over her after he'd saved her life. She had even helped pull him to safety afterward. He wasn't sure what to call the woman, but *enemy* didn't seem to fit the bill. "You go back to the Serpents. You tell them *Yingtao Mu* and the Chou family is off limits. They are under my protection, and I will defend them with every fiber of my being if needed."

"You should have let me fall. I will come back. Kill you in your sleep."

"You can try. Want to bet I can stop you?" Lionheart wrinkled his nose into a snarl. "Maybe you can turn invisible, but I can smell you coming a mile away, and you can't turn that off."

She said nothing.

"Go. Deliver my message. And then go away. Leave Aberdeen forever. I don't care where you go, but you're not welcome here." He spread his claws wide. "What's it going to be, Kobura? We going for Round Two or what?"

Kobura pulled her facewrap back up over her mouth and nose, leaving her eyes in a narrow slit of fabric. "A fallen blossom does not return to the branch."

Lionheart blinked. "What?"

"*Rakka eda ni kaerazu.*" Kobura turned and bolted once more for the end of the boom.

Lionheart pelted after her, but she had too much of a step on him. He stopped at the edge of the crane and saw as she knifed into the water below like a blade into a melon.

He watched for a long time, but she never came back up.

Chapter Twelve

*"Success depends upon previous preparation, and
without such preparation there is sure to be failure."*
—*Confucius*

Lionheart had attracted far too much attention along
the docks for his liking. Longshoremen stared at him or
shouted in Cantonese as he descended the tower from
the crane. Others were diving into the filthy ocean
waters, searching for Kobura in vain. A man in blue
coveralls with a white helmet labeled with hanzi
characters marched right up to Lionheart and
proceeded to unload a lifetime's worth of fury and
dismay upon him. From the man's furious gesticulating
and the way the others were grinning at his antics,
Lionheart suspected he was facing a supervisor. He'd
encountered many others of that class over the years.
To a man, they all detested anyone who interfered with
the flow of work in their jurisdiction, and woe was to
he who they decided was to blame. It didn't matter to
the supervisor that Lionheart had a monstrous,
inhuman countenance, or had possibly thrown a
woman to her death off his crane. No, he was angry
about the fact that everyone had stopped working to
watch the duel on the crane, and now they were still
not working. Lionheart didn't need to speak Cantonese

to understand. He bowed repeatedly, muttering "*Wo hen baoqian*" over and over, which he was pretty sure meant "I'm sorry."

The supervisor wasn't having any of it, and he stuck his finger in Lionheart's face more than once, either too brave or too foolish to worry about the lion-faced man biting it off.

"Yeah, yeah. Go tell it to the Marines, buddy." Lionheart spotted an Aberdeen Municipal Police car pushing its way onto the docks, red lights flickering against the pre-dawn sky. That was all the impetus Lionheart needed to stop being polite. He put a bruised hand upon the supervisor's shoulder, which elicited an entirely new level of anger from the man. Lionheart shoved him aside and ran down the pier. Excited shouts followed him and the police car's siren switched on, although the docks were crowded enough the car couldn't pursue him very quickly.

Lionheart spotted a hooded poncho hanging from the corner of a stack of crates and grabbed it as he ran past. More angry shouts rang in his ears as he yanked the poncho over his head and turned away from the docks back toward the rest of Aberdeen.

A few turns later and he was in an unfamiliar part of town. The police car was somewhere back on the docks and for the first time, he felt like he could catch his breath. The poncho didn't have pockets or he'd have stuck his hands in them. Instead, he kept his arms as far underneath it as he could, keeping the hood pulled well forward to hide his face. He would need daylight to figure out where he was in relation to *Yingtao Mu*, and that mean holing up somewhere for a couple of hours until it was light enough to see the streets and landmarks.

He found his way into a narrow alley filled with reeking garbage. It was the kind of stink common to the exotic realm of New Jersey, and when the wind was right, it blew right across Manhattan and made Lionheart's eyes water. The garbage in the alley seemed to be mostly the remains of foodstuffs—rotting fish carcasses, moldy rice, and decaying vegetables. They were the kind of odors that would stick in his mind for hours, but unlike manmade chemical smells, Lionheart's brain could filter out the organics over time. He needed to rest, to clear his head. His entire body ached from his chase, climb, and fight with Kobura, and he still hadn't figured out how he felt about her throwing herself off the crane. Had she died in the water? He couldn't be sure. He knew cliff divers could and did survive plummets like that on a regular basis, but it didn't follow Kobura would have.

Still, he told himself he wouldn't be surprised if he ran across her again someday in the future. He could only hope their next meeting, if it ever came to pass, wasn't as strenuous as their first. He closed his eyes, just for a few minutes, he told himself.

The peculiar crawling on his skin of someone staring at him awakened him from his slumber with a start. He sat up amid the pile of garbage that had become his bed to broad daylight and a pair of young Chinese boys staring at him with wide eyes and mouths. At his motion, one of them squealed and ran up the alley toward the street as fast as his stubby legs could carry him. The other boy popped a thumb into his mouth and stared in silence. Lionheart waved at him and after a moment, the boy's other hand came up in a similar wave. Lionheart yawned and the sight of his teeth sent the other boy running away.

"Always something." His belly rumbled despite the rotting garbage around him. He'd burned a lot of energy during the night's activities, and he needed to get outside of some calories or he'd be useless for the next inevitable confrontation with the Five Deadly Serpents. The sky was bright enough that stealing anything from a street vendor would be out of the question. The last thing he needed was to attract the attention of the authorities after he'd worked so hard to avoid them. He figured the best thing he could do would be to get back to *Yingtao Mu* and Lihua. He hoped she wasn't out looking for him in Aberdeen, leaving the school undefended. Hong Kong law was a dangerous unknown to him and if anyone could turn it against the Chous, it would be Lian Kui.

He looked around where he was. The narrow alley lay between two three-story buildings. Getting up to the rooftops might make finding his way across town, and it also might mean answering fewer questions about who he was, why he looked like a lion, and why he didn't speak more than half a dozen words of Cantonese.

His finger and toe claws made short work of the crumbling mortar and he was on the building's roof in seconds. His purloined poncho flapped in the breeze behind him like the cape of a far better superhero than he. It reminded him for a moment of Stormcloud—although he'd always think of Tommy as Tornado instead—the way his black and gray cape fluttered around him like the angry clouds from which he'd taken his name. He pulled the hood up over his head in case anyone from a nearby building spotted him. It only took him a moment to locate the crane where he and Kobura had battled each other, which meant the school should be off in *that* direction.

He trotted across the rooftop, using his powerful leg muscles to spring over the alleyways between buildings. It made for quick transit across the buildings facing the long Aberdeen docks. The giant crucifixes of the industrial cranes gave way to the rickshaws of the small, independent vessels. Carefully-manicured stacks of containers became small piles of crates and bushels. The stink of fish replaced the eye-watering Diesel exhaust and industrial solvents.

Lionheart startled one rooftop denizen on his journey, nearly bowling over an old woman who was tending to a chicken coop on one roof. She shrieked in terror when Lionheart landed next to her. He bowed to her, showing as much respect to an elder as he could, and apologized. "*Wo hen baoqian.*" Her hand flew to her mouth as she took in his leonine face, but before she could say anything, he was off again, flying from rooftop to rooftop.

He spotted the walls of the Cherrywood *siheyuan* and smiled. It might not be the best sanctuary, and indeed could already have been overrun by the Serpent Warriors. If it had, Lionheart would battle all of them until either they had been evicted or he was no longer able to throw a punch. If the walls were still sacrosanct, Lihua would be there, and thoughts of her made his heart beat a bit faster. The buildings around the school were all of single-story construction, and traversing their rooftops would be much more noticeable to passers-by, so he dropped back down to ground level in a narrow alley between two tenements. He pulled the poncho hood as far forward as he could and kept his head bent down. He could keep his hands under the edge of the poncho, but he could only hope nobody noticed his bare feet with the thick cat-like toes and golden fur.

He covered the two short blocks quickly, keeping near to the walls. He wasn't so much worried about the locals seeing him; most of them would have known about him since he'd been in town for several days, staying at the school. He was more concerned about running across any police, or getting blindsided by Serpent Warriors. The former could lead to an international incident, embarrassing Just Cause and Lane Devereaux. The latter might get him killed.

He reached the door to the school without incident, raised his hand to the vermilion door, tapped the copper knocker against it, and waited. "Come on . . . Be in there." He knocked again.

The sound of the door bar being raised carried through the painted wood and a moment later it swung open a few inches to reveal the swollen, worried face of Yaoting. He brightened up as soon as he saw Lionheart. "Shi Xin! *Jinlai, gankuai! Gankuai!*" He waved to indicate Lionheart should hurry.

Lionheart followed Yaoting inside. The housekeeper shut and barred the door again and led Lionheart past the spirit wall—called such because evil spirits weren't supposed to be able to turn corners—into the training courtyard beyond. "*Chou xiaojie! Chou xiaojie! Shi Xin you huilaile!*"

Lihua appeared at the entrance to the family courtyard. She had dressed in clothing more befitting of her brother, wide-legged trousers, a long tunic, and a vest. Her hair was caught in a long braid hanging down her back. The practical attire was far more suited to a potential fight than being a proper hostess, but Lionheart couldn't have cared less. Seeing her was like a tonic to his spirit. He pushed his hood back. "Lihua."

She threw herself at him, nearly bowling him over with the ferocity of her embrace. She clung to him as if he were a life preserver on a rough sea, which he realized wasn't far from the truth. "I was so worried about you. I feared the worst when you did not return."

"There were a few scary moments, but it takes more than a single ninja to keep me from coming home for breakfast." Lionheart glanced toward Yaoting, who was beaming like a proud uncle. "Is there any?"

Lihua turned her head. "Yaoting, *zuo zaofan.*"

Yaoting bowed and bustled off toward the kitchen, his slippers shuffling across the tiles.

As soon as he'd vanished behind a sliding screen, Lihua's embrace turned into a deep, passionate kiss, and Lionheart felt perhaps he wasn't as tired or sore as he'd thought. He lifted her and her legs wrapped around him as well as her arms. Just as he decided he'd carry her back to his side house, she pushed herself away. For a moment, he couldn't understand why, but then Yaoting slid open the door and called to them.

"Good timing." Lionheart licked his lips. He could still taste Lihua's sweet kiss upon them.

Two bright spots of red burned on Lihua's cheeks, but her eyes were bright and she smiled as if all was right in the world and there was no Triad aiming to destroy her family's home and reputation. "Years of training." She motioned toward the kitchen. "Please, let us eat and talk about our next move."

"Yes, I've been thinking about that. Let me get outside some food and I'll clue you in." Lionheart followed Lihua into the kitchen where Yaoting had bowls of hearty noodle soup topped with a spicy stewed beef, peanuts, and fresh parsley. Lionheart bowed his gratitude to the housekeeper and dove right into the bowl, stabbing pieces of beef with his chopsticks when he couldn't manage to pick them up in the customary fashion. After he'd taken a few bites, he set his chopsticks down across the top of his bowl. "Officially, the police have closed the school. Unofficially, though, we're still here."

"You think we should open the doors to students again?" Lihua offered Lionheart some *douzhi*, but he shook his head politely, having no taste for the sour mung bean juice that so many Chinese folks enjoyed with their breakfasts.

"I said before and I'll say it again. Nobody closes this school but you and your brother. If you say it's open, it's open. Even if that means we have to put the word out quietly, I think you should accept students again as soon as possible." Lionheart raised a finger to forestall questions. "But, we need more than just students. We need our own private army. The Five Deadly Serpents have their warriors, their *Dashe Yongshi*. We can't keep facing them on our own, Lihua. We're going to be overrun. Somebody's going to get killed, and I'm worried it will be us."

"Finding warriors is not such a simple task. We cannot go out in the street and ask for them to come fight for us. If they have skills, they may already be associated with the Triads. If they have no skills, what would you have them do, die for us?" Lihua crossed her arms. "I will ask no one to do that."

"What if we offered something in return? Something special?"

"What do you suggest?"

Lionheart picked up his chopsticks again. "*Shizi Hou*. I will teach anyone who wishes to stay here Tibetan Lion's Roar. In return for their aid in defending this school, they will learn a rare and esoteric art. Surely that's got to be worth something to the right people." He wound noodles around his chopsticks and raised them to his lips, careful not to dribble sauce into his chin fur.

Lihua kept her arms crossed. She looked unconvinced. "You would bribe students to assume such a risk? I am not sure how I feel about that."

"If we're upfront about the risks and what we're offering, I bet we'd find at least a handful of those willing to step in. Maybe they won't be hardened fighters, but even a raw recruit can learn useful skills in a short time frame with the right instruction."

"How would my father feel about you passing along his training in this fashion?"

"You tell me, Lihua. I was a raw recruit that he took under his wing when he had no need to. Should his legacy end with me or should I pass along his knowledge to those who would help defend the school he built? Wouldn't he want us to use whatever means we could to save it?"

"*Yuanliang wo, Lihua xiaojie. Zheng shi zhe zhong ta benlai xiang yao.*" Yaoting bowed his head toward Lihua.

"What did he say?"

Lihua relaxed and a faint smile crossed her lips. "He said *forgive me, Miss Lihua. It is what he would have wanted.*"

Lionheart slapped his thigh and grinned. "You sly devil, Yaoting. You understand a lot more English than you let on."

Yaoting bowed to Lionheart and said nothing.

"He's right, you know. This is what your father would have wanted. We are honoring him by passing along his legacy."

Lihua sighed. "Yes, I suppose you are right. I wish Qiao were here. He should be part of a decision like this."

"Once we get our first batch of students here, and get this place secured enough so we can feel comfortable leaving for a couple of hours, we'll go talk to the police and see what we can do to get him released. Surely there's got to be a way to bail him out." Lionheart raised his bowl to his lips and drained the hearty, flavorful broth. It was every bit as satisfying as a good, strong cup of coffee, and the injection of protein rejuvenated him.

"I do not know. I am not familiar with the law. We have never broken it before."

Lionheart's nose wrinkled into a snarl. "And you still haven't. He's being railroaded for sure, probably by cops who are on the Five Deadly Serpents' payroll. We'll sort it out, one way or another." He offered the others some tea and then poured it for himself when they declined. "Should we put up a sign on the door of the school saying we're open for business?"

"No. We will spread the word at the market. It is the most effective way for news to reach people. Whatever students we will discover will arrive within an hour or two. Or perhaps not, if none wish to take part." Lihua pushed her bowl toward the center of the table. "I will go myself. Shi Xin, you stay here to protect Yaoting and the school."

Lionheart grimaced. "I don't like that at all, you being out there by yourself."

"You were out there by yourself all night, and here you are, eating noodles and drinking tea as if nothing had happened."

"I was lucky."

"You were prepared. As am I, Shi Xin. Do not fear for me." Lihua reached over the table and took his hand in hers. "I will be cautious."

"You better be."

狮 和 五 致 死 蛇

Lionheart fretted all morning, pacing back and forth like a caged version of his namesake as he waited for Lihua to return. He knew she was out, spreading the word through the local markets, keeping things away from official channels. He knew she was a talented warrior in her own right, who could take care of herself if things went south.

Even so, he worried, because the Five Deadly Serpents had shown their willingness to go beyond simple threats. They had violated the sanctity of the Cherrywood walls, they had attacked the Chous with intent not just to intimidate, but to kill. It felt like they were winning, and Lionheart didn't know how to battle an enemy that had so many weapons at their disposal.

He recalled a street battle between rival gang lords back in New York. Two heavily-armed groups of young men had gone all out, firing submachine guns indiscriminately at each other without regards to the risk to civilians. The bullets had flown as thick as hail in a tornado, and the heroes of Just Cause had to charge into that storm to save as many lives as they could. It had been a complex, fluid situation that changed every few seconds. Gangsters who had only moments before been shooting at each other turned their guns upon the heroes, seeing only the opportunity to increase their own juice, to strengthen their reputations by being known as the one who'd taken down Javelin, or Stormcloud, or Pony Girl. Javelin's armor was proof against anything less than a fifty-calibre bullet, and Stormcloud surrounded himself with a swirling funnel cloud of protective winds and debris picked up from the dirty streets. Pony Girl seemed to be everywhere at once, disarming gangsters as fast as she could, faster than anyone else in the world. The others had fought without fear, for they had faced the worst New York City had ever offered in the form of Destroyer. A bunch of snotty punks with popguns were nothing compared to the terrible behemoth built by a thirteen-year-old boy.

The new breed of gangsters were more likely to be packing pistols and Uzis instead of knives and bicycle chains, and Lionheart had learned the hard way they weren't nearly as easy to cow through fear. They were more likely to stand and shoot at him instead of flee, trusting their lives to their bullets than to their feet. He'd been forced to change his tactics in the wake of the new violence of the streets. Instead of charging in like a rampaging beast, he lunged at them from the shadows, from behind, using stealth to his advantage. He could disarm one in a single blow, drop them with a second. It was fast and brutal, and he sent a lot of victims to the hospital with his new battle strategy, but it was effective. There was a lesson to be learned there, he realized as he paced through the Cherrywood training courtyard.

Fighting a many-headed beast wasn't a question of open confrontation. That would only get him killed. For success in a battle against a much larger force, the key was to attack in such a way so defending was difficult, or impossible. Taking down the entire Five Deadly Serpents at once would be impossible, but perhaps if he wore it down piece by piece, warrior by warrior, he could carve away enough of the center mass that the entire structure would collapse, like hewing down a mighty oak tree.

It was only a question of finding the right shadows from which to strike.

That realization gave him a new purpose, and he began to form the first outline of a plan. He needed to focus, to free the conscious portion of his mind so it could wander, working upon solving the quandary of the Five Deadly Serpents. He went to the old, worn training circle in the courtyard, placed his hands low and high, and walked the circle until at last Lihua returned with a handful of students in tow.

"Five? That's it?"

Lihua shrugged. "Not many students are willing to risk earning the attention of Wu Zhiming She. I could have looked longer, I suppose, but I felt it more important to bring this group in so we may begin."

Lionheart looked them over. They were all young. Had Lionheart himself ever been that young? The eldest among them—the girl who'd held Qiao's attention at his last class, in fact—might have been twenty or twenty-one, although he doubted it. The youngest was a gangly teen with acne on his face and hair that had gone so long without washing it was matting itself. In between there was a hefty young man with a roll of fat hanging over his waistband, a muscular young fellow with the chapped hands and windburned face of a sailor, and a short, unassuming man with wire-framed glasses and an overbite.

"Well." Lionheart couldn't think of anything else to say. He'd dared to hope for a few rogue warriors, highly-trained fighters who sought justice and a chance to ply their trade in its service. Instead, all he'd found was a handful of misfits. "I suppose it's too much to hope that any of you speak English?"

The five students looked at each other, confused, before returning their attention to him, staring in wide-eyed wonder.

Lihua shook her head. "I will translate for you, Shi Xin."

"What did you tell them to get them here?"

"The truth. The Five Deadly Serpents intend to steal the school away from me and my family, and an American superhero has come to teach those who are willing to defend it."

"That's it? Because they're looking at me like I'm the Second Coming."

Lihua gave him a sly smile. "I may have exaggerated your abilities a bit. Be sure to give them a good show."

Lionheart's smile became a pained grimace.

Chapter Thirteen

"To see the right and not to do it is cowardice."
—Confucius

After a couple of hours working with the students, Lionheart was feeling a little less terrified about the prospects of defending the school than when he'd started. All of them, it turned out, had some previous training, and they each had some skills and physical qualities they could take advantage of through proper training. Lionheart had forgotten the young woman's name from the first time he'd seen her, but Lihua reminded him it was Jinjing. Jinjing, though small, had very fast hands and her fists were hard from years of stabbing her hands into the water to pull up fish.

The youngest boy was named Tengfei, and he'd come to Hong Kong from the north, where his uncle had taught him some beginning northern forms. His leg muscles were surprisingly powerful, and he could manage some wicked kicks and jumped much higher and farther than might have been expected for someone of his age and size.

Jian was only a bit older than Tengfei, but he was built like Lionheart, with broad shoulders, a narrow waist, thick arms and legs from many hours spent hauling nets full of fish onto boats. He was the opposite

147

of Tengfei in his own training as well. He'd studied a southern style Lionheart identified as Hung Gar, crammed into the narrow streets and alleyways of Guangzhou, where straight-line fighting was the norm and flashy leaping kicks were more the province of theatrical acrobats than fighters. His low stances drove his powerful, short-range punches.

The eldest of the students was an angry young man with the defiant shadow of a mustache on his upper lip and the slick moves of a well-trained Wing Chun fighter. His ability to flow from attack to attack, chaining them together in a flash, was one of the best Lionheart had seen. Somehow, though, Bingwen had neglected to work on the toughening aspects of his training, and by the time they'd spent a few minutes sparring, his arms were covered with bruises, his knuckles swollen, and a large mouse had risen underneath one eye from a blow Lionheart pulled just in time to avoid doing serious damage.

The fat boy's name was Hong, and his cheeks turned crimson and sweat dotted his brow with the slightest effort on his part. Being overweight in China was a sign of idle wealth, as most people worked too hard and ate too little to pack on any extra pounds, but somehow Hong had managed it while working in a bindery. Lihua whispered to Lionheart the boy was rumored to eat paste, but one look at the boy was enough to convince Lionheart it was unfounded. He was just one of those people who gained weight easily. Despite his bulk, he had a credible background with Leopard-style fighting, and he was deceptively fast. When showing his skills against Lionheart, he was never where Lionheart punched or kicked, and his counterstrikes came in from unpredictable directions and almost faster than possible for a non-parahuman.

After working with all five students for the better part of an hour, Lionheart determined Hong was the most dangerous of the lot.

After getting a sense of the skill levels and abilities of the five students, Lionheart called for a break and encouraged the students to get to know one another on a personal level, as they could be called upon to defend each other as well as the school, and it was easier to fight for someone whom you knew and cared about personally than a complete stranger. Yaoting brought out tea and sticky rice balls from the kitchen, and he looked happier than he had been at any point during Lionheart's stay in the school. The presence of the students was like a salve upon his soul.

Lionheart appropriated a clay mug of tea and a pair of rice balls and ate them methodically while devising a training schedule optimized for each student's abilities. It was far more complicated a process than he had thought, and asked Lihua for a pencil and paper so he could figure it all out. She bent down and kissed his broad feline nose. "You worry too much, Shi Xin. My father never wrote down his training plan. Nor does Qiao. There is no need when one knows what must be done."

Lionheart looked up at her. "But how do I know what must be done?"

"They must be trained, each to the best of his ability. Or her ability." She sniffed. "I still do not like Jinjing."

"They're all so different, with such different backgrounds and training. I don't know where to begin."

"Where did my father begin with you?"

"Stances. Then a health and strength form."

"Then begin with those."

"But they all know stances. They've all had a lot more training than I had when your father found me."

149

Lihua placed a warm hand upon his cheek and he clasped his fingers over it. "They came here to learn *Shizi Hou*. Teach them as you were taught. They will accept the training." She smiled down at him. "Or they will not."

Lionheart drank down the last of his tea, letting it invigorate him. The gentle breeze through the courtyard carried within its grasp the salt of the ocean, the spice of the cherry blossoms, the stink of fish, and the smoke of dozens of cooking fires. It smelled nothing like the miasma of New York City, and the longer he breathed in the scents of Hong Kong, the less he missed the great towering titans of steel and concrete. He was beginning to feel like Yingtao Mu was his home, instead of being a guest within its high walls.

It felt good.

狮 和 五 致 死 蛇

After three hours of training in the first rudiments of Shizi Hou, Lionheart's students were sore and sweaty, but remained surprisingly cheerful considering how hard he'd beaten them up with a low stances workout, learning and repeating the first strength form, and closing out with a round-robin sparring session where he encouraged each of them to work to their strengths. As much as they sparred with each other, Lionheart studied their styles and abilities, learning the best ways to train each of them.

Hong's skill with Leopard Style would have frustrated the others into anger had he not been so cheerful and quick to deflect an opponent's rising fury with an honest smile and laugh. Even so, Lionheart thought he might have to put Bingwen on the ground to keep him from losing his temper, but the Wing Chun fighter barely managed to keep his cool. Jian's Hung

Gar made him a tough opponent for all of the others, and he gave Hong the hardest time. Tengfei was poor at sparring, but his youthful energy kept him bouncing back up every time someone knocked him down. Jinjing could hold her own against Tengfei and Bingwen, but she went all to pieces against Jian and Hong, as one was tough enough to take her best blows and the other avoided them.

Lionheart brought them back to the center of the training courtyard and asked Lihua to translate for him. "I'm pleased with you all. If you all put forth that kind of effort every day, learning Shizi Hou will be a rewarding experience for all of us. That being said, the Cherrywood School is in danger, and the cost of my instruction is your help in defending it from the Five Deadly Serpents, should that arise. Twice they have come over our walls, once in a large group and once with a single assassin. Twice we have fought them off, but it could happen again at any moment. Do I have your commitment to protect this school in its time of need?"

The five students didn't hesitate. They each made a fist with their right hands and pressed them against the open palms of their lefts, bowed their heads. " *Women jiang, sifu.*"

Lihua looked at Lionheart. "They say *we will, Master.*"

"Good. There are five of you, each as different as the fingers on a hand, but the fingers together form a fist. Therefore, I name you *Yingtao mu quan.* The Fists of Cherrywood." Lionheart smiled as his students grinned at each other. He knew by bringing them together under the banner of a team name, they would be even more ready to defend not only the school, but each other. The lessons he'd learned being part of Just Cause, something far greater than just himself, served him well here as he stood before the hopeful youngsters. He saw Yaoting standing by the main house, awaiting directions. "Yaoting, can you help them get settled in and prepare dinner? Then later, if you can, maybe you can put together some kind of patch or something that they could wear? Something to identify them as the Fists of Cherrywood."

Yaoting bowed and called the students to follow him toward the front house, which would have been used for the servants if the Chou family had been much wealthier. Lihua took Lionheart's hand and squeezed it. "It is nice to have students here. I wish Qiao were back so he could teach them as well."

"I've been thinking about that. We should go talk to the police and see about getting him released."

"I do not think they will. Many of the police are paid by the Five Deadly Serpents. They can use Qiao as leverage against us."

"The Serpents can't own the entire police department. Someone in there is honest and will see it's a railroad job. All we have to do is find that man and lean on him until he breaks."

Lihua clutched her own shoulders, as if trying to warm herself against an icy breeze only she could feel. "I hope you are right."

狮 和 五 致 死 蛇

Lionheart had an irrational fear that the police station would close at dusk, the way many of the stalls along the Aberdeen thoroughfares did. He needn't have worried, though. Crime, and the business of stopping it when possible, was a twenty-four-hour occupation. Officers regularly entered the large, gray British-built office building, either alone or escorting their most recent arrest. He watched the traffic going in and out of the offices and felt butterflies start to spin their circles in his lower belly. "Maybe this wasn't such a good idea."

"Are you having second thoughts?" Lihua had walked beside him all the way from the school, her hand clasped in his. She'd dressed in a smart-looking cheongsam in a muted navy blue with a subtle floral print upon it. The dress hugged the contours of her body but flowed outward into bell-like sleeves and skirt, lined with white silk beneath the navy print. Her feet were encased in simple rubber-soled silk slippers. To avoid undue attention on the streets, Lionheart had to borrow clothing from Qiao's closet. Yaoting had made some quick alterations to allow Lionheart to squeeze his thick shoulders into the dark jacket with the mandarin collar and silk knots instead of buttons to hold it shut. He had on wide-legged trousers of the same color as his jacket that swished around his bare feet. The trouser legs kept his furry toes well-hidden. A conical straw hat sat low over his face, hiding as much of his mane as possible beneath its woven texture. Even so, on the trip to the police station, one street urchin had looked right up into Lionheart's tawny-furred face and ceased his plaintive begging.

Lionheart winked at him and the boy ran away. He sighed. "I don't know if I'll ever get the hang of kids. They're all terrified of me."

"They just do not know you as I do." Lihua's smile was soft and compassionate. "Do you have a plan?"

Lionheart smiled back down at her from under his conical hat. "No, but if you hum a couple bars, I'll fake it."

"I do not understand."

"Don't worry about it. I guess bad jokes are bad in all languages." A police car rolled past, its underpowered engine straining to carry it through traffic, burping the blue smoke of burnt oil in its wake.

153

Lionheart wrinkled his nose at the chemical odor. This far from the docks, he couldn't smell even a hint of the ocean in the air. It was nothing but cooking smoke, smog, and the stink of human and animal waste curing in Aberdeen's insufficient sewers. "Let's do this."

They walked into the police station through the front doors, Lihua a step behind Lionheart. As he entered the building, lit by buzzing overhead fluorescent lights, he removed his conical hat and handed it to a surprised clerk. Curious muttering transformed to concerned questions and then frightened shouts in Cantonese and English as Lionheart strode through the station toward the back offices. He could smell the stink of fear upon the officers, the sweat upon unwashed bodies, the empty boxes of noodles crammed into wastebaskets. He kept his hands out from his sides, his claws tucked away inside their sheaths, showing himself to be unarmed. The *click-clack* of guns around him was like hail falling upon a tin roof. His heart pounded and adrenalin flooded through his system. Keeping himself calm and collected in the face of such danger meant focusing upon his internal strength, the *xi* which Master Chou had tried so hard to get him to find.

Keeping his voice calm and his hands in plain view, Lionheart spoke. "I want to speak to the Chief."

A door opened and an older white man in a police uniform stepped out. His hair was cut into a short, graying brush, and his eyes were framed by wire-rimmed glasses. He smelled of aftershave and scotch. He had a pistol holstered on his belt but his hands were empty, like Lionheart's. "I'm Station Sergeant Montgomery. I'm the highest ranking officer in this facility. What do you want?" His accent was of British aristocracy, the sort that made him sound like a villain from a James Bond movie.

"For starters, I'd like your officers to stand down. I'm not here to start a fight or cause any trouble. You know who I am, Station Sergeant?"

"You're the American superhero. Lionface, isn't it?"

"Lionheart."

Montgomery smiled, using only his lips. "My mistake. Terribly sorry. What can I do for you, Mr. Lionheart?"

"May we speak in private? In your office?" Lionheart glanced to either side, noting that guns were trained on him from multiple directions. The officers weren't paying attention to their fire lines and if somebody shot and missed, he was likely to hit one of his fellow officers. "I assure you, I am not here to cause any trouble."

Montgomery stared at Lionheart as if he were trying to divine the superhero's intentions, but Lionheart kept himself centered, peaceful, introspective. At last, the Station Sergeant relented. "Stand down. *Fangxin, jingcha.*" The officers in the station grumbled but lowered their weapons. "You may join me in my office." He turned his back upon Lionheart and led him and Lihua into his office. One more officer, a native, followed the two into the office and closed the door behind him. Montgomery motioned to the chairs in front of his desk. "Please, won't you sit? This is Sergeant Yang, my second-in-command." Yang was a stocky man who smelled of the beef noodles he must have eaten for dinner. He stood beside the desk and folded his arms in a stance suggesting he was expecting trouble and was ready to respond in kind. "May I offer you a drink, Mr. Lionheart?"

"It's just Lionheart, and no thank you." Lionheart could practically hear the other station officers piling up outside the office, their ears pressed up against the frosted glass and the walls, trying to hear anything from within. "This is my friend, Chou Lihua. Your men came to her school and arrested her brother, Chou Qiao. We've come to ask you to release him."

Yang tensed up at the request, and Lionheart caught a distinct scent of nervous sweat wafting off his uniform. Montgomery, on the other hand, only looked bemused and politely apologetic. "I'm terribly sorry, Lionheart. I'm afraid Mr. Chou is the subject of a criminal investigation, and he will have to remain in custody."

"And what are the charges?" Lionheart rested his hands on the arms of the chair, giving every indication of peacefulness. He didn't have to see identifying marks upon Sergeant Yang to know he was taking pay from the Five Deadly Serpents. Any false move and he'd be the first to act.

"He is accused of murder."

"What?" Lihua's strident cry made Yang nearly jump out of his shoes. "That is ridiculous! It was—"

"Hush, Lihua." Lionheart's rumble wasn't quite a growl, but it carried the point nevertheless. If Lihua said the wrong thing, it could give the police exactly the ammunition they needed to press charges. He knew whatever charges the police intended to file wouldn't stick without evidence or corroboration. "Murder's a serious crime, Station Sergeant. I'm not really up on Hong Kong laws, but when and where is this alleged murder supposed to have happened?"

Yang stamped his foot. "Why you here, American? This Chinese matter. You not Chinese. Where you papers?" He pointed at Lionheart as if he could make the superhero vanish by simple force of will.

Montgomery sighed. "My colleague, indelicate as he is, does have a point. I'm going to need to see your papers before proceeding further. After all, we can't have you here in the country illegally. That would be most improper for a heroic individual such as yourself."

Lionheart smiled. He'd expected someone to play that particular piece in the game. He reached into his jacket and pulled out his passport and a letter from Lane Devereaux authorizing him to act on behalf of Just Cause. It might not have carried much weight in most countries outside of the United States, but it looked official, and if it got a local constable to see him as a representative of the law instead of a civilian, it meant he could get things done a lot more efficiently. He handed the documents to Montgomery. "I'm sure you'll find everything in order."

Montgomery took several minutes to thumb through the pages, his eyes scanning text, not missing a thing. At last, he passed them back to Lionheart. "Indeed, they appear to be. According to my officers, Mr. Chou killed the victim in his courtyard three nights ago. We have corroborating witness statements identifying him."

"So sorry. You waste trip here." Yang grinned a dull, snaggletoothed smile.

Lihua fidgeted in her chair. Lionheart could tell she was aching to jump up, punch both the policemen, and then to battle her way through the rest of the station to free her brother. He wasn't sure she couldn't pull it off, but he planned to avoid that eventuality if possible. "Station Sergeant, that's simply not possible. I came here to Aberdeen to pay my respects to Mr. Chou's father, who trained me for many years. While staying in the Cherrywood School, I've been training with Mr. Chou. I was in the school three nights ago, training with him, as I said. I don't recall him killing anyone. He may have worked his students hard, but that's hardly fatal."

"You lie! He kill one, no, two man!" Yang actually pounded his fist on Montgomery's desktop and Lionheart caught a clear glimpse of the hanzi tattoo on the back of his hand.

Lionheart rolled his eyes and smiled at Montgomery. "So now it's two men? Murdered? Are there bodies? How were there witnesses if this alleged act took place in the courtyard? The walls at *Yingtao Mu* are tall enough that nobody could see over them by accident. For witnesses to have seen something, they would have needed to be in the courtyard itself, which would be impossible unless they were there illegally." He rested his elbows on the chair arms and clasped his fingers under his chin. "I think somebody is lying to you."

"You lie! He use spear!" Yang was nearly frothing at the mouth.

Montgomery stared at his assistant. "Sergeant Yang, stand down! Go get a cup of tea or something and compose yourself. I will not tolerate this kind of behavior."

Yang, offended to the core, stomped out of the office, nearly tripping over a couple of the other station officers who were huddled by the door.

"Dreadfully sorry about that." Montgomery sighed. "He doesn't usually get so worked up. Odd people, these Chinese. Sometimes things set them off for no apparent reason."

"Station Sergeant, please. I don't know what may have actually happened, but I'm positive you've got the wrong man. Mr. Chou is a martial arts instructor, nothing more. I wouldn't be at all surprised if this is some kind of trumped-up charge intended to remove him from his school. There's a local . . . organization that has been trying—unsuccessfully, I might add—to purchase the Cherrywood school, if not steal it outright. What better way to move that along than to remove the primary owner from it over legal troubles?"

Montgomery raised an eyebrow like Mr. Spock, looking so natural with the act that he must have practiced it in front of a mirror for hours. "You're telling me he's been set up?"

"And your police department is the . . . what is the word? Patsy." Lihua uncrossed her legs and then crossed them once more. She was still on a hair trigger beside Lionheart. He wanted to reach out and comfort her, but didn't dare take his attention away from Montgomery even for a moment.

Now that Yang was out of the room, Lionheart leaned forward, taking a more conspiratorial tack in the conversation. "I'm from New York City, Montgomery. We may not have invented police corruption, but we damn sure perfected it. I know you guys are working hard to root out the corruption in your own department, but it's like finding . . . a snake in the grass. You get what I'm saying here?"

Montgomery clasped his hands over his blotter. "I believe I understand your message, yes."

"There's a wrong side and a right side to this thing. I can't tell you which to choose, but you can either be the chick fed to the snake, or the mongoose that kills it. What do you say, sir?"

Montgomery opened a drawer of his desk, pulled out a coffee mug and a bottle of scotch. He offered it to Lionheart and Lihua, both of whom declined. He poured himself a generous splash in the mug, downed it, and then refilled the cup once again. "You've made an excellent point, my American friend. I'm going to order Mr. Chou released. See that he keeps his nose clean."

Lihua gasped with delight and Lionheart smiled. "I will do my utmost best."

"I don't want a war. Nobody does. Not in my town." Montgomery finished his second cup of scotch, looked at the bottle as if he were considering a third, but then put it away. "But if it happens, you should believe that I will stop at nothing to bring to justice those who breach the peace." He looked over his glasses at Lionheart. "At that point, anyone is fair game. Anyone, Lionheart. Do you, as you say, get what I'm saying here?"

Lionheart's smile was as dry as the Sahara. "I believe I understand your message, yes."

Chapter Fourteen

*"The opportunity to secure ourselves against defeat lies
in our own hands, but the opportunity of defeating the
enemy is provided by the enemy himself."*
—Sun Tzu

Qiao stank of barely-repressed fury when the police brought him out from the holding cells. Lihua threw her arms around her brother, holding back her sobs. Qiao's arms returned the embrace, but Lionheart could see his cold, calculating eyes were focused far away. Lionheart was sure Qiao only had eyes for the Five Deadly Serpents, and the war that Station Sergeant Montgomery had feared would come to pass. It was only a matter of time.

The three walked out of the police station through the silent air, the weight of every eye upon them like bricks piled in tall stacks. Lionheart kept an eye out for Sergeant Yang, but he was nowhere to be seen. Given his earlier actions, he must have been reporting to his masters. It wouldn't be long before Lian Kui marshaled his forces and came for the school once more. What warriors would he send? What weapons would they face? Lionheart was afraid, really afraid for the first time since coming to Hong Kong. The Triad was well-armed, not just with martial artists, but with guns to bring down the school, and enough money to sweep the incident quietly out into the harbor.

He remained lost in his thoughts as they walked through the streets of Aberdeen. He'd left his hat behind in the police station, and the sea breeze toyed with his mane and tickled his nostrils. On the busy streets, civilians flowed around him and the Chous like water rushing past rocks in a streambed. Even so, they shrank away from him, unwilling to touch the *gweilo* with the lion's face, lest whatever curse had touched him would pass itself along to them.

They reached the school. The doors were shut, as Lionheart expected, and also barred on the inside. Lihua made some joke in Cantonese that earned a wry smile from Qiao as he reached up to bang the copper knocker. They heard the sounds of the door bar being lifted out of the way and the vermilion door swung inward to reveal three of the Fists standing ready to defend the school from soldiers, police, Serpent Warriors, or demons. They had their backs against the spirit wall, but they relaxed when they saw Lionheart and the Chous.

"Qiao!" Jinjing threw herself against his chest and hugged him, almost exactly the same way Lihua had in the police station. Disapproval settled across Lihua's face but she said nothing.

Qiao met Lionheart's gaze over Jinjing's head and gave him the smallest of nods of approval. The motion was so much like the same nod Lionheart had received from Master Chou during his years of training that it brought a lump to his throat. Like father, like son. Lionheart cleared his throat. "Let's get inside."

Jian and Hong shut and barred the door behind them and escorted them into the courtyard like they were Secret Service agents protecting the President. The rest of the Fists joined them, presenting themselves to Qiao for his consideration. Qiao walked around the five students and Lionheart noticed they all wore head sashes with hanzi characters. Qiao read them. "*Fists of Cherrywood School.*" He looked at Lihua and Lionheart. "This is your doing?"

Lionheart bowed his head. "After the police took you, we realized there weren't enough hands on deck to keep things shipshape. Lihua and I talked it over and we made an arrangement with these students."

"I am curious to know the details of this arrangement. They are staying here, I presume?"

"Yes. That was the deal. They will help guard and defend *Yingtao Mu* for as long as required, and in return for their efforts, I will train them in Shizi Hou."

Qiao stared at him. "So you are staying as well. This is not your fight, Shi Xin."

"I've made it mine."

"So you have."

Yaoting bustled out of the main house, all smiles and a tray brimming with *youtiao*. "*Huanying hui jia, Sifu Chou!*"

Qiao looked at the Chinese doughnuts and smiled. "Is it breakfast time, Yaoting?"

"Anytime good time for *youtiao*." Yaoting distributed the fried snacks. Hong ate his in record time and watched the tray like a dog hoping for an extra treat.

"I suppose so." Qiao took one. "Better than jail food."

"What is our next move?" Lihua hesitated, then entwined her arm around Lionheart's. He was glad she took that step. He didn't want to keep hiding their mutual attraction from Qiao. The way Jinjing fawned over him, perhaps he might not notice his sister's behavior. Or if he did, he might not be quite so disapproving of it.

"We should take the fight to the Serpents. They have entered my school twice . . . no, three times now without my permission. They have dishonored my father, my family, and my guests. It is time we taught them the error of their ways." Qiao repeated himself in Cantonese for the benefit of the Fists.

"I don't disagree that they deserve some retribution, but we really ought to think it over before we go rushing off without due preparations." Lionheart licked a spot of grease from the *youtiao* off one finger. "They are very well armed, and I think they could hold off an army up there in that mansion of theirs. I'm just worried that they'll take those weapons and overrun the school." Lionheart took a deep breath. This was the part he'd been dreading; he'd spent the walk from the police station trying to determine the best way to deliver it, but in the end, there had only been one real option. "I think you should leave."

Lihua pulled herself away from his arm. "What?"

"Have you been up there, where the Serpents are headquartered? I have. Lian Kui was careful to show me everything, so I'd know exactly what we're up against. The number of men he's got, the number of guns . . . We can't defend against that, should they decide to turn them loose upon us. All it'll get us is shot and a burial at sea." A ghost of a smile crossed his face. "We can join all the other bodies out there in the harbor. There's no honor in letting yourself be murdered. Or your family. Or your students."

"Our father built this school." Lihua's tone was frosty. "He worked very hard to give us a place to train, to live."

"It's a building. Yes, you have history here, but there are many places you can live, many places you can train and teach. Places that aren't under the scrutiny of a Triad like the Five Deadly Serpents."

"No. That is not an option. There will be another way. We stay here. If honor demands our death, so be it." Qiao pounded his fist into his palm.

"Dammit, Qiao, I wish you'd stop being so fucking . . . Chinese. I'm trying to save your life. Lihua's life. Yaoting. All of your students. You can't take on the Wu Zhiming She. It would be like trying to fight the ocean itself." Lionheart lowered his voice. "And there's something more. They've got parahumans. People like me. People with powers. You don't have enough to fight back against something like that."

Qiao sighed. For the first time, Lionheart saw a crack in his armor. On one hand, he felt like he ought to go to work on that crack, widening it until Qiao relented. On the other, breaking down the man who had become his friend would be one of the hardest things Lionheart had ever done. "I wish I knew why this is so urgent for them now. Our school has been here for years. So have the Triads. Why now?"

Jian, who had been listening intently like the other members of the Fists while Lihua translated into Cantonese for them, sat up suddenly and spoke quickly, with growing excitement.

Lihua nodded at what he said and then turned to Lionheart. "He says there is a boat that has been moving around the harbor, never anchored in the same spot, but never docking either. It is a small private cargo ship people say belongs to the Five Deadly Serpents." She asked Jian a question and he replied. "He says it is called the *Kowloon Seadragon*."

"I'll bet it's got a delivery for them from the continent. But why haven't they docked? Do they have to have the school to unload a cargo of heroin?" Lionheart rubbed his jaw.

"Maybe they are being watched? They cannot own all the police. They might need the school so they can unload the cargo and transfer it off the dock right away, before a customs official or police inspector can look at it." Lihua sighed. "I do not know how smuggling works."

"I doubt any of us do." Lionheart smiled at her. "If we did, we'd be in the business ourselves. I hear it's pretty lucrative."

Qiao slapped his hand upon the table, making Jinjing jump. "We should go destroy their cargo. Tonight. Take the fight to them. If they do not have their heroin, they may leave us alone, at least for the time being. They will have other problems."

"Hold on, Qiao, let's not go running off all half-cocked. Do we know for certain the *Kowloon Seadragon* is smuggling heroin?" Lionheart fixed Qiao squarely in his gaze.

Qiao wouldn't look back at Lionheart. "No."

"If it is, do we know what kind of guards are on board? If they have guns? If they have parahuman abilities?"

"No." Qiao drummed his fingers on the table.

"Look, I agree with you that destroying a heroin shipment would put the Serpents on the hot seat in a lot of ways. It would cost them a lot of money and credibility within their own supply chain, but we need more intel. Here's what I think. We've got a couple of sailors in the Fists. Why don't we take a sampan out and pass by the *Seadragon* in the morning? If you get me close enough to the ship, I'll be able to tell if there's heroin on board, and guns. That would at least give us an idea of what we're up against."

Qiao glared at him. "How will you know that? You see through walls?"

Lionheart tapped his nose. "The nose knows, man. When I visited the Serpents' headquarters up in the hills, I could smell the stink of heroin all over the place. One of my teammates used to, uh, indulge from time to time. I know the smell of it, believe me. And gun oil? That's easy."

"You would do this?"

"Of course I would. It's why I'm here, Qiao. Let's get some rest tonight and come morning, we'll go gather our intel. Then we'll be able to plan our next move with some real data backing us up instead of just going by the seat of our pants."

Qiao stood, his jaw standing out in sharp relief. "Yes. Rest now. Gather data in the morning." He offered a stiff bow to the members of the Fists, to Lihua, and to Lionheart. "Until morning, then."

The others watched him leave. Lihua turned to the Fists and ordered them to take turns on watch overnight, in case the Serpents came in the darkness again. They dispersed, three heading for their bunks in the front house and the other two dividing up the two courtyards for watch duties. Lihua sighed and moved into Lionheart's arms, squeezing him tight, nestling into him. "I want to sleep with you tonight, Shi Xin, but I cannot. Not with Qiao here. I should speak with him."

Lionheart closed his eyes and inhaled, drinking in the faint floral tones in her hair. "You're right. I wish you weren't, because I think . . ."

She looked up, her dark eyes reflecting the warm glow of the courtyard lanterns. "What do you think, Shi Xin?" Her whisper barely carried across the inches between her lips and his ears.

"I think . . ." He stopped, the words jamming up inside his throat. How could he tell her he was falling in love with her? They'd barely known each other for more than a week, and yet she'd pushed her way into his heart with the unstoppable patience of a waterfall. It couldn't be love. It had to be mere animal attraction. He was, after all, as animal as they came. And yet, he felt like baying at the moon, roaring his feelings to the entire harbor. Somehow, this young Chinese woman had completely swept him off his feet. He didn't know what terrified him more, finding out she felt the same way about him or discovering she didn't. Either way, it was a distraction neither of them could afford given their current circumstances. "Go to Qiao. Try to convince him to leave. There is no dishonor in protecting his family. Passing along his training is the best way to honor Master Chou."

"I will speak with him." Lihua stretched up and kissed him, her lips soft and warm. Then she whispered in his ear, "*Wo ai ni.*" She pulled away and fled, her hair down over her face as if she were hiding.

Lionheart didn't have to speak Cantonese to know what she had said, and the muscles in his chest tightened from the grip of unfamiliar emotions. She disappeared into the main house and Lionheart tasted blood where he'd bitten his lip. "I love you too."

Chapter Fifteen

"If ignorant both of your enemy and yourself,
you are certain to be in peril."
—*Sun Tzu*

"Shi Xin?"

The soft voice awoke Lionheart with all the urgency of the emergency klaxon back in Just Cause Headquarters. A faint odor of chrysanthemums brushed across his nose as he lurched off his pallet. The fresh, green scent immediately brought Jinjing to mind, and sure enough, the young woman stood in the door to his room, backlit by the moon. "Jinjing? What's the matter? Oh, shit. You don't speak English. Um . . ." He struggled to find the words in Cantonese but the language was still too new to him. "Yaoting. I need Yaoting."

Jinjing turned to look back in the courtyard and called to someone there. "*Dai lai Yaoting.*" She faced Lionheart again and grimaced, knowing the communication barrier was a problem. "*Eh . . . Sifu Chou he Lihua dou bujianle.*"

"Master Chou . . . That's Qiao. Qiao and Lihua . . ." Lionheart lit the lamp beside his pallet, bathing the room in its warm yellow glow. He turned to Jinjing and saw her eyes wide and worried. "*Dou bujianle.* What's *bujianle*?" A chill ran down his spine as Jinjing made a fluttering motion with her hands. "Gone. They're gone?"

"Yes. Gone." Yaoting came up to the bedroom door. "I no know when they leave. Qiao give tea to Tengfei. He fall asleep." He held up the offending mug for evidence. "*Menghanyao.*"

Lionheart took the mug and sniffed it. A sharp, chemical odor hid amongst the drying tea leaves, almost unrecognizable. "Slipped him a Mickey Finn. And now they're both gone."

"Where you think they go?" Yaoting looked worried and Lionheart couldn't blame him. He doubted the poor old housekeeper had slept a full night since before Master Chou had died.

"Where else? They must have gone after the *Kowloon Seadragon*. Dammit. I should have kept watch over Qiao myself. Should have known he wouldn't sit still even for a night."

"You must go find them." Yaoting's voice trembled like he was on the edge of tears. "Wu Zhiming She kill them."

Icy claws dug their way into the small of Lionheart's back. He didn't want to think about what kind of torment Lian Kui and his men might put Qiao and Lihua through. Especially Lihua. God, if anything happened to her . . . "Jinjing, uh . . . *Yingtao Mu Quan.* Get them up. I need all of them here."

Jinjing must have understood his intent, for she scrambled to obey.

"Tengfei still sleep. Cannot wake." Yaoting shook his head.

"He's been drugged. Nothing to be done but let him sleep it off." Lionheart pulled on a pair of jeans and a t-shirt over his matted chest fur. "I've got to go find Qiao and Lihua. I'm afraid they're going to get in a lot of trouble."

Jian stepped forward and smacked his chest with his fist. "*Wo jiang gen ni zou.*"

Yaoting looked at Lionheart. "He say he go with you."

"I gathered that much. I can't have him come along. I need all of the Fists here to defend the school."

Yaoting translated as best he could to Jian, who pointed and unleashed a torrent of Cantonese at Lionheart.

"He say you no know where boat is. He know. He take you on sampan."

Fierce pride swelled in Jian and Lionheart knew the young man had a point. "All right, he can take me, but he's only the taxi service. I want him to come straight back here after bringing me to the *Kowloon Seadragon*. I need all five of them here to protect the school." He dragged his claws through his mane, tearing through the worst of the tangles and pushing it back out of his face. "If Qiao and Lihua get captured . . . or worse . . . the Serpents will have no barriers to overrun the school except the five of you."

"Six." Yaoting put his hands on his hips. "I fight too."

"Yaoting . . ." Lionheart smiled at the old housekeeper. "I can't stop you, but I can ask you not to. You're a great man and very good at what you do, but you're no warrior. I would hate for anything to happen to you."

"I make no promise." Yaoting looked resolute and brave.

Lionheart nodded. He knew he had no chance of convincing the housekeeper to be less heroic. He turned to Jian. "Do you speak any English at all, Jian?"

Yaoting translated for Jian. The fisherman showed his crooked teeth in a wide grin. "Mickey Mouse. Sumbitch."

Lionheart sighed. "Yaoting, can you please tell him I expect him to come straight back here to the school after he takes me to the *Kowloon Seadragon*?"

Yaoting nodded. Jian asked him a single question and Yaoting looked back at Lionheart. "He want know if you need sword or knife or any other weapon?"

Lionheart popped his claws out of his fingertips, drawing a murmur of excitement and appreciation from the Fists. "This is all I need."

狮 和 五 致 死 蛇

It was still early enough in the wee hours that activity on the Five Deadly Serpents' dock immediately behind the school was minimal, but Lionheart spotted the two men watching the entrance to the dock right away by the cherry-red glow of their cigarettes. The way the breeze was blowing, he just caught a gentle whiff of gun oil. Guns weren't common in the area, and it didn't take a genius to know they were most likely Lian Kui's men, which meant the leader of the Five Deadly Serpents was expecting trouble at his docks. Lionheart wasn't surprised, given the battle he'd fought with Kobura only a couple of days before. He grabbed Jian's arm, pulled him into a shadow, and pointed. Jian squinted into the darkness until he nodded. He looked back at Lionheart, who drew his finger across his throat in a gesture that transcended language boundaries.

The two guards weren't very good. Between smoking and talking, they were far too inattentive for their own good. Lionheart and Jian crept through the darkest part of the entrance to the docks, freezing whenever one of the guards happened to glance in their direction, but the two Serpent Warriors were more interested in the entertaining story one was telling the other. He animated himself with broad arm gestures as he told his tale, and the other chuckled.

Lionheart rose up out of the shadows behind the listener and tapped him on the shoulder. "Excuse me."

The man whirled in open-mouthed surprise only to get a hard fist driven into his face followed by a knee to the abdomen and a finishing elbow strike to the back of his neck. He fell into an unconscious heap. The man who'd been telling the story fumbled at his belt for a pistol tucked into the waistband of his jeans but Jian clapped his hands over the man's ears from behind, making him yelp in sudden pain as his eardrums ruptured. His pistol clattered to the cement of the dock as Jian finished him off with a solid uppercut to his chin.

Lionheart nodded his approval and they dragged the two unconscious Serpent Warriors behind a stack of crates. It felt like a good, solid start to what Lionheart hoped would be a straightforward rescue-and-retrieval operation. He wanted to ask Jian where his boat was, but it would have been pointless. The fisherman's English vocabulary was limited to "Mickey Mouse, sumbitch," and Lionheart hadn't managed to get a good grounding in Cantonese in such a short time period. He motioned to Jian to take the lead and the young man headed down the docks and out across the boats tied together in the harbor. They crossed the floating bridges of other boats until Jian stopped on a sampan and unlashed it from its neighbors.

Sampans were slender vessels, built from only a few planks of wood. Jian's boat was some twenty-five feet long, with a low, arching canvas cover over his fishing supplies and storage crates in the center portion. The young man took his position at the prow and indicated to Lionheart that he ought to get beneath the canvas. Lionheart did as he was asked and Jian took hold of the long pole attached to the aft oar and began to work it in a rocking, twisting motion. The oar paddle moved like a fish tail beneath the water, sculling the slim craft away from the floating village and out into the harbor proper.

The storage area of the boat stank of spoiled fish, blood, and some kind of sharp-smelling paste that Jian must have used to treat his nets. The oar whispered as the sampan glided over the water. Lionheart peeked out from beneath the canvas cover, watching as Jian steered them past more anchored sampans and junks into deeper water. Soon he spotted the boat that had to be their target. He could see a couple of human-shaped shadows on the top deck and he knew he'd only have one chance to get on board the boat unseen, and to do so he would have to get in the water. Wet fur was unpleasant enough on its own, but when he was dragging it around during a fight, it made for a real struggle. Nothing to be done about it, though. He wished he could tell Jian what to do, how to approach beside the *Kowloon Seadragon* without making it look like that's what he was doing. Instead, he had to trust the fisherman wasn't an idiot, and it was making his stomach hurt.

The *Kowloon Seadragon* was a dark shadow against the water, although Lionheart could see the top deck, which was painted white. The vessel was a tramp freighter with a large forward hold, two masts with cranes hanging from them, and a smokestack rising from the aft. Lionheart hadn't ever spent any time on boats and had no idea what size crew to expect. He guessed, given the amount of deck to cover, that the two men on the top deck, by the pilot cabin, were probably assisted by a third and maybe fourth on the main deck, and possibly even one to two more on the aft deck. That didn't even begin to cover how many might be belowdecks in the hold.

Lionheart began to wonder if Qiao and Lihua had come to the *Kowloon Seadragon* after all. He neither saw nor heard any indications of a fight going on, indeed nothing to suggest one had happened at all. Surely if they'd come to attack the boat, the guards wouldn't be hanging around like nothing had occurred. They'd have more guards if the boat had been attacked, or it would have been moved. Could the Chous have gone somewhere else? With a shiver, Lionheart wondered if Qiao would have the nerve to go straight to the Wu Zhiming She headquarters. If so, Lionheart feared, it would be his final journey.

He saw that the sampan was almost close enough to the *Seadragon* for him to make his move. He picked up a piece of dark wood he'd selected for flotation assistance and glanced toward the prow. "Jian, good luck. Get back to *Yingtao Mu* quick as you can."

"Mickey Mouse, sumbitch. *Hao yun, sifu Shi Xin.*" Jian kept his eyes forward, humming to himself as he sculled onward.

Lionheart rolled off the side of the sampan into the chilly water, clutching the board against his chest. He had a difficult time floating in water at home as his muscle mass and fur tended to drag him downward. He was much more buoyant in seawater, but hadn't been willing to risk going into the ocean without some kind of insurance. He lay in the water on his back, only his snout and fingertips poking out as he held onto the plank like it he was the surfboard and it was riding upon him. He didn't know why he'd thought the water would be warm. The weather had been mild, with afternoon rains, and it was still early spring. The cold seeped in through his fur to his skin and he started shivering. The water was far more dangerous than he'd considered, and he hoped it wouldn't wind up killing him in a wasted death.

Keeping his legs below the surface, he kicked his legs like a frog, spreading them apart and then pulling them together through the water. Each kick brought him a foot closer to the *Seadragon*. As he neared the vessel, the black hull rose above him, blocking out the stars and moon. His nostrils were full of salt and diesel fuel and he couldn't smell anything else useful. All he could hear was the water slapping against the hull in slow, regular rhythm. He felt lost, alone, more than he'd been since before he first met Master Chou, all those years ago. The way the water moved along the hull of the boat, it kept trying to alternately pull him underneath or bash him against the wall of metal.

Then his hand found a rung and he realized there was a column of them climbing the side of the hull, a way on board. He released the plank and pulled himself out of the water to perch on the lowest rung. It was neither restful nor relaxing, but he wanted to give the water time to drain from his fur before ascending to the deck. He could fight wet if he had to, but one slip on a wet floor could spell his doom if he faced a skilled opponent.

At last, the steady stream of seawater reduced to scattered droplets, and he didn't feel like he'd flood the deck simply by climbing onto it. He reached for the next rung, then the next, and then the next.

Chapter Sixteen

"The quality of decision is like the well-timed swoop of a falcon which enables it to strike and destroy its victim."
—Sun Tzu

Lionheart waited on the ladder, just below the line of sight for the deck. He kept himself pressed up against the black paint of the *Kowloon Seadragon*'s hull, trying to be as invisible as Kobura had been when she attacked the school. He couldn't hear anything besides the creaking of the boat and the rhythmic slapping of waves gently breaking against its side. He knew there was a guard nearby because the man's cigarette laid a trail like a beacon on the breeze. There could be others not in immediate view of the ladder, and because of it he'd have to work fast. His fur was still dripping wet and it would slow him down.

But first, he needed to deal with the closest guard. He could smell the hint of gun oil on the gentle sea breeze, suggesting if Lionheart went over the rail at the wrong moment, it would be the last mistake he made. An idea occurred to him. Maybe he didn't need to get over the rail faster than the guard could pull the trigger. He started scratching his claws on the hull. They made a faint but shrill squealing sound. It made Lionheart's fur stand on end. Surely the guard had to hear it. After a half a minute of persistent squeaking of claws on metal, Lionheart smelled the cigarette smoke getting stronger. He braced himself with one hand and readied the other. A moment later, a head appeared over the railing, looking down at Lionheart in open-mouthed surprise.

Lionheart lunged upward, grabbed the man's shirt, and yanked him downward. The man's head rang off the railing with a dull thud and he collapsed to the deck. Lionheart held his breath, focusing with all his senses. Was anybody else approaching? Had the alarm been raised?

After a half minute, he decided he was safe—well, safe enough to continue with his one-man assault on the boat, at least. He pulled himself up onto the deck, keeping low but feeling horribly exposed all the same. He kicked the guard's weapon, a small submachine gun with a large suppressor over the muzzle, into the water. The splash was quiet enough he didn't worry about it being overheard by anyone else on board. He considered for a second whether to send the guard tumbling after the gun, but he might awaken in the water and shout for help, and although Lionheart knew it was only a matter of time before he was spotted on board, he wanted to maximize his stealth time. He moved aft, slipping underneath the deck of the rear superstructure. No lights came from the cabin windows as he hugged the wall, trusting to his ears and his nose to warn him if anyone was approaching.

He reached the corner of the superstructure and stopped right beside it, eyes shut, concentrating on the scents in the air. Diesel fuel, of course, and old exhaust. The salt of the sea air. The tang of heroin. Fresh urine. He smiled. There were few ways more embarrassing to be caught off guard than while one's pants were down. He rounded the corner. The guard's gun rested against the rail while the man pissed into the harbor, humming quietly to himself. Lionheart retrieved the gun, and turned it around to hold it butt-first. The guard finished his business and reached down for his gun. When he couldn't find it, Lionheart cleared his throat. The guard looked up at him and his eyes grew to the size of saucers. He took a deep breath to shout a warning but before so much as a peep could escape, Lionheart smashed him in the face with the butt of the gun. The guard collapsed, blood leaking out from the ruin of his shattered nose. Two down.

Lionheart looked at the gun in his hand. He'd handled plenty of them over the years, taking them away from criminals and the like, but he'd never actually fired one. He wondered if it might be time to learn, but then thought better of it. He was a killer, no question about that. He had plenty of blood on his hands, but killing low-level soldiers in a criminal organization was a wasted effort when the boss was the only one who truly mattered. That boss was Lian Kui, and he would be the figurative serpent's head that needed to be cut off in order for the body to die. The gun went over the side.

He continued around the aft of the *Kowloon Seadragon* until he found a stairwell leading up to the poop deck. He started up it when he heard a shout of alarm from somewhere forward. Someone must have found the first man he'd taken down. At least he'd gotten to take out two of the ship's guards before the alarm was raised. He ran up the stairwell, planning to get to the bridge and work his way downward. A door opened at the top of the stair and a man stuck his head out, presumably to see what the commotion was. Lionheart grabbed him by his shirt and threw him over the side. The man hollered all the way down to the water.

Floodlights at the top of the forward crane flipped on, bathing the main deck in sickly yellow light. Another man jumped down to the poop deck from the navigation deck up above. He raised his submachine gun and Lionheart ducked behind the lifeboat as bullets chewed into it, spattering him with splinters. He waited until the gunfire stopped and then took a running leap at the aft crane boom. His momentum carried him up and over the boom like a gymnast until he was perched atop it. The gunman slammed a new clip into his gun and opened up on Lionheart once more.

Lionheart leaped, twisting through the air to make himself harder to hit, and landed on the navigation deck, which was small and only held the captain's ready room and the wheelhouse. He heard a hatch below open and the footsteps of two more men emerging from belowdecks. The others were converging upon the stairwells and Lionheart had run out of higher ground. He shouldered through the door into the wheelhouse.

The man in the cabin already had a pistol up and he fired point-blank at Lionheart. The bullet creased his shoulder with a line of fire. Before the pilot managed a second shot, Lionheart grabbed his hand, pistol and all, and smashed it against the throttle box, shattering bones. The man yelped as Lionheart raked his claws across the man's face and followed up with a vicious elbow strike across the chin. To his credit, the pilot made an attempt to fight back, but his counterstrike was fully ineffective and Lionheart knocked him unconscious with a solid blow to his temple.

He heard the sound of a gun being cocked behind him and whirled around, holding the unconscious man before him like a shield. Another man stood in the doorway of the wheelhouse, his face twisted into a rictus of intense fury as he emptied the entire clip of his submachine gun at Lionheart. Bullets slammed into the body of the man he held and a line of fire raced across his trapezius as one bullet carved a groove in it. Later, Lionheart might take the time to feel bad about the man in the wheelhouse, but it was clear the guards were playing for keeps, and working to keep them alive would come back to bite him in the end.

He hurled the bullet-ridden body at the man in the doorway as he struggled to change clips. The grisly missile knocked him back down the stairwell. Lionheart leaped after him and landed hard, driving his feet downward in a kick that shattered the man's pelvis with a sickening crack. Vomit sprayed from his mouth as he shrieked in agony. Lionheart grabbed his head and twisted, severing his spinal cord and killing him instantly in a merciful act that was probably more than he deserved.

Lionheart's nose and ears told him there were still two men out on the deck. He peeked out from the cover of the quarterdeck door at the top of a stairwell leading down to the main deck. One of them spotted him and his gun spat bullets into the wooden walls as Lionheart ducked for cover. The man yelled something in Cantonese and his companion answered. They split up, apparently trying for some kind of containment. Lionheart smiled. That was their mistake. Even though they both had submachine guns and he had only his claws and teeth, he'd faced far worse opponents. Fighting one on one was something Lionheart could do all day long. These guards didn't seem to be proper Serpent Warriors. The few he'd faced already didn't have a whit of training. They put all their stock in their guns, and without those guns, they were useless.

He glanced around the top of the stairwell and spotted an emergency fire axe hanging on the wall. He retrieved it and crouched down, straining his ears and nose to the limit to detect the man approaching from the starboard side of the ship. The scent of the man's sweat came to him first, followed by the reek of his gun and the sourness of his breath. A soft footstep touched the bottom of the stairwell. Frantic, heavy breathing hissed off the stairwell walls as the man moved up, step by step, closer and closer.

The tip of the gun appeared at the entrance to the stairwell and Lionheart lunged with the axe. He chopped it down upon the barrel. The man fired in reflex and then yelled as it backfired thanks to the blocked barrel. Lionheart smacked the man across the face with the flat of the axe blade, opening a furrow in his cheek from the force of the impact. He followed it up with a knee into the man's side and then as the fellow collapsed, smashed his elbow down onto the back of the man's neck. He'd be out for hours.

A gun cocked behind Lionheart. A triumphant voice crowed, "*Gweilo.*"

Lionheart twisted around, jumping up and away in what he hoped was an unexpected direction as he sidearmed the axe at the man. Bullets whistled beneath him for a moment until the axe head buried itself in the man's throat just above his sternum. He dropped his smoking gun and clawed at the weapon protruding from his throat, making horrible gobbling sounds. Lionheart only needed a moment to determine the man would no longer be a threat to him, or anyone else after a minute or two. He allowed himself another moment of mercy and killed the critically-injured guard.

No further attacks came, and Lionheart stepped out onto the aft deck, adrenalin coursing through his system as he concentrated on his senses. Blood dripped from his fingertips. Only a bit of it was his. His shoulder ached and burned where the bullet had grazed him, but the pain served to keep his senses sharp. He couldn't smell anyone else on the main deck or above. If there were people belowdecks, they weren't moving to engage him. He worried about the presence of the guards on the ship. Although they'd been heavily armed, they hadn't seemed like they were expecting trouble. If the Five Deadly Serpents had suspected they'd be facing Lionheart, he wondered why they wouldn't have had far more guards who were much more competent on hand. Both the lifeboats were still clamped to their berths on either side of the quarterdeck. Unless someone had left on another boat or swam away, anything that happened on the *Kowloon Seadragon* might not have reached the Five Deadly Serpents yet, especially if there hadn't been time to issue a radio message.

A hint of heroin crossed his nostrils and he smiled a ferocious, predatory grin. Maybe he hadn't completely wasted his time. He found the aft stairwell to the lower deck and descended into the darkness below. The engine room was a filthy pit of oil and Diesel spillage, with numerous kludged-up repairs Lionheart imagined violated every possible maritime safety protocol, if there was even such a thing in Chinese shipping.

The odor of heroin grew stronger as he moved forward toward the main hold, and then a familiar scent crossed his nostrils and he froze.

Lihua had been here.

Her scent had imprinted upon his mind when they'd first slept together. He'd know it anywhere. She had been on board the *Kowloon Seadragon*, and that meant Qiao had been as well. Another step forward and more familiar scents assailed him—the coppery sting of blood, the dark stink of fear, the wet stench of death.

All of it was overlaid with the tang of heroin and the salty rot of bilgewater. He reached the pressure hatch at the main hold. It was open and a faint light came from within. He looked inside.

The hatch was larger than he'd expected, some twenty feet across and twice as long. A few crates were tied down inside nets against the walls. An inch of seawater sat on the floor of the hold. The only light in the room came from a shop light, hanging from a hook on a chain that dangled from the top of the hold where the overhead doors were still tightly shut. Beneath the light sat a single solitary figure, tied to a chair, a black sack covering its head. Lionheart's blood ran cold as he stepped into the hold. He stepped through the puddle on the floor, hating the way the cold seawater seeped through his fur.

Lihua's scent still danced in his nose as he moved around the figure in the chair. The stink of death almost overpowered the remaining hint of his lover, and when he saw the hooded person was male, his rejoicing was short-lived.

He knew it was Qiao even before he removed the blood-soaked hood.

The young warrior had been savagely beaten. His jaw had broken, and splintered ends poked out through the flesh of one cheek. Only a couple of broken teeth remained in his mouth, and only a bloody, ragged stump remained where his tongue had been. Someone had gouged out both his eyes, and pinkish fluid was drying upon his cheeks. If Lionheart had any question about whether Qiao was still alive, the deep cut across his throat answered it. Sweat, vomit, and blood stained his tunic, and bits of teeth were still stuck to the fabric.

"Oh, goddamn. Goddamn." Lionheart turned away. In all his years of training and fighting, he had never seen such brutality upon another person.

But where was Lihua? He hadn't been mistaken; her scent remained behind. Had she suffered the same beating as her brother? Was she dead as well? He shook his head. No, this had been an object lesson for her. He replayed the scenario in his mind the best he could figure. Qiao and Lihua had come aboard the *Kowloon Seadragon*, much as he had himself, with the intent to destroy its cargo. Instead, they'd found a trap awaiting them and were captured. The Serpent Warriors had tried to force them to sign over the right to the Cherrywood School, but they had refused. Then the Warriors had attempted to convince them. Qiao was tortured, certainly while Lihua watched. They would have told her they would stop if she gave up the school. She had refused, and because of it her brother had paid with his life. He must have still been in the hold because they wanted to dispose of his body where nobody could see. Keep their noses clean, Lionheart thought bitterly.

The Serpent Warriors were gone, and so was Lihua. They must have taken her back to Lian Kui. Lionheart didn't know about Chinese law, but he suspected that if Lihua died without transferring ownership of the school, it would go into some kind of probate, which meant that it could be even longer before the Five Deadly Serpents could acquire it. They needed a legal transfer, which meant they'd hold Lihua until they could get her to sign it over. She might not be safe, but they wouldn't kill her right away. Lionheart had a chance to get to her before that happened, and if he had to fight his way through the entire Triad, so be it.

As for the *Kowloon Seadragon*, he figured it belonged at the bottom of the harbor. He considered what to do about Qiao's body. Bringing it back to the island would be difficult at best if he used one of the

Seadragon's lifeboats, and it would only take one bystander to see the body to open a whole new can of worms. Would it be dishonorable to him to be buried at sea, the way so many great sailors and soldiers had been throughout history?

Then Lionheart realized he didn't care. Honor was what had gotten the Chous mixed up with the Five Deadly Serpents in the first place. Honor was why Qiao had been killed. The men who'd done this didn't believe in honor. They dealt in firm, tangible commodities like bullets and drugs. Honor was a tradition that meant nothing anymore. Trying to be the better, more honorable man against such villains would only serve to get Lionheart killed. The time for honor was past.

It was time for justice.

"Be at peace, Qiao. I'm going to go find your sister." Lionheart pulled the hood back over Qiao's ruined face. It was the closest to a burial shroud he had available. He lowered the shop light and shone it around the hold until he spotted two things that should make it easier for him to send the vessel to the seabed. A spare anchor was hanging from a heavy hook in one wall, and a stopcock jutted from the wall just beneath it. He splashed across the floor and hung the light from the same hook as the anchor. He got his hands beneath the curved metal crossbeam, groaning at the solid weight of it. It moved little by little as Lionheart's muscles shivered and creaked with the effort. At last, with a rasp of metal on metal, he got the anchor off its support hook and let it fall onto the stopcock below it, jumping back to avoid getting his toes smashed.

The heavy anchor broke open the stopcock and seawater rushed into the hold like Lionheart had turned on a firehose. If nothing else, the Five Deadly Serpents would have to find a new boat to smuggle their drugs, and he would call that a victory. He turned toward the hold exit, as he would need to get to the surface before the vessel took on too much water.

A nude man with nearly translucent skin pulled the hatch shut, sealing them both inside the hold.

Lionheart wasn't surprised he hadn't heard the other man enter the hold—he'd been making a lot of noise moving the anchor—but even though he could see the man's pale flesh glowing in the faint shop light, he couldn't smell him. Everyone had a scent, no matter how often they bathed or disinfected themselves, but this newcomer had no smell at all. Despite his white skin, his features were Chinese and his dark eyes squinted at Lionheart. He wasn't even five feet tall, and he didn't have so much as a scrap of body hair. He grinned, showing a mouthful of fangs, and something peculiar rippled along the sides of his neck. Lionheart gasped as he realized they were *gills*.

Seawater swirled around his knees and he knew he was in trouble.

Chapter Seventeen

"Quickness is the essence of the war."
—Sun Tzu

The pale man took a step toward Lionheart. Although he was nude, he appeared devoid of any external genitals. He spread his hands and smiled and Lionheart saw the webbing between his fingers. "I am Ai Haishe, the Dwarf Sea Snake. I have been waiting for you." His voice was soft and indistinct, as if he spoke with marbles in his mouth. It could have been the fangs distorting his words or it could have been the rushing of water through the shattered stopcock in the forward hull.

The water had already risen above Lionheart's knees. He was running out of time. Ai Haishe had gills and surely wouldn't have locked the two of them in the hold if he couldn't have survived underwater. Lionheart had no such benefit. Niceties such as introductions would have to wait for another time. He charged toward the pale man in great splashing leaps.

Ai Haishe dropped into the water, for a moment giving Lionheart an unblocked path to the hold exit. He went for it, but a pale hand closed around his ankle and dragged him backward with surprising strength. Lionheart whirled and tried to drive his elbow down upon Ai Haishe's back, but the man lashed a foot

189

through the water like it was air and swept Lionheart's feet off the deck. He fell backward and the seawater closed over his face.

Ai Haishe was on top of him in a flash, pushing him down against the deck, his fangs flashing in a monstrous grin. Lionheart braced his shoulders against the hold floor and thrust upward with his knees. Ai Haishe flew up and over his head to splash down several feet away.

Lionheart struggled to get back upright again. The water was midway up his thighs and the *Kowloon Seadragon* was starting to tip forward as more seawater rushed into the hold. Ai Haishe whipped through the water like a dart, propelling himself with his webbed feet. He flew out of the dark seawater like a flying fish and raked Lionheart's side with tiny claws on his fingertips. Lionheart twisted to counterstrike, but the fish-man was already looping around behind him and a powerful blow to the back of one knee sent Lionheart careening forward into the deeper part of the water.

Ai Haishe came at him like a missile and savaged him with his teeth and claws, pushing Lionheart into deeper and deeper water. The boat was canting forward far enough that Lionheart lost his footing and slipped completely under. Ai Haishe sliced at him, sending bits of fur swirling away into the dark water. Lionheart kicked at him but the water fought every motion, making it slow and awkward. Ai Haishe dove into the deeper water, spiraling around Lionheart faster than he could turn. Lionheart's mane swirled around his face as he tried to swim upward. The dark hold and slanting floor would have made it difficult to tell which way was up if he wasn't also fighting for his life. His lungs burned and it took every erg of effort not to gasp for a breath of air that wasn't there for him to take.

Something solid bumped against Lionheart's back. It felt like wood, and it moved, which meant it was floating. He took a blow from Ai Haishe and swiped at the fish-man with his own claws, opening furrows in his flesh. Ai Haishe might have drawn first blood, but Lionheart's claws were sharper. Lionheart kicked away, spots dancing in his eyes as he sought air beyond the floating wooden object. Then his head broke the surface and he drew in a deep breath of sweet, sweet air. Before he could take another, Ai Haishe pulled him under again.

A hard fist into his gut sent what air was left in Lionheart's lungs rocketing toward the surface. Water rushed into his nose and only by biting his own tongue did he keep from reflexively inhaling. He flailed about, blind in the dark water, trying to catch Ai Haishe with any kind of defensive blow. Hands closed around one of his feet and instead of panicking, Lionheart used the contact to determine where the fish-man was. He stomped downward with his other foot and caught the man in his face.

Lionheart shot upward against the floating wooden object and he scrambled around it, digging his claws into the wood for purchase until he reached open air once more. He was hanging on a crate, riding it upward as seawater carried it closer and closer to the hatch at what was quickly becoming the top of the hold instead of the aft. Ai Haishe jumped him from behind and sank his teeth deep into Lionheart's shoulder, which was already hurting from the bullet graze. He roared in pain and smashed his head back against Ai Haishe's. The man didn't release his bite and in fact dug his fangs deeper into Lionheart's flesh. Lionheart tore a board away from the crate and drove the splintered end back toward Ai Haishe. The fish-man shrieked and tore away a chunk of Lionheart's shoulder as he recoiled.

An overwhelming stink of heroin filled his head and he knew what was in the crate he'd torn open. The Serpents must not have finished unloading the *Kowloon Seadragon*, however covertly they'd been doing it, before Qiao and Lihua came aboard. He shoved his arm into the crate, ignoring the pain of splintered wood scratching his flesh. His fingertip claws snagged a plastic baggie just as Ai Haishe lunged out of the water, dug his hands into Lionheart's mane, and yanked his head back, exposing his throat even as he tugged him beneath the swirling surface yet again. The fish-man spun around Lionheart and opened his mouth wide to tear open Lionheart's throat.

With no other weapon handy, Lionheart pushed the baggie against Ai Haishe's gills and crushed it. It burst apart in a murky cloud of powder around the fish-man's head. Ai Haishe's reaction was swift and satisfying as he released Lionheart and lurched backward, his eyes bulging and his hands grasping at his throat in a futile attempt to clear the heroin that he'd inhaled through his gills.

Lionheart popped his head above the surface for a moment, taking a deep breath, and then plunged back into the water where Ai Haishe was shaking, perhaps beginning an overdose seizure. Lionheart closed one hand around the fish man's wrist and used that leverage to wrap his other arm around Ai Haishe's throat. With one firm twisting motion, he broke Ai Haishe's neck across his chest. The man stopped his thrashing and Lionheart let him fall away into the watery darkness.

He took a moment to look around, astonished that the shop light hadn't yet shorted out despite being fully underwater. It couldn't last much longer, and at the rate the water level was rising in the hold, it wouldn't need to. As near as he could tell, the *Kowloon Seadragon* had tilted itself at least forty-five degrees nose-down into the water, which meant not only was the hold filling, but water would be leaking in through the main deck as well. He might not even have minutes to get out before the *Seadragon* gave up all pretenses at flotation and headed for the seabed.

His shoulder burned from the cold saltwater in the bullet wound, and his entire body ached from the stress of combat in and under the water. Nevertheless, he made his way to the steeply-tilted floor of the hold not yet submerged and crawled up it, using finger and toe claws to get whatever purchase he could find. He reached the hold entrance and hesitated. If there was water behind it, turning the wheel would send a cascade down upon him, probably dislodge him from his perch, and drown him. His only hope would be to swim upward against the current and try to find the stairwell to take him back to the main deck, which could also be flooded. It would have been much easier to fall back and let the water take him, but Lihua was probably already in the Five Deadly Serpents mansion. He didn't doubt she could hold off a great many attackers, but the Serpents were many and she was one. Eventually she'd get worn down, and he didn't want to think about what they might do to her.

"I'm coming for you." He said the words aloud, hoping whatever Great Powers of the Universe were listening might find it in their hearts to lend him a helping hand. Then without further ado, he braced his feet against the wall of the hold, fast becoming a ceiling at the angle of the sinking ship, and twisted the wheel.

The light burning in the water beneath him winked out just as the door swung open and a torrent of water rushed into the hold. Lionheart hung onto the door with grim resolve in the darkness. His ears popped as the seawater pushed air out through the nooks and crannies. He shut his eyes, knowing they'd be useless in the darkness of the submerged lower deck. He needed to find the eye of calm at the center of the storm around him. His *xi* was tangled up with the stress of external combat and threats from the environment. He wasn't good at meditation at the best of times, but he knew it would be the one thing that could get him back to the surface. He had to trust himself.

Master Chou would have been proud the way he relaxed even as he dangled from the door, even as the rising waters touched his toes. He let himself become as empty as the void, a vessel ready to be filled with the entirety of the cosmos. He filled his lungs with air again and again, taking in the scents of the water and the detritus which it carried into the hold, focusing on each hint of odor and cherishing it. The water rose above his waist, then his chest, and still he relaxed, breathed, waited. Somewhere above him was the light of day, and beyond that Lihua, and beyond her the entirety of the universe.

The water reached his chin and he took one final breath before it fully engulfed him. With nothing but the air in his lungs, nothing to guide him but his fingertips and memory of the deck layout, he pulled himself upward into the main deck corridor, now more vertical than horizontal. His blood pumped in his ears like the pounding of war drums. His outstretched hands found the gap in the corridor where he'd expected it to be, and he knew it was the stairwell to the main deck and open water. His lungs burned and he longed to open his eyes, but with the *Kowloon Seadragon* well on its way toward the bottom of the harbor, he knew he couldn't trust them. Likewise, the water currents swirling around the vessel as it flailed and tossed in its death throes were confusing and contradictory. Only the light within him could be trusted as it sought its partner, a beacon in the shape of Lihua on the opposite side of the barrier between sea and sky.

The *Seadragon* fell away from him, trying to drag him down in its embrace, but instead he swam up and away from it, and as the last whisper of air escaped his lungs, he breached the surface like a whale in the North Atlantic. The stink of Aberdeen Harbor had never smelled so sweet. His head filled with the scents of saltwater, of rotten fish, spilled Diesel fuel and oil, and the underlying tang of heroin. The sun was still below the horizon, but the sky had gone from black to a grayish pink, suggesting a bright and clear morning on the way. The *Kowloon Seadragon* still wallowed with its stern sticking out of the water, stubbornly refusing to have the good graces to sink the rest of the way. A field of floating debris surrounded the vessel, and Lionheart found a broad piece of wood that could hold his weight. He heaved himself up onto it, sprawled onto his back, and rested. Exhaustion permeated every strand of muscle, every pore of skin.

His opportunity to rest was short-lived. The sound of approaching motors made him open his eyes to look toward the island. He saw a speedboat and four jet-skis heading from the throng of the floating village toward the *Seadragon*'s watery grave. At first, he thought they might be police, but squashed that notion. The police wouldn't know about the sinking vessel yet, but the ship's crew might have radioed to the Five Deadly Serpents to report they were under attack. Or they were coming back to retrieve the final cargo of heroin. Whatever the case, Lionheart couldn't risk being seen. With a weary sigh, he slipped back into the water, muscles protesting their chilly submersion once more.

Worried shouts came from the jet-ski riders and half dozen men on the speedboat as they circled the debris field. More than once, they called out for Ai Haishe, and Lionheart knew they were his enemies for certain. The speedboat came to a halt beside the corpse of the beleaguered *Seadragon* and the men aboard had an animated discussion about what they should do. The three jet-skis poked through the floating debris, stopping beside the larger pieces, presumably looking for the missing crate of heroin. Lionheart kept himself beside the drifting plank, holding himself beneath the lapping water but for his nose and eyes.

A jet-ski punk swung around the plank. He stank of gun oil and unwashed sweat and a submachine gun hung from a strap around one shoulder. The morning sun peeked over the edge of the world, highlighting the man's red-rimmed eyes and slack jaw, suggesting he'd been partying pretty hard when called out to do a job. He nudged the jet-ski throttle and came within inches of Lionheart without noticing him.

Lionheart knew he wouldn't have a better chance. He reached out of the water, hooked his claws into the man's leg, and yanked him off the jet-ski. The man's surprised yell cut short as his mouth filled with water. Lionheart grabbed onto the jet-ski and pulled himself onto it. The man he'd just dislodged raised his dripping gun out of the water, pointed it right at Lionheart, and pulled the trigger.

Nothing happened.

Lionheart lashed out and kicked the man in the face. A chatter of gunfire splattered across the water beside him as one of the other jet-ski punks fired at him, an open-mouthed look of shock plastered across his face. Lionheart twisted the throttle and yanked the steering yoke over. The jet-ski leaped forward. More bullets whistled past him as he zigged and zagged, making himself harder to hit.

The other two jet-skis leaped over the water as they charged toward him. Behind him, the powerful outboard motor of the speedboat rumbled to life, and the chase was joined.

Chapter Eighteen

*"The general who advances without coveting fame and
retreats without fearing disgrace, whose only thought is
to protect his country and do good service for his
sovereign, is the jewel of the kingdom."*
—*Sun Tzu*

Lionheart took the jet-ski around the *Kowloon Seadragon*,
using the swell of the hapless vessel's aft to give him some
cover from the pursuing Serpent Warriors and then
opened the throttle wide. The jet-ski leaped over the
surface like a gazelle. Its quick responsiveness reminded
him of the one time he'd raced a course on a superbike
instead of his preferred motorcycle. He was far enough
ahead of the other jet-ski drivers for them to forgo
shooting at him, instead focusing upon keeping up. The
speedboat would be a problem as it had more power and
extra hands on board to take shots at him. He'd have to be
more strategic to avoid getting killed that way.

Ahead of him was the maze of the floating village,
and the speedboat's advantage would be nullified by the
cluttered waterways, but first he had to get there.

He whipped the jet-ski around a buoy and then past
a tramp freighter not unlike the *Kowloon Seadragon*.
The crew gaped at the lion-headed man racing on the
jet-ski, and then ducked as the pursuers passed, waving
their guns and shouting to one another.

The early morning sunlight made the long shadows of the floating village deceptive, and Lionheart had to be careful not to run into anything innocent sitting in a shadow. He jerked the yoke to avoid a collision with a bundle of wooden traps gathered in a net and found himself heading directly for a sampan with a wide-eyed couple clutching at one another in surprise. With no time to do anything else, he tilted the jet-ski's nose into the water and dove. Seawater battered his face as his head passed just beneath the sampan's keel. The jet-ski came back out of the water at a steep angle and went airborne, actually flying up and over another sampan before splashing back down onto a long open stretch between rows of boats lashed together. He glanced back to check whether he'd made any progress escaping.

The pursuing jet-ski riders attempted to duplicate his feat. One matched his dive-and-jump move for move, passing beneath the first sampan and over the second. The other rider mustn't have dived deep enough, for the jet-ski popped back out of the water without anyone upon it. Then the speedboat crashed right through both sampans, rendering Lionheart's acrobatics to waste. No, it wasn't wasted, he told himself. He'd done his best to avoid them. Now, with Serpent Warriors chasing him through the cluttered maze of the floating village, he needed to bring the chase to a close and quickly before more people got hurt. At least they weren't shooting at him for the time being. Trying to hit him would have been a waste of bullets. In his experience, bad guys with guns weren't normally concerned about such a thing, but perhaps the Serpent Warriors were a slightly higher class of thug.

He angled his jet-ski close to another sampan and snapped off the long sculling oar, giving himself an eight-foot-long bamboo pole, which was a better weapon than nothing. He wasn't sure what he would do with it, but grabbing it had been almost instinctual, and so he kept hold of it. Then he spotted a way to use it, and steered the jet-ski toward a narrow gap between sampans that led to another wide-open waterway beyond. It would take expert timing and a healthy dose of luck, neither of which seemed to be in great supply for Lionheart. As he reached the gap in the boats, he nosed the jet-ski down into the water once more, and as it dove under the surface for a moment, he reached up and wedged the pole across the gap. The tough bamboo pole bent but didn't break as each end embedded itself in the hull of the sampans on either side. He glanced back again to see the results of his handiwork.

The rider behind him didn't react in time and the pole caught the Serpent Warrior just beneath the chin, yanking him off the jet-ski and flipping him up in the air, trailing blood and bone fragments from a shattered jaw. The speedboat flashed through the gap, shattering the bamboo pole and catching the unfortunate jet-ski rider like a bus running down a pedestrian. The man broke against the sharp speedboat prow and was borne beneath it.

Lionheart didn't have time to see if the man resurfaced, nor did he care. He'd found himself in a wide waterway sparsely populated with larger vessels sailing toward the docks and very little cover besides them. The pops of gunfire began to sound behind him as the men on the speedboat decided it was worth the risk. A bullet cracked through the plastic fairing just beneath Lionheart's right arm. He began sweeping the jet-ski back and forth at random, never staying the same course for more than a second or two, keeping his movements as unpredictable as he could, but it would only take one lucky shot to disable his ride or catch him in the back of the head. He needed to find some better cover.

Or, he thought as an idea occurred to him, eliminate the advantage of his pursuers' guns.

He swung the jet-ski toward a tugboat churning its way in toward Aberdeen. The crewmen aboard the ship stared in shock over the gunwales as the lion-man swung around their stern and then twisted back in a tight u-turn. With no time to gauge his distance, Lionheart leaped with pure instinct, claws splayed as he flew across the churning waves toward the tug. He caught one of the tires lashed along the outer hull, nearly tearing through it with his razor-sharp claws before he dragged himself up onto the deck. The crewmen yelled in fear and surprise at his sudden boarding maneuver. "Get down, get down!" Lionheart waved at them as he scurried across the deck, but it took a trail of bullet holes across the forecastle for them to realize they were in more danger from the men in the speedboat. They hit the deck, still yelling in frantic Cantonese.

Lionheart had spotted something on the deck he could use to even the odds, but he needed to keep the guys on the speedboat honest before they pulled alongside the tug and swarmed over the gunwales. He grabbed hold of a coil of thick rope that would have been a heavy load for a strong man but was manageable with his parahuman strength. He twisted his hips and shoulders, ignoring the burning pain in his wound, and hurled the coil toward the speedboat. It flew through the air in an amorphous mass like some giant amoeba until it hit the boat, enshrouding its occupants in its coils.

One of the men got tangled in the rope and fell overboard, losing his gun and shouting frantically for help as the twisting rope kept him from staying afloat.

Lionheart grabbed a wicked-looking three-pronged gaff from the edge of the deck and hurled it at the speedboat while the men were taking a moment to untangle themselves. Although the metal hooks curved back toward the handle instead of pointing forward like a spear or trident, the man who got struck in the face would have argued in favor of its effectiveness as a weapon. He blubbered as his nose burst open from the solid impact. For a few seconds, nothing but chaos ruled upon the speedboat, and those precious seconds were enough time for Lionheart to get on top of the forecastle and unlimber the firefighting cannon. He'd seen how effective they'd been controlling riots in America, and figured it would be an efficient way to put an end to the pursuit so he could get back to the real work of finding Lihua and taking down the Five Deadly Serpents. The problem was he'd never actually operated one before.

The deluge gun looked simple enough. It had a screw nozzle that adjusted like a lawn sprinkler, allowing for a fine, powerful stream or a broader fan. There was a trigger that did nothing when he pulled it, suggesting he needed to turn it on. He spotted a pull handle like one for a lawnmower and yanked it. Somewhere beneath his feet, a generator coughed to life and a moment later, water began to dribble out of the nozzle tip.

The speedboat was coming around for another pass, the men having divested themselves of the rope Lionheart had hurled upon them. They raised their submachine guns at him and Lionheart grinned back at them. "Let's go." He pulled the trigger and a satisfyingly powerful jet of seawater shot from the tip. He swung it to point at the boat and adjusted the aperture to make a thin, needle-sharp spray. He aimed for the men's heads, figuring if they were smart they'd jump overboard to save the potential losses of teeth, eyes, or worse. The first two men didn't figure that out and their heads snapped back as the water jet hit them. They tumbled back off the boat. The other three ducked down, trying to find cover behind the edges of the hull. At his higher angle, Lionheart brought the jet down upon their backs full force, filling the hull faster than it could drain.

The speedboat sank lower into the water. Lionheart released the trigger and called down toward them. "Had enough? Throw your guns overboard." He watched them toss their weapons into the water and nodded in satisfaction. "Out of the boat. I don't care where you go, but you're not getting on this tug and you're not staying in the speedboat. I'll tear the throat out of any man still in that boat when I board it." He paused. "Anybody doubt I can do it?"

The three men looked at one another. One of them muttered to the other two, perhaps translating the gist of his threat into Cantonese. All three went over the side and swam several yards from the boat where they waited, treading water, looking thoroughly cowed.

Lionheart smiled at the cowering crewmen. "If you gentlemen would pull your tug alongside that there speedboat, I'll be on my way." He turned to glare down at the Serpent Warriors in the water. "And as for you lot, if you happen to get out of the harbor before I do, go to Lian Kui and deliver a message for me. You tell him I'm coming for him."

狮 和 五 致 死 蛇

Lionheart drove the speedboat back to the docks controlled by the Wu Zhiming She. He could have gone anywhere along the Aberdeen harbor; all docks would eventually get him where he needed to go, but he was hoping to find any evidence of Lihua. Perhaps the Serpent Warriors who had taken her might not have gotten around to removing her from the docks yet. With them clearly in the process of removing heroin from the *Kowloon Seadragon* on the sly, they would have been concerned if the crew had managed to send a radio alert. It was no wonder he'd run afoul of so many of them, armed and ready to fight a war. If his little distraction had done enough, they might have waited to remove Lihua from the area.

But instead of finding the woman who'd stolen his heart, he found Station Sergeant Montgomery waiting on the docks along with half a dozen officers. They were as heavily-armed as the Serpent Warriors had been, including some odd shotgun-type weapons with bulky packages at their muzzles. Lionheart suspected they were nets, and the idea of them wanting to trap him like a wild animal made his fury brim to the very top. If they wanted to face an angry beast, he'd be more than ready to oblige.

However, Montgomery's hands were empty and the officers with him held their weapons at the ready without pointing them at Lionheart. Sergeant Yang, who might as well have walked around carrying a sign saying *Paid for by the Five Deadly Serpents*, was nowhere to be seen. Maybe he was of a mood to converse instead of merely to arrest.

Lionheart bumped the speedboat up against the dock, careless about whether or not he damaged the finish, and jumped up onto the wooden boardwalk. A couple of the officers cursed under their breaths at his size and apparent strength, but kept their weapons away from him. "Mr. Lionheart. I'd say I'm surprised to see you here, but in fact a call came into the station about you, and it was so unbelievable that I had to come and see for myself." Montgomery's smile was as pale as the morning clouds over the harbor. "What are you doing here?"

"Returning this boat." Lionheart nodded toward the speedboat, already starting to drift away from the dock. Nobody had made a move to lash it in place.

"It belongs here?"

"As far as I know."

"And how did you come to acquire it?" Montgomery had his arms crossed and Lionheart suspected he already knew most of the answers and was instead fishing to see what truths and lies would be forthcoming. With his cheery British accent, he managed to sound like both a buffoon and a James Bond villain all at the same time.

"It was adrift in the harbor. Nobody was on board." Lionheart smiled. That was true. More or less.

"What were you doing out in the harbor?"

"Looking for a way back to shore. Lucky for me, I found one."

"And what of the reports of gunfire?"

Lionheart spread his hands. "As you can see, Station Sergeant, I'm quite unarmed."

"You're hardly that."

The men behind Montgomery shuffled their feet, swaying back and forth and fingering their weapons with the kind of nervousness that came from men who were outclassed and knew it. "So what happens now? Are you going to detain me? Because I don't have time for that."

Montgomery raised his hand and said "*Wang hou zhan, guanyuan.*" The officers dutifully lowered their weapons and stepped back to give him some space. "I'm afraid I'd find it rather difficult to detain you legally,

Lionheart, given your status here, unless you'd committed a crime." He fixed his gimlet eye upon Lionheart. "Have you committed a crime?"

"Not yet." Lionheart didn't back down. He didn't have time with Lihua's life possibly on the line.

"Let us speak candidly. Five minutes, Lionheart. I suspect you have superheroing to do." Montgomery strolled over to the dock beside the drifting speedboat, retrieved a gaff from a rack, and pulled on the vessel to bring it back to the slip. "You're going after the Five Deadly Serpents, aren't you?"

"Yes. They've taken Lihua Chou. They murdered her brother Qiao aboard the *Kowloon Seadragon*."

"Which is no longer in the harbor? My men reported losing it somewhere overnight. Yes, I've had men I trust watching it." Montgomery succeeded in pulling the loose speedboat back to the dock and proceeded to moor it. "You probably see us as provincial buffoons out here, but as much as I believe in keeping the peace being my primary function, it galls me that the Triads are bringing heroin into Hong Kong through my city. My docks. This section is my responsibility, Lionheart, and aside from the few I have who are above reproach, the Wu Zhiming She practically owns my department. As long as they keep the money flowing into the pockets of my officers, they will look the other way when heroin is carried ashore."

"Corruption is the same everywhere in the world. It'll continue unchecked, unless someone puts a stop to it." Lionheart gnashed his teeth. Every minute he spent conversing with Montgomery was one more away from finding Lihua. They could be torturing her even now. Beating her. Or worse. Much, much worse. "I plan to."

"You can't fight the Serpents by yourself. They're far too well organized and equipped. And unfortunately, I cannot assist you. If I lose the few honest men I have in a misguided assault, the Triads will only further cement their power base here in Aberdeen. You see my quandary. And after I told you nobody wants a war."

"You want to put a dent in the heroin trade here or not? Be a good cop, Montgomery. Make that badge mean something." Montgomery's lips twitched but he said nothing. His eyes glanced downward toward the badge pinned to his uniform. "I'm a superhero, Montgomery. With all due respect, fighting against impossible odds is the first thing in my job description. Maybe there's another way you can help."

"I can't simply order up a search warrant for their premises. They own the magistrates as well."

"What about probable cause? Do they have that here?"

Montgomery raised an eyebrow. "Please elaborate."

"If you have reason to believe a crime is being committed on private property, or you witness something indicative of it, you can enter without a warrant, right?"

"Why, yes. But in the case of the Wu Zhiming She, it would have to be a rather significant event. Something not even a corrupt officer would dare to ignore."

Lionheart glanced into the speedboat and saw the flare gun beside the emergency kit. He reached down and removed it from its clips. Montgomery watched him tuck it into the back of his trousers but said nothing. "You want a significant event? I'll give you a significant event. I'll give you something that not even Sergeant Yang could overlook."

The barest hint of a smile crossed Montgomery's lips and Lionheart knew he'd found the right button to push. "I see. Well, I suppose it wouldn't be entirely unwarranted to have the men doing some sort of drill up in that area. How will I know your signal?"

Lionheart's voice was grim. "Trust me, you'll know."

"Then I had better send you on your way."

Montgomery's hand moved as if to shake Lionheart's hand, but Lionheart shook his head. He was certain Serpent Warriors were watching the proceedings unfold. "Eyes are everywhere, Montgomery."

"Indeed. I believe I did see that monstrosity of an American car parked on the street just beyond the docks."

"I thought I was the only American monstrosity around here. Perhaps I should go say hello."

Montgomery smiled. "Time, as they say, waits for no man. Good luck and good hunting, Lionheart."

"I make my own luck, Montgomery. But when it comes to hunting . . ." Lionheart extended his claws and flashed his fangs. "I always catch my prey. Now I've got to get out of here and go do my job." He closed his hand into a fist. "I'm sorry about this. I'll be careful."

Montgomery sighed. "Make it look good."

Lionheart socked him across the jaw.

Chapter Nineteen

*"Thus, what is of supreme importance in war
is to attack the enemy's strategy."*
—Sun Tzu

For a few moments, Lionheart was afraid Montgomery's men would actually shoot him. Bullets whistled past him as he zigged and zagged across the docks toward the exit. One spalled off a shipping container far too close to his head for his liking and he ducked around the corner of it. He suspected the officers had strict orders to put on a good show, but a couple of them weren't quite the marksmen they could have been, and they were the ones whose shots were getting uncomfortably close to him. He decided to forgo the exit altogether and went into the maze of containers, using his claws to pull himself up tier by tier until he could run along the top. By disappearing among the containers, Montgomery's men would have justification to stop shooting and start searching, giving him the time he needed to get to the Five Deadly Serpents' mansion up in the hills.

But first, he had a bit of unresolved business.

He reached the main thoroughfare beyond the docks and spotted the Pontiac Firebird parked beside a noodle stall. The stocky figure seated behind the wheel, slurping noodles like a vacuum cleaner, had to be Lang She.

Lionheart glanced around the street, trying to spot any other Serpent Warriors. He was clearly identifiable without anything to put over his head, and people were already staring at him. If he didn't spot the *dashe yongshi* before they saw him, he might never see the killing shot before his life was leaking out onto the cobblestones.

There, that fellow up on the rooftop above the noodle stall with the binoculars. He was sweeping them back and forth across the docks. He had to be Lang She's second, still trying to find Lionheart on the docks and watching the police in their search.

Lionheart ducked into a narrow alley and did a chimney ascent, feet and shoulders pressing against opposite walls until he reached the roof. He trotted past birdcages, evoking disturbed cooing from the roosting pigeons and doves in their nests, rounded a couple of chimneys, and found himself perched above and behind the Serpent Warrior with the binoculars. He stepped off the ledge and dropped a few feet to land right behind the man, snaking one arm around the Serpent Warrior's throat and covering the man's mouth with his other. The man kicked as Lionheart dragged him back, squeezing his arm across the man's throat until his kicks grew weak, then stopped altogether. Lionheart pulled him well away from the edge of the rooftop, near the pigeon cages, figuring if he awakened prematurely, the birds' alarm might give Lionheart a bit of warning if he was still nearby.

He dropped back down into the alley and went back onto the street. Without any cover or disguise, he knew he had to work fast. He ran up behind the Firebird, watching the reflection of Lang She in the driver's side mirror to see if the Serpent Warrior looked in his direction. Luckily, the man was far too engrossed in shoveling noodles into his mouth to even notice when Lionheart came right up beside him. "Hello, Lang She."

Lang She, startled, turned to look with his chopsticks halfway to his mouth. His eyes widened as he recognized Lionheart's snarling face, but before he could even react, Lionheart drove a hard fist right to the center of his face. Lang She's nose flattened like a deflated playground kickball with a wet crunch. Shrimp noodles exploded across the car's interior like a bomb had gone off. A stunned Lang She reeled from the blow and Lionheart dragged him right out of the car through the window. Passers-by shouted in surprise as Lionheart bounced Lang She's head off the car's hood and then hurled him across the street. Lang She crumpled into the gutter that doubled as a sewer with a splash and lay still.

Lionheart pulled open the door, saw the keys were still in the ignition, and sat in the driver's seat. He swiped his hand across the windshield interior, wiping away the noodles clinging there, and started the car. The engine, unmuffled and poorly tuned, roared into life in a wreath of blue and black smoke. Lionheart shook his head and clucked his tongue in annoyance. It was a shame Lang She hadn't taken better care of such a fine piece of Detroit machinery.

It would be a crime what Lionheart was about to do to it.

He leaned on the horn, scaring pedestrians out of his way, hammered the accelerator down, and popped the clutch. The engine's roar turned to a high-powered shriek as the rear differential locked and both wheels spun together, adding the tang of hot rubber to the stink of burned oil and raw gas. Even though poorly-tuned, the Poncho still had enough power to make for an impressive launch, and Lionheart drove it right down the center of the street, one hand on the wheel and the other on the horn. People jumped out of the way and then stared open-mouthed in its wake.

Being shortly after dawn, the streets were busy but not as crowded as they could have been. Had it been later in the morning, Lionheart might have been forced to navigate the crowds while riding the brake the entire time. Instead, he managed to keep his velocity up and got clear of the harbor area after a few minutes, and then out of the busiest part of Aberdeen shortly thereafter. He could see his destination, the mansion of the Wu Zhiming She, perched high up on a hillside. If he got there quickly enough, he hoped he'd arrive ahead of any warning that he was on his way. Surely they were expecting him. Ai Haishe had been waiting for him aboard the *Kowloon Seadragon* and Lang She was watching for him at the docks. Until someone reported to Lian Kui that Lionheart had been permanently dealt with, the leader of the Triad would have to assume he was still at large.

On the way up toward the Wu Zhiming She mansion, Lionheart spotted a road repair crew working to patch a large pothole with gravel and mud. He stomped on the brakes and the Pontiac fishtailed to a halt right beside the rickshaw of the crew's equipment, eliciting angry and fearful shouts from the workers. Their words died on their lips as the lion-faced man stepped out of the car. He raised his hands in what he hoped was a peaceful gesture. "I need to borrow a couple things from your cart."

Most of the crew backed away, uttering placating prayers to their ancestors and warding away evil spirits. One man stood his ground, probably the supervisor. He raised an angry finger toward Lionheart and unleashed a blistering Cantonese tirade upon him. Lionheart took it for almost a minute before he remembered who he was. He took a deep breath and let loose with a snarling roar that shook the petals off a nearby cherry blossom tree. The supervisor went white as a sheet and his rant died in the middle of a sentence. Done communicating in anything resembling words, Lionheart raised a clawed finger and pointed in the direction of the rest of the crew, who were already fleeing back down the road to Aberdeen. The supervisor focused upon the sharp claw at the end of Lionheart's finger before his eyes returned to Lionheart's face. Lionheart raised an eyebrow and nodded his head in the direction of Aberdeen and let a low growl rumble from the pit of his throat.

The supervisor fled.

Lionheart selected a shovel and pickaxe and set them on the seat beside him. Thus fortified, he set out once more, careless around the corners, enjoying the blast of greenery-scented wind in his face mixed with the stink of hot metal. When he came to the drive of the mansion, he cranked the wheel over and the Pontiac responded with a magnificent T-stop, ending with the nose pointed up the hill toward the house.

He only had a few seconds, because the car would be in sight of the house and the inevitable armed guards around it. He jammed the handle of the pickaxe through the steering wheel, using the picks to hold it in place and wedging the handle underneath the seat. He let go of the wheel and crouched on the seat, pushing the shovel head against the accelerator and the handle against the headrest. The Pontiac jumped forward, fighting the pickaxe holding the steering wheel in place. Lionheart watched through the open T-top, waiting for his chance. As the Pontiac passed beneath a tree with low-hanging branches, he sprang from the seat.

A branch caught him solidly in the chest, hard enough to hurt. Nevertheless, he pulled his legs up as quickly as he could and hoped nobody had seen him exit the vehicle. The Pontiac roared along, its exhaust leaving a distinctive reek in the air as it struggled to turn off its headlong course. In a few seconds it would hit something, causing enough of a distraction for Lionheart to enter the Wu Zhiming She territory, if not the mansion outright.

He scrambled through the branches until enough foliage blocked direct view from the mansion, and then dropped into the soft heathery ground cover below. Once he had feet on the ground, he raced through the greenery, keeping as much of it as possible between him and the mansion. The sound of the car crashing against something echoed off the hills, and men shouted at the surprise intrusion. Lionheart kept to the periphery, dropping to all fours when he saw, heard, or smelled a guard. Many of them had abandoned their post to go see what had caused the ruckus up front of the house, and Lionheart was trusting his distraction to get himself into the house.

Real lions tended to hunt in the open, in groups, letting their prey flee one lion only to run right into the jaws and claws of another. Lionheart felt more like a jaguar, stalking his prey from cover and preparing to ambush, and only a minute after he'd escaped from the driverless car, he had his opportunity. A guard had drifted too close to the edge of the property so he could see what was happening at the front of the house. Lionheart peeked from beneath some foliage and saw the Pontiac had actually hit something hard enough to roll, and smoke poured from the bottom of the engine, currently facing the sky. The guard gawked at the ongoing incident, his gun dangling from one hand while the other shielded his eyes against the sunlight.

Lionheart lunged out of the trees and wrapped one hand over the guard's mouth while delivering a powerful blow to the vagus nerve behind his ear. The hapless guard never had a chance. He went limp immediately as Lionheart dragged his unconscious body back into the heather. He ejected the clip from the gun and threw it away, then focused his energy and delivered a devastating blow to the weapon itself, breaking it apart and bending many of the pieces into uselessness. Satisfied with the first blood he'd drawn, he glanced around the Wu Zhiming She property. No other guards were nearby. He'd created a hole in coverage. He charged across the field, feeling horribly exposed for the few seconds before he reached the relative safety of the mansion's wall.

The smell of smoke grew stronger and more acrid as the flipped car out front burst into flame. Shouting grew in volume and excitement as well. If they hadn't already realized nobody had been in the car, they would any moment. Better he should get inside the house. He looked up. Three floors aboveground, possibly with an attic, and certainly with a cellar. Where would they keep Lihua? In the cellar, certainly. That was the most likely spot, but he couldn't risk making a beeline for the basement and winding up falling into another trap. Ai Haishe had nearly beaten him in the hold of the *Kowloon Seadragon* and he couldn't risk getting cornered that way again.

So be it; he'd start at the top and work his way down.

He'd seen martial arts movies where heroes did corner ascents, bounding up the side of a building by pushing off the opposing corners faster than they could fall. They also most likely had wires. They didn't, however, have claws. Lionheart dug his toes into the brick, finding plenty of purchase in the mortar between them, and went right up the corner between the chimney and the wall. He reached the overhanging roof with its curved-up corners and lunged for the eaves. For a precarious moment, he dangled beneath the wood, only held up by his finger claws. The bullet wound in his shoulder twinged painfully, reminding him that he had done nothing to treat it short of letting his own fur mat it into an improvised bandage. He reached out, stretching further than was safe, and hooked his fingers over the edge of the rooftop. Facing away from the wall, he contracted his waist and pulled his legs up and over his head, getting onto the roof like a gymnast going over the uneven bars.

He sprawled on the roof for a couple of minutes, regaining his strength after the frantic, harrowing ascent. Nobody would be able to see him on the roof unless they had a helicopter. Although he wouldn't put it past Lian Kui to have his own chopper parked somewhere offsite, there wasn't one flying anywhere nearby. The roof smelled of the pitch used to glue down the tiles, just starting to bake in the morning sun. There were skylights, clearly not part of the original construction given their incongruous appearance amid the patterned tiles, and it was through one of those Lionheart gained access to the building's interior.

He peeked down past the edge of the skylight into the room below, shielding his eyes and trying to see anything despite the glare from the rising sun. Unfortunately, he could only see a little bit of the room below due to the low angle of the sun. If anyone was down there, they'd see him the moment he dropped into the room, so he'd have to work fast. He dug his claws into the edges of the skylight and lifted. For several seconds nothing happened as his legs and shoulders quaked with the effort. Then with a splintering of wood, the skylight tore loose from the framework of the roof and an overwhelming smell of gun oil and cordite. There could be a dozen guns pointed at him even as he shoved the skylight aside, but he'd made his commitment and would stick to it. Lihua had to be somewhere in the house, and he'd be damned if he let them kill her after they'd killed Qiao.

No hail of bullets came his way as he dropped through the open skylight and hit the floor ten feet below. His knees complained at the impact but he couldn't accede to their request for a break. He took a risky moment to glance around his surroundings before seeking cover, and what he saw amazed him.

He was in an arsenal.

The first time he'd visited the Five Deadly Serpents' mansion, he'd noticed a pervasive smell of gun oil and mineral solvents, and it appeared he'd discovered the source of that odor. Gun racks covered two walls of the room, packed to brimming with everything from single-shot rifles that must have been over a century old to modern submachine guns and semi-automatic pistols. Some of the firearms were clearly military in origin, with enough ammunition to fight a wide-ranging and protracted war with whatever opponent crossed the Triad the wrong way. Cases of grenades lined the walls beneath the gun racks, ranging from standard explosive to a variety of smoke and even tear gas canisters. The third wall held an array of swords, spears, and exotic weapons like butterfly knives, chain whips, and tiger forks. There were blades shaped like circles with additional blades protruding from them; blades shaped like deer antlers; even blades that had so many odd forks and angles that Lionheart couldn't begin to imagine how to fight with them. Quivers of arrows framed bows from short bows all the way up to the huge bows designed to be used on horseback. A forest of crossbows hung from pegs, including the famous repeaters that had been part of Chinese military history for centuries.

The final wall held a workshop for cleaning, maintaining, and repairing weapons of all sorts. Sitting upon the bench was something Lionheart tentatively identified as a disassembled minigun, something he hadn't seen except in movies, and leaning up against the bench was an honest-to-god rocket tube, an anti-tank weapon of some kind. He shook his head. No wonder the police didn't want to have a gang war. If other Triads were only ten percent as well armed, it would be like World War III.

He wondered if maybe he should take some of the weapons for his continuing assault. But no, he'd never fired a gun and it wasn't the time to learn. He already had the weapons he was most intimately familiar with at the ends of his arms and legs. He would trust to them to get him through the day. Still, he couldn't leave all these weapons behind him as he headed deeper into the building. The moment the alarm was raised, the Serpent Warriors would be racing for the armory. He needed to do something to ensure they couldn't rearm and gain an advantage not only numerically, but through superior firepower as well.

The obvious solution was, of course, to blow it all to hell and gone.

He was just starting to peruse the selection of grenades when he heard the sound of a key in the armory's lock. He whirled away from the arms and sprang across the room to crouch just beyond the arc of the door. It swung open to reveal four Serpent Warriors, none of whom appeared to be armed with anything more serious than a pistol. The man who'd opened the door found himself staring at a snarling Lionheart and urine flowed down the front of his trousers.

In one smooth motion, Lionheart grabbed the man by the back of his neck and smashed his head against the doorframe. He collapsed into a puddle of his own piss even as Lionheart launched himself into the midst of the men in the hallway. They yelled frantic warnings in Cantonese and tried to protect themselves, but in the confines of the corridor, they were more of a danger to each other than they were to Lionheart. A lot of times when he fought against unpowered opponents, he held back, not wanting to be viewed by the public as the monster he appeared to be. He no longer had that compunction after the events that had occurred since his arrival in Aberdeen.

Every blow he delivered was powerful enough to shatter bones, to explode internal organs, to kill. He crushed the wrist of the man who had the pistol, then yanked the man toward him while striking with a hard palm strike to the point of the man's chin. The man's skull cracked and the ends of the broken hinges of his jawbone tore through the skin behind his ears, making the notion of eating solid food ever again an unlikely proposition. Lionheart followed up with an elbow to the sternum of another man, shattering his ribs and making him hit the wall so hard it cracked and masonry showered down in a frothy cloud.

A Serpent Warrior tried to lunge at him. He sidestepped the blow, took the man's wrist, and pulled back to break the man's elbow across his chest. Before the man even had time to shriek his agony, Lionheart twisted the broken arm and used the leverage to piledrive the man's face into the floor in an explosion of bloody tooth fragments. He braced his hand against the floor and drove outward with both feet in a solid double-kick that broke the last man's pelvis.

Lionheart rolled back to his feet, gore dripping from both his hands. He'd reopened the wound in his shoulder and it seared with pain as sluggish blood soaked his fur. His senses sang, open to all the sounds and smells of the Five Deadly Serpents' mansion. He heard excited voices, approaching footsteps of many warriors. Mineral oil and gunpowder and sweat filled his nostrils. They were coming for him.

He was ready.

He backed into the armory, leaving the men he'd just defeated where they lay, whimpering and bleeding. Let the other warriors see what they would risk by facing him. Perhaps they would have second thoughts. He shut the door and locked it, then stepped aside just as several bullets spalled through it.

Somebody screamed something in Cantonese outside the door and the gunfire stopped. Lionheart didn't have to speak the language to get the gist of it. *Quit shooting at all the explosives, dumbshits!*

"We know you in there, American." The voice was familiar: Wang Wen Mang, the lanky *choi li fut* fighter who'd come to crash Master Chou's funeral. "Come out and we make your death swift. Honorable."

Lionheart retrieved the rocket tube from beside the workbench. He thumbed off the safety and rested it on his wounded shoulder, letting the pain sharpen his focus. He aimed it right at the center of the door.

"Come and get me."

Chapter Twenty

"Pretend inferiority and encourage his arrogance."
—Sun Tzu

For a moment, Lionheart thought maybe the Serpent Warriors had thought better of their assault, but then bullets chopped through the door all around the handle, chewing the brass knob loose from the wood. The door was kicked open, and he pulled the trigger on the rocket tube.

He didn't know what it would feel like, whether there would be recoil or a jerk or anything, but the only thing he noticed was the flash of heat behind him as the initial rocket motor ignited with a cloud of flame and the tube suddenly getting lighter in his hands. The rocket flashed across the armory toward wide-eyed Serpent Warriors. He squinted into the flare of the exhaust as the missile cut between the men in the corridor even as they were throwing themselves to the floor. The rocket's tail glanced off one of them who wasn't fast enough to get out of the way. It tumbled in its flight for a moment before nose-diving into the floor. The explosion tore apart walls and men with equal impunity. The hallway focused the shockwave like the barrel of a shotgun and knocked Lionheart off his feet to crash back against the workbench at the far end of the armory. He couldn't hear anything but ringing in his ears and his eyes wouldn't focus. Fire blurred before him and the smoke seemed to fill his head. His face and chest burned from a hundred tiny shrapnel wounds, like he'd angered a swarm of stinging flies, and the stink of his own burnt fur mixed with the darker stench of roasted human flesh.

Get up, he told himself. You're not done yet.

He peeled himself away from the workbench that he'd shattered with his body, blowing out a flame he noticed lingering on the back of one knuckle like it was a candle wick. He felt dizzy and would have loved nothing more than to lie down on a cool stone somewhere and let the rain wash over him. Lihua, though. He focused upon Lihua, because he couldn't rest until she was safe.

Grenades had spilled out across the floor from the force of the explosion. Lionheart selected two of them and stepped into the ruined hallway. Bodies and pieces of bodies were strewn across the floor, where a huge burnt crater marred the wood, with the walls around it charred black and smoking. Further down the hall, small fires burned on the floor and walls. The smoke was enough to make Lionheart's eyes stream and he coughed as he stepped past the bodies. He took one of the grenades, a smoker, pulled the ring, and threw it down to the end of the hall. White smoke hissed and billowed forth from the canister. He couldn't tell if anyone was around the corner thanks to the ringing in his ears, so he wanted to give himself any advantage he could. The doors along the hall had all been blown off their hinges from the RPG blast. Nobody came from the rooms to challenge him; most looked like some sort of storage.

Then something grabbed his foot and Lionheart fell.

A boneless blackened tentacle had wrapped itself

around his ankle with surprising strength. He tried to free himself but to no avail, and a moment later another tentacle lashed out to wrap around his waist like a boa constrictor wrapping its prey. It had fingers at the end of it and he realized it was not a tentacle but an arm, stretched and flexible like a thick hawser, and it was trying to choke the breath out of him.

Wang Wen Ming came at him out of the smoke like some kind of human-serpent hybrid, his body bending and flowing like a snake's. His skin was blackened and charred, and half of his face was an angry splotch of raw bleeding flesh with burnt bits of skin dangling from it. Lionheart tried to tear away the arm wrapping itself around his chest but it was lengthening and thickening even as he struggled. Wang Wen Ming wrapped his legs around Lionheart's lower body, taking away all his leverage. It was like being stuffed inside of a bag made of living flesh.

"Kill you, *gweilo.*" Wang Wen Ming's voice bubbled like his own lungs were full of fluid.

Lionheart couldn't respond. He couldn't draw breath as the human constrictor squeezed the life out of him. The roar in his ears was like the wind racing around the edges of Just Cause Headquarters back in New York, when the fall storms came rolling across Manhattan, making the buildings shake and sending swirling cyclones of leaves from Central Park all the way out into the Atlantic. Wang Wen Ming's laughter seemed to come from a great distance.

Lihua. Stay focused upon Lihua.

Lionheart twisted his wrist so hard he felt a bone crack in it. His fingers closed around a fold of Wang Wen Ming's boneless arm and squeezed. He dug his claws into the serpent-man's flesh until they met, tearing a huge chunk of flesh from the arm. Wang Wen

Ming yelped as his blood sluiced from the wound. The strength of the arm wrapped around Lionheart's torso weakened from the wound he'd inflicted, and sweet oxygen raced back into Lionheart's lungs.

Revitalized by fresh air, even when filled with the campfire smoke of the smoldering wood around the RPG explosion and the roasted vanilla scent of the smoke grenade, Lionheart's strength returned. Assisted by the lubrication of Wang Wen Ming's blood, he managed to free one arm. He lunged up and clamped his fingers over Wang Wen Ming's throat. From there it became a battle of wills and strength and whose would fail first. The cracked bone in Lionheart's wrist ached as it sent shooting pains down his arm every time the broken edges rubbed against each other. Wang Wen Ming still had a lot of strength left in the rolls of boneless flesh he'd wrapped around Lionheart, but it, too, was failing as blood ran from the huge hole in his arm as well as the insistent pressure upon his own throat.

Lionheart decided to change tactics. He released Wang Wen Ming's throat and the man grinned as best he could around his wounds, sensing victory at hand. "Sorry . . . about . . . your face." Lionheart reached up, dug his claws into the raw and ruined flesh on one side of Wang Wen Ming's face and pulled.

He tore off the rest of it.

Wang Wen Mang screamed as blood ran down his twisted body like a waterfall. His looping curls of flesh fell away from Lionheart and Lionheart stepped free. He spun around once, using the circular momentum to drive a single straight kick to the ruin that had been Wang Wen Ming's face. The snake-man's head snapped back, tearing itself halfway free from his throat from the force of the blow. Wang Wen Ming collapsed and blood sluiced free from the ragged wound.

The fight felt like it had taken hours, but Lionheart knew it couldn't have been more than a couple of minutes since he'd fired the RPG. More warriors would be rushing up toward the third floor, or at least advancing with some caution through the smoke. His ears still rang from the explosion, and he'd have to depend upon his other senses to get him through the upcoming engagements.

The smoke by the stairs swirled as someone came running through it. Lionheart grabbed the nearest loose object at hand—Wang Wen Ming's boneless corpse, and threw it at the onrushing warrior. The serpent-like body flopped through the air like a thick, bloody rope to tangle itself around the Serpent Warrior. The man yelped at the grisly missile and then grunted as Lionheart drove a hard fist into the center of his face, sending half his teeth flying down his throat. He gagged and then collapsed following Lionheart's elbow to the back of his head.

He reached the edge of the smoke cloud at the top of the stairs. The burnt vanilla stink was almost overpowering enough to make his eyes water. He could feel the vibrations of people coming up the stairs in his bare feet. He would deal with them in a moment, but first he pulled the ring from the other grenade he'd grabbed, loaded with thermite that he could identify from its sharp scent. He hurled it down the hall through the open door and then plunged into the smoke.

A blast of flame pummeled him from behind as he ran down the stairs, nearly knocking him off his feet. The initial explosion was like a loud firework, but an infernal hissing followed it, rising into roaring thunder punctuated with reports like cannon fire as the thermite ignited magazines and other explosives.

A Serpent Warrior goggled in terror as Lionheart burst out of the smoke upon him like a demon riding upon a fountain of fire. Lionheart stiff-armed him in the throat and was past him before the man even hit the ground. A half-naked man, sweaty and stinking of sex jumped out of a room into the hallway with one of the ubiquitous submachine guns the Serpent Warriors seemed to favor. He was too close to Lionheart and as he pulled the trigger, Lionheart stuck his finger behind it, preventing it from firing. A knee to the stomach bent the man over and an elbow to the back of his neck finished him. The machine pistol clattered to the floor. Lionheart retrieved it. For a group of so-called warriors, the amount of actual martial training they'd done was pitiful. They were fighters of the new generation, more apt to reach for a pistol than a blade, to trust superior firepower over superior training. It would be their undoing.

A feminine shriek brought him out of his thoughts. Was it Lihua? The man Lionheart had just dispatched didn't have her smell upon him. If he had, Lionheart would have torn him open from stem to stern. Lionheart glanced into the room the man had just left. A Chinese woman he didn't recognize sat in a European-style four-post bed with a frilly canopy. She had the sheets drawn up to her chin and was screaming at the sounds of combat and explosions, the stink of gunfire, the monstrous creature filling her doorway.

Lionheart didn't know if she was there willingly or not, and didn't have time to care. "Get out of this house." He turned away, not knowing or caring if she'd even understood him. She wasn't Lihua.

He looked down at the machine pistol in his hand. He could use it. Even up the odds a little. It was a simple thing. Just pull the trigger and spit death from afar. He wouldn't have to bruise his knuckles on any more Serpent Warriors. He held the means to wound or kill ten, twelve, twenty men. The thought elated and disgusted him at the same time. Where was the artistry in it?

A door opened down the hall and Lionheart raised the pistol and pulled the trigger. It burped and spat its full clip in a couple of seconds, bullets chewing into the walls, ceiling, and floor. It was hard to aim, and the hot casings bounced off his feet and burned them. He didn't hit anyone, but then, he wasn't sure he'd intended to. He ran down the hall, the weapon still clutched in his hand. When a head poked out of the doorway to peek, he hurled the empty pistol. It whistled through the air like an oddly-balanced Japanese *shuriken* and the handle caught the fellow right above the eye. He dropped like he'd been shot.

Lionheart rounded a corner and found himself at the balcony overlooking the large front lobby of the mansion. A dozen Serpent Warriors stood down in the lobby, looking up at him in shock. Like they were all connected by one thought, a dozen arms raised a dozen guns. Lionheart threw himself to the floor and rolled. Bullets chewed through wood and walls, a lethal spray of fiery lead from below. Distant windows shattered as bullets found their way through seams and gaps to the outside. A gout of smoke wafted up from the lower floor, bringing with it silence as the men stopped firing, their clips empty.

The momentary lull was the result Lionheart had sought, and he charged at the railing at the edge of the landing like a linebacker going for the all-time sack record. It was a thick hardwood rod, pockmarked with bullets, but it couldn't withstand the force of Lionheart driving his shoulders into it. It broke free of the balusters supporting it as Lionheart went over the edge, a ten-foot section of heavy hardwood in his arms. He tumbled once as he fell and landed in a fighting crouch in the main lobby. For a long couple of seconds, nobody moved, as if they couldn't quite believe the American superhero was going to take on the bulk of the *dashe yongshi* on his own. Then somebody yelled his challenge and the others took up the cry and they charged in toward Lionheart, intent upon overrunning him and making him pay in blood for the damage he'd already done to the Five Deadly Serpents.

Lionheart had other plans.

A normal human couldn't have used the hardwood railing effectively as a weapon. It was too heavy, too ungainly, but wielded by Lionheart's parahuman strength, it became a lethal cudgel. He started it spinning around, working it with both hands like it was a helicopter rotor and he the engine. The ends whistled through the air and he caught the first man with a blow across the face so hard that the man flipped sideways a hundred eighty degrees to land on his head. Already unconscious from the first blow. Behind Lionheart, the opposite end of the pole caught another man across his chest, shattering ribs and knocking him down. A foolish Serpent Warrior raised his pistol only to get his entire hand crushed and split open from the splintered end of the pole.

Lionheart waded into the Serpent Warriors, who scattered before him like leaves in a typhoon. The railing had proven a frightening and effective weapon, for every time it touched someone, he would suffer a broken arm or hand, rib or skull. The floor became cluttered with wounded, unconscious, and possibly dead Serpent Warriors. Those who could were trying to crawl away on their bellies like their namesakes, doing their best to avoid being tagged by the whistling ends of the railing once more. Firearms and other weapons were forgotten in the panic to get away from the monster with the huge staff.

Then the end of the whirling railing struck the unyielding edge of a stairwell. It recoiled in an unexpected direction and Lionheart had to drop to the ground to avoid being brained by his own weapon. He'd lost track of where he was in the lobby. Master Chou would have chided him for being unmindful of his surroundings. The railing clattered down beside him and the remaining eight or ten Serpent Warriors closed upon him, ready to stomp him into bits of bloody fur.

He didn't have room to build momentum with the railing again, but he managed to grab it and lunge with it like a spear just above floor level. The end bent one warrior's foot horribly sideways and his full weight came down upon an ankle with nothing beneath it. His scream penetrated the foggy buzz in Lionheart's head. He braced his elbows against the floor and kicked another warrior's knees, breaking them sideways and dropping him beside his shattered-foot brother.

Lionheart rolled backward in a somersault, found his feet up against the stairwell, and used it as a launching pad to spring up and forward like a tiger leaping upon its prey. He uttered his most terrifying roar as he fell upon the *dashe yongshi*, none of whom had the foresight to be carrying a tiger fork. There were no niceties in this battle, no holding back for fear of causing irreparable damage. Lionheart went for every cheap and lethal shot he could take, crushing one man's windpipe, gouging out the eyes of another, breaking the neck of a third. And still they came, blindly loyal to the Five Deadly Serpents triad even as they threw themselves to their deaths upon Lionheart's fists and fangs. Perhaps their fates would be worse had they shown cowardice or retreat in the defense of their master's house.

Then all of a sudden there were only three opponents, and they were far more skilled than their brethren. Their attacks came in coordination, intelligently, like they'd spent many months training to fight alongside one another. One of them scored a painful blow directly upon the bullet wound in Lionheart's shoulder and followed up with a knuckle to a nerve cluster in his shoulder that made his entire arm go numb. Lionheart countered by flaying open the man's belly.

He paid for that one with a blow to the back of his neck that made the entire world go gray. He swayed, lost in space, as a knee was driven upward against his spine, making his legs seem to disappear. The room spun and Lionheart wound up on his back, holding up his one good hand in a weak attempt to defend himself. The two *dashe yongshi* looked down upon him and laughed, preparing to finish him off. Lionheart had nothing left, no strength, no energy. He'd failed.

Both men halted their laughter suddenly and expressions of confusion and surprise warred for space upon their faces. Each man had sprouted a gleaming extra appendage from the center of his chest, silvery but streaked with blood. The appendages disappeared back into the men's chests and each of them fell without a further sound.

Behind them stood a battered and bloodied Lihua, a sword clutched in each hand.

Chapter Twenty-One

*"If you are far from the enemy, make
him believe you are near."*

—*Sun Tzu*

"Lihua!" Lionheart was hurting. The last few warriors he'd fought had taken a lot out of him, and done some damage that would take some time to heal even with his parahuman metabolism. He struggled to stand.

Lihua transferred both bloody swords to one hand and lowered the other to Lionheart. He clasped it, feeling the warmth in her palm, taking the strength she offered him, and between them he found his feet once more.

They embraced, their bodies a litany of pain, taking solace in each other. "Shi Xin . . ."

She smelled of sweat and blood, steel and pain, heroin and hate. "Lihua . . . I'm so sorry. Qiao . . ."

"I know. They killed him in front of me."

"Why didn't you just give up the school? We could have found a new home for it."

Lihua leaned back to gaze into his eyes. One of hers was swollen, the white of it crimson with burst capillaries. "Our father would not have wanted us to give in to criminals. Better we should fight back, even at the expense of our lives." She looked around at all the wounded and dead Serpent Warriors in the lobby.

"Besides. We have done well for ourselves. I did not fight this many men myself, but there are seven in the basement who will never traffic heroin or slaves again."

"Slaves?"

Lihua's eyes flashed. "There are women. They force them to process the heroin. They must work in the nude. They force them to do other things as well, to please the *dashe yongshi*."

Lionheart's mouth went dry. "Lihua . . . they didn't . . . harm you that way?"

"No." She grimaced, the expression made worse by the bruising and cuts on her face. "They threatened it. Showed me what would happen if I refused to sign their documents. That was when we heard the gunfire, the explosion." Her grimace transformed to a sardonic grin. "They were distracted. I killed the first man, the rapist, with my bare hands. I found swords quickly, though. I knew you must have come for me. I came to find you, to help you."

"I'm glad you did. I was done. Finished." Lionheart embraced her once more. "Did you kill Lian Kui?"

"No. I lost him during the fight. He isn't among these?" She kicked at one of the men she'd run through.

"No. He must have found another way out."

"He will be powerless after this. Losing his Triad. Losing his mansion, his heroin. He is finished. His own suppliers will see to that, should he ever find them again."

Lionheart glanced up. Flames had spread to the second floor. Lihua was right about the mansion becoming a total loss. "Come on, babe. We should get out of here while we still can."

Lihua shook her head. "We cannot. There are still women in the basement, locked up, We cannot let them die there."

Lionheart nodded. It wasn't even a question in his mind. Saving people was what superheroes did, and even if she had no powers, Lihua lived by that tenet. "Let's go." Lihua handed him a sword. It felt awkward and light in his hand after swinging around a large, heavy railing, and was a weapon he had barely more familiarity with than a pistol. He gave it back to her. "You keep it. I'm better with these." He popped out his claws, blunted and broken from all the fighting.

They went back to the basement, passing several bodies on the way. With his warrior's eye, Lionheart noted all of them had died from stab wounds, professionally delivered to locations like the heart, the throat, or the eyes. He nodded his approval at Lihua's work.

He hadn't been to the basement on his initial tour, but he'd known it existed from the scents. It still surprised him to see how extensive it was. The heroin packaging and production facility was even larger in footprint than the mansion above. The Five Deadly Serpents must have dug several additions to increase their available floor space. Crates lined one wall, on their sides, showing stacked bricks of morphine base wrapped in plastic. The various tables in the basement contained the lab equipment and chemicals to turn the morphine base into heroin powder, then repackage it for distribution and transport. The air itself seemed fuzzy with toxic dust, and Lionheart was almost afraid to breathe, for he could feel the faint tingle of the drug as it insinuated its way into his system, like a low-grade fever.

The opposite wall held a row of steel cages, with bars and locks, where several women were imprisoned. Beside them were a couple of rooms with doors, presumably where the Serpent Warriors would take the women to be raped. The women, representing a variety of ages and body types, were all dressed in ragged shifts. They clutched at the bars with their filthy hands or reached through them, entreating Lihua and Lionheart to rescue them. In another place, another time, they might have been terrified at the bloody lion-faced man in their midst, but they'd seen and been subjected to the worst kinds of atrocities of which men could conceive, and compared to that, Lionheart didn't induce fear at all.

Lihua went to a peg on the wall near the cages and retrieved a set of keys on a large iron ring. "Here, I will let them out. You check the side rooms."

Lionheart nodded. He kicked open the door to the first room and found it empty. The second held a broken chair, some scattered documents, and two bodies. One man's neck was cleanly broken while the other looked like he'd gone through a shredder, brutally beaten with a chair leg that had finally been rammed through his throat, pinning him to the floor. His dead eyes stared up at the ceiling. The room smelled of Lihua, and he knew it was where she'd begun her own crusade of justice.

He returned to Lihua, surrounded by a gaggle of frightened women, all babbling at her in Cantonese. They shrank back from him as he approached and grew silent. "There's nobody else here. Get them out of here and I'll destroy the lab and inventory. The Five Deadly Serpents are ruined after today."

"The house is already burning. We can smell it." Lihua sniffed and Lionheart agreed the air was full of smoke.

"It might not reach the basement." Lionheart reached into his pocket and retrieved the flare gun he'd taken from the speedboat. "This will."

Lihua nodded. "Where should we go?"

"I met with Station Sergeant Montgomery briefly before coming here. He and I see eye-to-eye on this.

He'll be here. Go to him." Lionheart paused. "I trust him. I don't think I'd trust any other officers without him around though."

"I'm glad you came to find me. If you hadn't, I might be dead by now."

Lionheart smiled. "Oh, I don't know. You're pretty resourceful. I think you might have freed yourself anyway."

Lihua stole a quick kiss from him. "Be careful, Shi Xin. *Wo ai ni.*"

"I love you too. Get out of here."

Lihua led the women to the stairs. They fussed and babbled in Cantonese and she had to bully a couple of them up the stairs. They were clearly afraid of Wu Zhiming She retribution. Lionheart watched them go. Once the last woman had cleared the stairwell, he got to work putting everything he could find that might possibly be flammable—chemicals, bricks of opium, a couple of tables he broke apart into kindling—into a big pile in the center of the room. His head was pounding from the smoke from the fire in the mansion above, and the drug dust swirling through the basement air wasn't helping. He longed to be outside, to breathe the heady sea air once more, to bury his face in Lihua's hair and let her scent rejuvenate him.

Heat washed down the stairs, and he could hear the flames roaring overhead. It was time to make his escape. He pointed the flare gun at the pile he'd created and pulled the trigger. A hissing white-hot projectile spat sparks across the floor as it flashed into the pile. For a moment, he thought he'd have to find some other way to burn the drug lab to the ground, but then the pile ignited so fast it seemed to explode. He turned and ran up the stairs to find the mansion engulfed in an inferno. It looked like anyone who could walk, crawl, or otherwise drag themselves out of the building had already done so. One glance up to the second floor told him it was pointless to check up there for any survivors, but he made a quick circuit of the main floor and checked to see if life remained in any of the unmoving bodies in the lobby where he and Lihua had battled the last of the Five Deadly Serpents.

One man still had a pulse. It was tempting to leave him there to burn like the others, but someday Lionheart would have to tell his friends about the events in Aberdeen, and he didn't want to have to lie to them. How many of the *dashe yongshi* had been decent young men, corrupted by the power implicit in their training, their guns, their lifestyle? They'd made their choices, and he'd fought them because of those choices. That didn't mean he had to abandon a survivor to die in the fire. Perhaps that man could turn his life around. Lionheart hefted the man up onto his shoulders in a fireman's carry and turned to see the front door of the mansion engulfed in flames. Of course it was, he thought. Why should anything ever be easy?

Flames licked at his heels and back as he turned away from the door. He apologized to the man he was carrying, ran to a window, and hurtled through it in a shower of glass. He rolled across the manicured grass, doing his best to keep from further injuring the man he carried. When he got to his feet and turned to look back at the mansion, he realized how effective his assault had been. Fire erupted from the roof and walls with a deafening roar. One corner of the house, presumably where the armory had been, had already collapsed, and occasional pops of detonating cartridges shot sparks into the air.

All in all, it had been a good day's work.

狮 和 五 致 死 蛇

True to his word, Station Sergeant Montgomery had brought quite a few officers up the hill to check on the property of the Five Deadly Serpents when the fire broke out. One might have even said it was an excessive response, given the number of prisoner transport vans that accompanied the investigating officers. Lionheart and Lihua met with the Station Sergeant shortly after their escape from the confines of the burning house and announced they would bear witness to the charges of murder, attempted murder, drug smuggling, rape, and enslavement.

"I realize I might not carry the most weight as a *gweilo* here." Lionheart sat on the tailgate of an ambulance, letting a paramedic bandage the wound on his shoulder. He and Lihua had both suffered numerous injuries in the course of their fighting, although luckily none was more serious than the bullet wound he'd suffered early on in the day. The escaped women were likewise being checked over by medical personnel, given blankets and hot tea, and huddled together as they awaited their fates.

"You're more popular than you think." Montgomery watched as the fire brigade worked to bring the smoldering fire to an end. He'd ordered them to hang back until no more detonations came from the remains of the armory. "You Yankee superheroes carry a lot of weight. You're celebrities."

"I suppose so." Lionheart winced as the medic started stitching a cut closed on his back. The man was being a terrific sport about working on such an unusual specimen. It would be something to share with his grandchildren someday, Lionheart supposed.

"I'm sorry about the loss of your brother, Miss Chou," said Montgomery.

Lihua nodded. She had her arms intertwined with one of Lionheart's and rested her head against his undamaged shoulder. "He was a brave warrior. We will honor his memory."

Lionheart frowned. One of the women was sidling away from the group, hunched over with her blanket over her head, making for one of the parked police cars. Something wasn't right about the way she moved. He'd spent a lifetime learning how to observe motion in others, ostensibly to use it against them in combat situations. This woman wasn't moving like a victim at all. She moved like a man. "Montgomery . . . that woman there. Something's not right."

Montgomery followed Lionheart's gaze and likewise frowned. "Officer Hsiao, please stop that woman."

A police officer hurried over to the woman, bowed to her, and started to ask her a question but then stopped. His eyes widened and he opened his mouth to yell something. Before he could, the woman lunged out and brushed her hand across his throat. Lionheart leaped to his feet from the tailgate as the police officer fell back, clutching at his rapidly-swelling throat. Foamy spittle sprayed from his mouth. The woman glanced back and Lionheart saw he'd been correct in his assessment. It was no woman. "Lian Kui!" he shouted, and the head of the Five Deadly Serpents threw aside his blanket and ran for the nearby police car.

Lionheart bolted after him, his stitching forgotten. Lihua was only a step behind him as Montgomery bellowed for other officers to stop the fugitive. One more officer jumped in Lian Kui's path and got similarly poisoned for his trouble. Lian Kui reached the police car, jumped inside, and started it. Lionheart sprang at the bumper, trying to get a grip upon it, but his claws found no purchase on the slick metal and the car roared away, spraying gravel and exhaust in his face.

Pandemonium reigned as the police divided themselves into multiple factions. Montgomery ordered some after Lian Kui, others to assist the fallen officers, and still others to secure the area and make sure no other felons were hidden among the liberated women.

All thoughts of his own injuries forgotten, Lionheart scrambled to his feet and zeroed in upon a police motorcycle parked a few meters away. He leaped high and landed in the saddle, his foot striking the starter as he came down. The Honda engine sputtered to life. As Lionheart rocked it off its kickstand, Lihua slipped behind him, perching delicately upon the storage box between the saddlebags and wrapping her arms and legs around his torso. He almost told her to get off, but understood it would have been pointless to argue about it. Besides, he was man enough to admit that she was every bit as good a warrior as he, and Lian Kui had a poisonous touch. They would need every advantage they could get. "Stay there and hold tight. You need to be a part of me, to move when I move."

"I will always be a part of you, Shi Xin."

Lionheart twisted the throttle and took the bike through gear change after gear change, racing after the stolen police car. He flipped on the lights and siren, not just to warn civilians who might be heading along the roads to see the destruction wrought upon the mansion of the Wu Zhiming She, but to let Lian Kui know they were coming for him.

To Lionheart's surprise, Lian Kui headed further inland. Lionheart had expected him to run for the docks, perhaps to take refuge on a friendly vessel or to commandeer one and escape into the harbor, but instead he seemed intent upon losing Lionheart on the twists and turns of the hilly roads. Although the bike was faster than the car, Lian Kui seemed to know exactly where he was going and Lionheart had to slow down for corners when he wasn't sure how sharp they were. The other problem he discovered was the unsettling tendency for civilians to run out into the street after the police car flashed by to point and shout. He had to constantly weave back and forth to avoid killing anyone, even with his siren blaring its warning call.

"He is going north, toward Sai Wan." Lihua had taken his directions to heart and wasn't so much sitting behind him as she had wrapped herself around him until he was wearing her like a backpack. She was so sensitive to the movements of others that she instinctively leaned with him into every turn, and was so effective at it that they started to gain on the fleeing police car in spite of the unfamiliar road.

"What's in Sai Wan?" Lionheart had to shout over the roar of the bike's engine. He pushed it toward the redline every chance he could get. He swore to himself Lian Kui would not escape them.

"The Cross-Harbour Tunnel. He could be making for Kowloon."

"We'll see he never gets that far."

Chapter Twenty-Two

*"There is no instance of a nation benefiting
from prolonged warfare."*

—*Sun Tzu*

Traffic increased in volume as Lionheart and Lihua approached the Cross-Harbour Tunnel entrance on the north side of the island. Lian Kui had activated his stolen police car's lights and siren and was bullying his way through the massed cars, trucks, and motorbikes, even going so far as to knock them aside in his desperate flight.

"I didn't think there were this many cars on the island!" Lionheart had to shout to be heard over the growl of the Honda police bike.

"I have never been to Kowloon. I rarely come to this side." Lihua tightened her arms and legs around Lionheart and leaned with him as he whipped the bike around a stalled cargo truck. "I do not like traffic."

"I'm not real keen on it either." Ahead of them, Lian Kui finally ran into traffic tangle of cars, bikes, and people he couldn't push through. The police car rear-ended a sedan hard enough to jar its light bar loose. It skittered down the roof to smash the rear window of the sedan. A man leaped out of the car to scream at Lian Kui, who staggered out of the wrecked police car with a cut bleeding down one cheek.

He slapped the furious civilian and the man went down in convulsions from Lian Kui's poison touch.

Lionheart threaded the bike between cars, trying to close the distance between them and Lian Kui. If he'd been the only one doing so on a motorcycle, it would have worked, but it seemed everyone on a motorbike was likewise rolling between stopped traffic to get closer to the tunnel entrance. Lionheart darted between two delivery vans and then was stymied by a beat-up Datsun whose driver had decided to push into another lane despite there being no room. Lionheart grimaced and locked up the bike's brakes hard enough the rear wheel came off the ground a few centimeters. Lihua's weight left his back suddenly as she used the bike's deceleration to catapult herself up and over the Datsun. She hit the ground running.

Lionheart abandoned the police motorcycle and scrambled after Lihua. He couldn't see Lian Kui immediately, but the man was leaving a trail in the form of poisoned victims as he ran for the toll booths. Lionheart didn't know how long the tunnel was, but Kowloon couldn't have been more than a couple of kilometers across the harbor. Anyone in reasonable physical condition could run that on foot, especially if he hadn't spent the previous day fighting numerous opponents, nearly drowning, and then fighting even more. Lionheart's lungs burned as he sprinted between rows of cars. Lihua tried to keep pace with him but she was only human, and she fell behind as Lionheart closed the distance with Lian Kui.

Lian Kui slid across the hood of a Toyota and stumbled. He staggered back to his feet and snarled as he saw Lionheart approach. He hooked his fingers into claws and screamed, "You bastard!"

Lionheart only remembered at the last moment not to let Lian Kui touch him and he skidded to a halt only a few feet away. "Give up, Lian Kui. You're finished."

Lian Kui lunged at him and Lionheart jumped back, staying out of range. "I am finished? You can't stop me, *gweilo*. One touch—" He raised his hands like a menacing old black-and-white movie villain. "—and you will die like that dog Chou."

Lionheart snapped off a car antenna and brandished it like a rapier, making it whistle as he slashed at the air. "I'm going to cut you to pieces with this. I don't need to touch you to kill you." He laid into Lian Kui, cutting him across the forehead with a snap of his wrist.

Lian Kui ducked beneath a blow and lunged inward, slashing at Lionheart with his open palms. Lionheart had to dance back, using the broken antenna as a goad to keep Lian Kui from reaching him. He thrust the tip at Lian Kui and the antenna folded into uselessness. Lian Kui grinned through the bloody mask his face had become and reached for Lionheart.

Lionheart fell back, feeling Lian Kui's fingers hook into his mane.

"Shi Xin!" Lihua flew through the air and drove both her feet into Lian Kui's face, knocking him back to crash against a stopped car whose occupants stared in frank astonishment at the battle taking place before them. Lihua fell to the pavement beside Lionheart and for a moment all three combatants were down.

Lionheart held his breath, wondering if the poison coursing through him would hurt him, and then when he didn't seem to be suffering any ill effects, wondered why not. "Lihua!" He rolled over to look at her.

She smiled at him despite her bruised face. "I did not touch his skin. My shoes did."

"And my mane did." Lionheart sprang to his feet as Lian Kui did likewise. "We know how to beat you, Lian Kui. Give up."

"Never!" Lian Kui screamed and charged at them.

Lionheart yanked open the passenger door of a car beside him and ripped it from its hinges. He held it up like a shield to deflect Lian Kui and then swung it like Pete Rose knocking it out of the park. The door caught Lian Kui in his chest and he flew up and over the car he'd crashed into before.

Lihua jumped onto the hood and then had to back-flip high into the air as Lian Kui lunged at her legs, swiping a hand toward her unprotected ankles. Lionheart hurled the door at Lian Kui, who leaned back to let the whirling projectile pass over him. Lihua landed on the hood but lost her balance as one foot slipped into the gap between the hood and windshield. As Lian Kui struck at her, Lionheart leaped over the hood and drove both fists into Lian Kui's chest, still covered with a tunic.

The head of the Five Deadly Serpents fell to the pavement once more. Lionheart landed beside him, his hand raised to deliver a fatal strike. Lian Kui laughed through his bloodied lips. "Go ahead, *gweilo*. Kill me. Strike me down. I am defenseless. Your own death will not be nearly as quick or painless as mine. Like teacher, like student." Even as he mocked Lionheart, Lian Kui shot his hand out, grasping for Lionheart's ankle which had carelessly come within his reach.

Thunder roared in Lionheart's ears and the stink of gunpowder flooded his nose. Lian Kui's hand had vanished into a ragged, bloody stump with bits of fingers hanging from flaps of skin. Lian Kui's laugh became a shrill scream. Lionheart jumped back, his heart hammering in terror. Lian Kui's blood had splattered across his leg. He didn't know if he had been poisoned from it or not, and his eyes moved up to meet Lihua's.

She stood, still stuck on the hood of the car, holding a gun with a cavernous barrel pointed down at Lian

Kui. Smoke leached from the end as a single cartridge tumbled to the ground beside Lian Kui. "That was for my brother, Lian Kui, and this is for my father."

She fired again.

狮 和 五 致 死 蛇

"It's a right mess the two of you have made. Make no mistake about it." Station Sergeant Montgomery shook his head as he watched a couple of officers wearing hazmat suits bagging Lian Kui's body. Nobody knew exactly how his powers worked or if they would still function after his death, but Lionheart had recommended they take no chances. There were numerous victims of his deathly touch along his final escape route.

"I hope they can create an antivenin from his body." Lionheart had his undamaged arm around Lihua while the other hung in a sling. The paramedic had been thoroughly angry with him for the amount of activity he'd performed after being shot, and had given Lionheart a solid Cantonese rebuke. He'd taken it. Sometimes superheroes had to accept those kinds of things.

"I assure you, our people will make every effort to do so. If we can prevent anyone else from dying the way Ms. Chou's father did, we will. Now, I'm left with the question of what to do with the two of you." Montgomery folded his arms. "On the one hand, you've run roughshod all over my island. You've detonated explosives and burned down a rather expensive mansion that was nearly a century old. You've stolen police property and gunned down a man in the street without any sort of trial or hearing first."

"We have also destroyed an illegal cache of military-grade weaponry, rescued close to a dozen exploited women being held as sex slaves, brought down a major crime Triad, and put a big dent in the heroin trade, at least for the time being." Lionheart smiled, showing his teeth. "If you'd like to charge us, you can be sure those things will be brought up before a magistrate."

"No, I'm not going to charge you. Your record has been quite unimpeachable, Mr. Lionheart, and although I may not agree with your American cowboy antics, your results have been quite, shall we say, satisfactory. As for Ms. Chou, I understand that she has not only suffered the loss of her father to the Five Deadly Serpents, but her brother as well."

"That is a polite way of saying he was murdered in front of me." Lihua huddled beside Lionheart, a blanket wrapped around her shoulders. "I would bring charges against Lian Kui if he were still alive."

"I'm rather pleased that he is not. Sometimes police work can be an unconscionable amount of paperwork. Not having any suspects to interrogate or investigate does relieve some of that burden." Montgomery watched the officers load Lian Kui's body into a coroner's van. "Sergeant Yang has disappeared without leave. I shall have my men keep an eye out for him. There are a few questions I want to ask him concerning his allegiances." He paused as if to gather his thoughts. "I fear you've made far more enemies today than you realize. With the destruction of the Five Deadly Serpents, the remaining Triads will fight to possess this territory. You may have temporarily stopped the smuggling of heroin through Hong Kong, but it will certainly begin again."

"Then I'll be here to stop it."

Lihua pushed the blanket back. "Both of us will. I will see to it my father and brother did not die in the service of a hopeless cause."

Montgomery looked down his nose at her. "Your cause will be nothing but hopeless if you don't go home and spend some time resting and recuperating." He sighed. "Things will be quiet for a while. A few weeks. Perhaps as much as several months. I don't doubt there will come a time when we will once again find ourselves embroiled in a war with the Triads."

Lihua nodded. "We will be ready."

狮 和 五 致 死 蛇

Yaoting fussed over Lionheart and Lihua when they returned to the Cherrywood School like they were teenagers who'd stayed out past curfew. He gave them the kind of dressing-down Lionheart hadn't received since training with Master Chou. He wouldn't have been the least bit surprised if Yaoting would have wrapped up the ass-chewing with them being grounded, but instead the housekeeper made them each a cup of mint tea sweetened with honey and told them he'd better not see them up and about before midday.

The five members of the Fists were relieved to see Lionheart and Lihua alive and well after hearing the rumors and tales that had spread through the Floating Village population like the fire through the Five Deadly Serpents' mansion. They were equally as distraught to learn of Qiao's death, and Jian swore he would round up a crew to retrieve Qiao's body from the depths of the harbor so he could be properly honored in death. At first they were eager to hear Lionheart and Lihua's tale of how they brought down the Wu Zhiming She and defeated Lian Kui, but at last, it was Jinjing who bullied the other students into leaving the two wounded warriors alone. She pushed and shoved the young men away, shouting at them to leave Lionheart and Lihua time to grieve and to heal. Then she bowed and stole away, like the others, to handle the daily business of running and protecting a martial arts school.

Lionheart and Lihua sat beneath the cherry blossom tree in the family courtyard and watched the branches sway in the light sea breeze. Neither of them seemed to feel much like talking so they sat in silence, fingers intertwined, listening to the sounds of the world. Lionheart was more tired than he'd ever been in his life, and nearly jerked himself awake when Lihua spoke.

"It is difficult to see how he is gone. Nothing has changed. The school is still here. The tree still has blossoms upon it. Somehow I thought it would look different without Qiao here."

"He will always be here. In your heart. In your mind." Lionheart motioned to the courtyard. "In this place. His spirit will always be with you, reminding you to train harder."

Lihua smiled, even through the tears in her eyes. "Yes, that is what he would say. I will miss him so much, Shi Xin. He was more than my brother. He raised me. He was . . . my friend." She sniffled, bowing her head forward to hide her tears with her hair.

Lionheart brushed her hair back. "I will always think of him as a friend, and I will miss him as well." He raised his cup in salute and smiled at the cherry blossoms. "*Kong bei, niang yang.* Bottoms up, motherfucker." He drained his tea, letting its sweet coolness refresh him.

Lihua wiped her eyes. "Come, Shi Xin. Come with me now. Make love to me. Share yourself with me."

"Now? I mean, is this really the right time?"

Her voice was fierce. "We should celebrate that we still live, in the best way we know how. Our loved ones gave their lives for us, and we must honor that sacrifice. I want you, Shi Xin. Remind me how it feels to be alive."

Lionheart yawned. "It would be my pleasure, my love. There's just one thing."

"What is that?"

"Don't take it personally if I fall asleep in the middle. Babe, you wouldn't believe how tired I am."

He didn't, of course, because that would have been rude, but it took Yaoting almost half an hour of knocking to waken the two of them the following afternoon.

"Many times sorry, *sifu* Shi Xin. Man at gate ask for you. Say he wait long time if need."

Lionheart yawned and stretched. He'd hoped perhaps to take a lengthy bath followed by a large breakfast—or lunch, whatever time of day it happened to be—and then return to the comfort of Lihua's arms. He and Lihua had spent the evening and night in her house, but it would be for the last time. They would be moving into the main house. Given the way some of the Fists were hanging around the door when he emerged, wrapped in a silk robe, he expected the moving would happen sooner rather than later. "Who is this man?"

Yaoting's steps were measured as he padded across the courtyard path. "I do not know him, *sifu*."

They came to the main door. Lionheart worked his head from side to side, getting the kinks out of his neck. He was half expecting a fight, and that was no way to begin the day. Instead, the young man who stood on the steps immediately threw himself to the ground in supplication and began babbling in Cantonese.

"He says you saved his life." Lihua slipped her arms around Lionheart's. She was wrapped in a robe similar to his and still had sleep tangles in her hair, but her eyes were bright and her smile cheerful. Lionheart hadn't even heard her come up behind him. Hadn't smelled her. Or perhaps he'd grown used to her scent after being around it so much. He smiled down at her. "He says you had no need to. His life is yours and he is your servant. He would be very honored to train with the great *sifu* Shi Xin."

The man looked up and Lionheart recognized him. "You. I carried you out of the mansion. You're a Serpent Warrior. A *dashe yongshi.*"

"No!" The man spoke in English and held up his hand. Where he should have had a tattoo of the symbol of the Five Deadly Serpents there was only a bandage. He pulled it aside to show burnt skin. He must have held his hand to a flame for quite some time to obliterate the tattoo of his prior allegiance. He replaced the bandage and stood, keeping his head bowed. His words came slow but forceful, spoken with great emotion behind them.

"He says he understands if you do not accept him as a student. He swears he will guard this doorway from the street until the end of his days. He gives his life for you, for me, for this school." Lihua looked up at Lionheart. "He is very insistent."

"What is his name?"

Lihua translated and waited for the man's answer. "He says it is whatever you wish it to be."

"No. Stop that. His name. His real name."

"Ping. Ping Lao."

"Well, Ping Lao, it seems you won't take no for an answer, so I'm going to say yes. As busy as this place is going to be, Yaoting is going to need help. You will answer to him in all aspects of your work. You will serve him as you would me. And when you are done with your duties as he assigns them, you may train with the other students."

Ping Lao's eyes grew huge and he bowed repeatedly, saying "*Xiexie! Xiexie!*" until Yaoting took him firmly by the ear and led him toward the kitchen.

"It seems we have another mouth to feed," said Lihua.

"I'm sure we'll have many more before long."

"So you are certain? You will stay here?"

"Yes, I'll stay, Lihua. *Wo ai ni.*"

"I love you too, Shi Xin."

Epilogue

"People in their handlings of affairs often fail when they are about to succeed. If one remains as careful at the end as he was at the beginning, there will be no failure."
—Lao Tzu

November, 1984
Hong Kong

She came like a stranger, arriving at the gate of Yingtao Mu on autumn's breath and the swirling of dry leaves in the shortening dusk. Lao Ping came to Shi Xin, quiet and somber while the *sifu* finished his contemplation at the shrine built for Huizhong and Qiao Chou, and their faithful housekeeper Yaoting, who had succumbed to pneumonia two years before. It was a place of restful meditation, and Ping worked hard to keep it beautiful no matter what time of year.

"What is it, Ping?" Shi Xin would never quite achieve the melodious tones of a native Cantonese speaker, but over the years he'd become adept enough at speaking it to even find himself thinking in Cantonese far more than he did in English.

"You have a visitor, Shi Xin. From America."

Shi Xin looked up from the shrine in surprise. "America? Who is it?"

"She says her name is *Faejie*." Ping struggled with the unfamiliar name.

"Faith. Well, I'll be." Shi Xin stood and bowed to the ashes of his wife's family. "Please show her into the family room. See if she needs any refreshments. I'll join her shortly."

Ping bowed and hurried away to carry out his master Shi Xin's requirements.

Faith.

What in the world was she doing here?

Shi Xin tightened the sash of his robes and went to find Lihua and Bao. In the main courtyard, his senior students Jian and Jinjing were putting the current batch of trainees through their paces. The others—Hong, Tengfei, and Bingwen—were out, policing the docks as only the Yingtao Mu Quan could. The Fists had become as effective a shadow police force as any team of superheroes. Although they worked alongside of the law in the form of Chief Inspector Montgomery, whose rise through the ranks had been attributed to the downfall of the Five Deadly Serpents Triad, they mostly kept to the fringes, dispensing justice in the form of swift punches and kicks. They'd become feared enough that only the most desperate or foolish smugglers still attempted to bring illicit goods, slaves, or drugs through the Aberdeen docks.

Lihua was in Bao's bedroom, working patiently to comb mud out of Bao's fur. "It's like you're a dirt magnet. Does it seek you out while you're sleeping?"

"Daddy!" Bao pulled away from her mother's grasp to barrel across the room like a furry missile. She had her father's strength, her mother's grace, and the face of a kitten. It was only a month after her third birthday but she was already developing some great muscle tone and stamina beneath her lingering baby fat, thanks to the training regimen her father had implemented. Someday, she would grow into a powerful warrior in her own right, but for now she flung herself into Shi Xin's arms.

"Are you causing your mother trouble again?" Shi Xin scratched behind his daughter's ears the way his own mother had many years before. She twisted her head to and fro, making sure his claws caught all the best itchy places.

"No."

"Not any more so than normal." Lihua came over to Shi Xin and kissed him. "I saw Ping running through here like his tail was on fire. What's going on?"

"Faith is here."

"Your . . . friend? From Just Cause?" Lihua frowned. She knew about the history between her husband and the speedster superhero. "Why?"

"I don't know. But she wouldn't have come all this way if it wasn't important."

"You're going to meet with her?"

"We are. I want her to meet you and Bao." He didn't say it was because he knew he still had feelings for Faith, even though he'd pushed them aside for many years. He needed her to see Lihua and Bao, his wife and daughter. He needed her to see he was happy, that he didn't need her in his life the way he'd once thought he did. It had been years since he'd seen her; perhaps she'd managed to repair the damage the two of them had done to her own marriage for so long. He shifted Bao onto his hip and she giggled as she twirled her claws in his mane. Lihua stood and Shi Xin took a moment to admire her lithe grace. She still brought out the best in him, and he wondered every day how he'd managed to find her from halfway around the world.

"What is it?" She looked down at her house robes. "Do I look too frumpy? Like a housewife? I could throw on some training clothes. Something befitting a warrior."

"You look beautiful. And fortunate."

"Fortunate how?" Lihua wrinkled her nose in suspicion.

"Fortunate that you're not undressing to change, or Faith might be waiting longer than expected."

Lihua gasped and her cheeks flushed, but she smiled and slapped at Shi Xin's shoulder where he bore the white streak of a scar in his fur. "You scoundrel. Not in front of the baby."

"She knows we love each other. That is a good thing."

"Mommy loves Daddy and Daddy loves Mommy and Mommy loves Bao and Daddy loves Bao . . ." Bao sang as Shi Xin and Lihua walked from their room to the main family room.

Faith looked even more amazing at thirty than she had a decade earlier when Shi Xin had first met her. She'd cut her hair short into a practical bob that hung around her face like a frame. Instead of her Pony Girl costume, she wore jeans, sneakers, and a neon-green sweatshirt with some kind of angular pattern upon it. She was seated on a low couch with a tray of tea and dumplings. She smelled of airplanes, sweat, and coffee. When Shi Xin and Lihua entered, she jumped to her feet and crossed the room in a flash. "Lionheart!" She stopped when she saw Bao in his arm, who laid her head on her father's shoulder and popped her fingers into her mouth, eyes as wide as tea saucers. "Oh my God, is she . . . ?"

Shi Xin smiled. It had been awhile since he'd spoken much English, and the words sounded odd in his own ears. "Faith, it's wonderful to see you. This is my daughter, Bao, and this is my wife, Li'ang Lihua."

Faith smiled. "She's gorgeous, Lionheart. It must break your heart every time you look at her." She turned to Lihua. "And it's nice to meet you, Li'ang."

"Lihua, please. Li'ang is my family name. The name of my husband." Lihua's voice was tinged with frost.

"I'm sorry. Lihua. It's a lovely name and you have a lovely home. Thank you for seeing me." She looked at Lionheart. "You've really gone native. You look like you belong here."

"I do belong here. This is my home."

Faith smiled. "I'm so very glad you've found one. Things are . . . better between me and Bobby. I thought you ought to know that."

"I'm pleased to hear it. Why are you here, Faith? It's not that I'm not happy to see you, but it's a very long flight just to exchange pleasantries."

"It's Tommy. He's, um . . ." Tears sprang to her eyes. "He's sick, Lionheart."

Shi Xin narrowed his eyes. The way she said *sick* had an awful stink of finality about it. "Sick?"

"It's AIDS, Lionheart. He's got AIDS."

Shi Xin sank to the couch in disbelief. Tommy, who had once gone by Tornado and then later Stormcloud, was an old friend. They'd played poker together Wednesday nights in Just Cause Headquarters, often enough that crime rates dropped in the middle of the week, because woe be unto the criminal who interrupted a winning streak. Tommy was the beautiful, soft-spoken man with flowing hair like Sean Cassidy that every woman wanted to sleep with, except he was gay and none too cautious about it. Shi Xin didn't know much about AIDS beyond it being a death sentence. "How long does he have?"

"The doctors say maybe a year. He's been sick for a while now." Faith wiped her eyes.

"Daddy? Why is the lady sad?" Bao didn't speak English, although Shi Xin had been meaning to start teaching her soon.

"She has a friend who's very sick."

"Does she need medicine? We could get medicine for her friend." Bao slipped out of her father's lap.

"I'm not sure what he needs, Little Leopard."

Bao pulled her own kerchief out of her sleeve and offered it to Faith. "Don't cry, lady. We'll get medicine."

Faith accepted the kerchief. "Thank you, sweetie." She dabbed at her eyes. "I'm sorry. I didn't think it would be this hard. We've known for weeks. John Stone thought someone should tell you, but news like this needs to be delivered in person."

Shi Xin bowed his head. "I'm glad it was you who came, Faith. What is it you need from me?"

"We need you to come home. At least for awhile. Tommy's going to die. Nothing could stop that now. He needs to be surrounded by his friends. It's going to be hard enough for him going through it, but he's our teammate. He deserves our compassion. Plus we need your experience. We've got several new folks coming on board, and we could use you to help whip them all into some kind of team."

"I don't really belong there anymore. This is my home now. This is my family, Faith."

"I'm not asking you to come back for me. I'm asking for Tommy. He could die tomorrow, Lionheart, and I'm here instead of there. Don't you at least want the chance to say goodbye?"

That was the one tactic he knew he couldn't avoid. He had barely had the opportunity to say farewell to Master Chou. He never did get the chance to say farewell to Qiao. It was a privilege to see the dying one last time before they passed. Once, he would have said he didn't believe in an afterlife, but after years of living among the Chinese, he could see how the belief in it, in the supernatural, could put many minds at ease. Tommy was, and had been his friend for many years. To deny that friendship by not returning to America would be spitting in the face of honor.

But how could he leave his wife? How could he leave little Bao behind when she was just starting to get her first forms correct?

Then Lihua was beside him, Again, she'd moved without disturbing the least bit of air, which he'd decided was the mark of her high-level training. One moment she wasn't there and the next she was, and her hand slipped into his. "Of course you must go," she said to him, speaking in soft Cantonese. "This should not even be a question for you, my love."

"It's so hard to say yes. I want to go, but my heart is here with you and Bao."

"She is a piece of you. She is an anchor. When the time is right, you will come back to her, and to me."

"I will, I promise. I can't imagine being without you for very long."

Lihua gave him her best demure smile. "When you return, I will do my best to give you a son."

Shi Xin grinned back. "Sounds enjoyable." He turned to look at his daughter and his heart crumbled into razor-sharp shards of glass as tears matted the dun-colored fur around her eyes.

"Daddy leaving?"

He swept her up, holding her tight, smelling the sweetness of her fur. "Oh, Bao. Little Leopard. I have to leave for a while. My friend who is sick needs to see me."

"Are you going to make him better?"

Shi Xin swallowed a hard lump in his throat. "I will try."

"I'll have Mommy teach me to write and I'll write you letters. I'll write them for your friend too."

"I'll write back to you, Little Leopard. I promise." His own eyes were wet and he was glad of the fur around them. He looked up at Lihua. "I'll stay in touch. Have Ping arrange to get a telephone here. I know transpacific calls are dicey at best, but I'm going to go crazy if I can't hear your voice."

"I will." Lihua came over to embrace him and Bao together. "Remember that wherever you go, we will have a piece of your heart here to call you back home."

Shi Xin looked down at his family. He'd been an outsider for a quarter of a century, thanks to his inhuman looks and parahuman abilities. Only in the past few years had he found a peaceful sanctuary in the world, a home he would only leave for great need. "I'll be home soon. Before your next birthday, Little Leopard." He planted a kiss atop Bao's head, his eyes shut, drinking in her scent as if it would tide him over until he returned. He stayed in the tight embrace with his wife and child for a good long time, while Faith shuffled her feet and looked at the floor. At last, with painful pangs of regret, he stepped away from his family. "*Wo ai ni, Lihua. Wo ai ni, Bao.*"

"We love you too, Daddy!" Bao buried her face in Lihua's robes and sobbed.

"Hurry back, my love."

Shi Xin nodded and turned to Faith. "I'm ready now."

THE END
狮 和 五 致 死 蛇

*Lionheart mentions the first meeting between Master Chou and himself a few times during the course of this tale. Presented here is the original story as it first appeared in the **JCU Omnibus Vol. 1***

Pride

The day Richard Lyons was born, the doctor said it would have been more of a kindness to let him die. His face was disfigured, with a bifurcated upper lip and a highly placed, squished nose that gave him a catlike appearance. Downy soft blonde hair covered him from head to toe, and he had no nails at the ends of his tiny fingers. It was 1953, and a difficult time for children with any sort of disabilities, but Richard's mother had a different philosophy.

Her husband, Richard's father, died in Korea, never getting to see his baby son. Jennifer Lyons was unwilling to part with the last vestige of her husband, and so despite the triple-threat hardship of being a single mother of a disfigured child, all while trying to support them both in the small military town of Mercury, Nevada, she rose to the occasion of motherhood like a prizefighter to a championship belt.

Growing up in Mercury made for a peculiar life for young Richard. Established to support the teams handling atomic weapons testing, the town was packed full of military and science families. To some, Richard's deformity was a curiosity, especially as his body hair never stopped growing, claws appeared at the ends of his fingers, and his teeth came in sharp, like a cat's. To most families, though, he was shunned and outcast, and that made for a hard life of bullying and beatings by older, bigger children. If they'd lived in a larger town, perhaps there might have been other options, like private school or tutors. But all of those things required money, and as a single working mother, Jennifer Lyons didn't have the luxury. She couldn't just keep Richard at home; the boy needed schooling, because she was determined that he would have better options in his life than she'd ever had in her own. "It's your education, Ricky," she would tell him when he balked at going back to the torment of school. "It's your future. Someday, you'll understand. Someday, you'll thank me."

Many were the days when a heartbroken Richard would run to the Post Office where his mother worked, to hide beneath her desk, sobbing at the latest round of brutality perpetrated against him. Some days it was physical, and he had bumps and bruises from being punched or kicked, or cuts from when rocks were thrown at him. Other days, the torment was far simpler and cut deeper, when he'd find himself in the middle of a pack of students who taunted him without mercy until often as not, he lost his temper, lashed out, and then wound up getting beaten anyway. He could tolerate the jabs at his appearance, when he was called *catface* or *pussy*, but when the kids discovered they could get to him by implying his mother had sex with a circus freak, or a lion in the zoo, that became the brunt of their attacks. No matter what she was doing, Jennifer would stop her work, gather him up in her arms, dry his tears, and tell him she loved him.

Sometimes, it would make him purr.

Jennifer suffered her own ostracization, as the mother of a disfigured child, but where Richard's bullying often came right at him head-on, hers was in the form of whispers just out of her hearing range, stares from other women who would quickly look away if they caught her looking back at them, and a constant exclusion from any and all social activities and circles.

Then one day, everything changed when Richard finally fought back against a group of bullies. He was eleven, and got cornered by four boys from the high school. They pushed him around, punched him, spat on him, until one of them said "I seen his momma's pussy, man, and you know what? It looks just like him. I heard that for twenty bucks, anyone in town can see her pussy."

Something in him snapped. He popped his claws—something his mother had absolutely forbidden him to do—and waded into them, snarling and hissing like a wild animal. He slashed and bit, tossing the boys around like they were little more than balsa wood models. All four wound up in the hospital, and Richard wound up in the police station while his mother desperately tried to talk the chief out of taking away her little boy and locking him up.

"He's a menace, your son. He's a monster. We don't want him in Mercury," said the Chief. "He belongs in a cage. Or a circus, the freak."

"Then I'll take him and we'll leave," said Jennifer.

The Chief nodded. "See that you're leaving by tonight, or I'll take him out and shoot him like the beast he is. Waste of a bullet, if you ask me."

The Lyonses left Mercury as the sun set behind the mountains, Jennifer at the wheel of her old beat-up Packard. They didn't know where to go, or what they would do when they got there, but at least they still had each other. The Packard's trunk held all their worldly belongings, which after years of struggling, didn't amount to much more than a couple of suitcases' worth of clothing.

Tired and hungry, they arrived in Las Vegas sometime later, and Jennifer checked them into a motel for the evening. The room had a color television, the first one Richard had ever seen. He spent all night staring at it, flipping channels until every single one showed a test pattern. The last thing he saw before one channel went off the air was a late-night news report about a group of costumed superheroes in New York City called Just Cause. They had battled The Mob and come up victorious. He especially felt inspired by the team leader, Lady Athena. She seemed so regal and powerful, so self-assured. He wondered if he could ever aspire to be like her.

Richard popped his claws out and studied them in the glow from the cathode ray tube. He was more cat than human, with his claws and needle sharp teeth and the fur that his mother shaved off him every week. He was also so much stronger and faster than the other boys, even those in high school. Maybe he was like the ones in Just Cause.

Jennifer dashed those hopes the next morning. "No, dear, you're not a superhero. You're just my son, but that's all the hero I could ever want. You stay here in the motel today while I go see about finding a job. Don't leave the room."

"I won't, Mama." Richard was an obedient boy and stayed in the motel room all morning, looking at the television and hoping to find something more about Just Cause. All he ever saw were soap operas and commercials, though.

Around lunchtime, Jennifer returned with a bag of sandwiches, a quart of bottled milk, and news that she'd obtained a job at the same diner where she'd bought them. "We'll be back on our feet soon, darling."

"Yes, Mama."

They stayed in Las Vegas for the next several years. The Sixties became the Seventies and as he entered high school, Richard stopped cutting his hair. It grew out into a magnificent mane of tawny gold and ruddy brown, and when he stopped shaving, his entire face became covered with fur. He was still bullied, but it only took some judicious use of his strength, carefully metered, to convince others that he was no easy prey.

He found a peer group of sorts in the gearheads and motorcycle gangs. They were surprisingly tolerant of his oddities, and for the first time in his life, Richard had friends. They wore motorcycle boots, leather jackets, and dirty t-shirts. They cut classes and smoked cigarettes and wrenched on their cars and bikes.

And then one day, they went looking for trouble and they found it in a group of Hell's Angels only too willing to bring knives, chains, and guns to bear. None of Richard's friends came away unbloodied, and two of them wound up in the hospital. For his own part, Richard got sliced up on one arm by a bearded man who outweighed him by a good hundred pounds.

He ripped the man's face to shreds.

Richard knew he couldn't go home again after that. People knew about the cat-man in Las Vegas, and he was afraid the Hell's Angels would come looking for him. He hit the road that night, hitching a ride with a cross-country trucker who took him as far as Phoenix. The trucker gave Richard a hat to help hide his features, and five dollars to help him on his way, wherever it was that he was going. It killed him to leave his life and his mother behind. She had been in his corner since the very day he was born, and without her, he was once again a frightened and lost little boy, except now he couldn't run to find her in the post office and hide beneath her counter. Sometimes, in the dark, when he was huddled up in the corner of a railroad car, or a five-dollar flophouse, where nobody could see or hear him, he would allow the tears to come.

Richard drifted east and north, working odd jobs where he could find them and being hungry where he couldn't. He didn't want to stoop to stealing or mugging people, even though with his abilities it would have been so easy. He sent his mom postcards when he had a few cents extra to spend on them, but other than that he stayed on his own on the road. Sometimes he'd stay in a town for only as long as it took to find a ride. Other times he stayed for a week, or even a month. There was work to be had, and he forced himself not to be too proud to do anything. He paved a highway in New Mexico, he harvested corn in Colorado, and he roughnecked in Oklahoma. By then, he'd made enough money to buy an old Indian motorcycle, and his spare money went into fixing it up.

When he had a chance, he stopped by newsstands and bought magazines or papers that had stories about Just Cause or the other parahumans in them. He knew he belonged with them, and after a couple of years wandering, he set New York as his destination goal.

One thing he learned in his travels was that for every decent, kind-hearted soul willing to help out a man down on his luck, there were ten more eager to kick him while he was down. More than once, Richard had to run from the law, or from angry friends or family members in pickup trucks and guns, who hated hippies, bikers, and freaks. More than once, he left them bleeding by the roadside.

And then one day in the fall of 1972, everything changed for him.

He was washing dishes in a small town an hour outside of Chicago. A cold rain was battering the glass of the diner, and fallen leaves blew against it like bomb shrapnel. He'd been working there for only a week, sleeping at the town's YMCA and saving up money for a new front wheel. He'd blown a tire and wiped out on the bike. He'd been fortunate enough to land in soft heather and ferns along the roadside, but the sliding bike plowed into a stone and bent the front wheel into a pretzel.

The bikers roared into town, oblivious to the elements, and parked their steeds in a row in front of the diner. The waitresses, cooks, and patrons looked out at them nervously as they swaggered across the sidewalk and pushed open the diner door with a bang.

They weren't Hell's Angels, Richard observed, but that didn't make them less dangerous. By the patches on their sopping jackets, they were a group called the Demon Lords, and their leader was more like Richard than like everyone else in the diner.

The gang leader was huge, near seven feet tall, with muscles that strained to burst through his denim vest and t-shirt. His skin was a burnished bronze color, knobbed with hard bumps that looked like alligator hide. The skin condition continued up his face, where several of the knobs sprouted short ivory horns. A heavy brow ridge hooded his eyes, which burned with sulfurous intent. Thick claws decorated his fingers, and overlong canine teeth poked out of his mouth above and below.

The other seven Demon Lords were normal humans, but they had a sense of casual violence about them that made Richard's hackles rise. They sauntered through the diner like they owned it, leering at women and children, casually picking mouthfuls of food off patrons plates, being generally rude and boisterous.

"You, uh, gentlemen need to leave," said the oldest waitress, who'd spoken up on Richard's behalf when he asked for a job. "I don't care if he's ugly," she'd said, "so long as he can sling a mop and a rag." Her name was Alice, and Richard was pretty sure the diner had been built around her.

"Whatever happened to *the customer's always right?*" sneered the scaly Demon Lord.

Richard set down his sponge and wiped his paws off on his apron.

"What you doin', man?" asked the black guy working the fryer. His name was Jimmy, and he made the best fried chicken Richard had ever tasted.

"I can't just let them push everyone around," growled Richard.

"Man, there's ten of them and one of you. I don't care what kind of teeth and claws you got. They'd skin you alive, kid. Hush up and maybe they'll leave after they get what they want."

"Hey, the lady asked you to leave," said a brusque man in a hat with earflaps and a quilted vest. "Why don't you clear on out? We don't want your kind in here."

"My *kind*? What kind is that?" The Demon Lord's voice grew sly and quiet.

"Scum. Lowlifes." The brusque man clenched his fists.

"Scum. Lowlifes," repeated the Demon Lord. "I had no idea. Boys, did you know that we're scum and lowlifes?" The other bikers snickered. The Demon Lord bowed to the brusque man. "Thank you, kind sir, for your kind words. Nobody has ever complimented us quite like you have."

"I s-said clear on out." The brusque man lost his bravery as he realized he had the full attention of all the Demon Lords.

The leader lashed out his hand quick as a flash and knocked the man's hat off his head. The others laughed as it sailed across the diner toward an Oriental man sitting at the end of the corner, eating a bowl of soup.

Without moving a muscle more than necessary—indeed, without even looking—the man caught the hat before it could upend his soup bowl and set it gently on the counter beside him. Then he sipped another spoonful of soup as if nothing had happened.

The Demon Lord, already bored with the formerly-brusque man, stalked across the diner toward the man and his soup. Richard tore off his apron and threw it aside.

"You gonna die, man," said the fry cook.

"He's an old man. He's not bothering anyone," said Richard. "They can bother me instead." He came out from behind the prep tables and around the corner of the counter.

The Demon Lord paid Richard no mind. He had a new interest in the old man and his soup. "Well," he said, drawing it out. "What do we got here? Some kinda kung fu guy? Kwai Chang Cocksucker?"

The other Demon Lords laughed like it was the best joke any of them had ever heard.

"Hey, ugly, leave him alone," called Richard. "You want to mess with someone, mess with me." His claws were out and he didn't even remember popping them.

The Demon Lord turned to see who was addressing him in such a tone. He caught sight of Richard and looked him up and down. "Ugly? Well if that ain't a case of the pot calling the kettle black, I don't know what is." His ugly face grew hard. "You think you can take the Demon Lord, pussycat?"

The other Demon Lords laughed and made miaowing noises.

"You want to step outside?" asked Richard, eliciting even harder laughter from the bikers. They mocked his words, flinging them back at him like flying daggers.

"You know? I don't. It's raining, and I don't want to mess up my hair." The Demon Lord ran a palm across his bumpy, hairless scalp. "I see it's already too late for yours, though. Pussums got all wet in the rainy-rain."

"Hey Joe," called one of the others. "Maybe it's time to put the cat out for the night."

"Don't bother," said Richard. "I'll leave." The look of condemnation on Alice's face cut Richard to the marrow. He could almost hear her yelling *coward* after him in that same time she used when the line cooks messed up an order.

"And that's that," said the Demon Lord, apparently whose real name was Joe. "Now, where were we? I believe we were about to do some kung fu fighting with Bruce Lee, here."

Richard stepped out into the rain. He hated how the cold water seeped through his mane, matting it down against his thin t-shirt and enhancing the musty smell he never could quite eradicate. He looked back at the Demon Lords in the diner, about to cause even more trouble, then over at their bikes, parked diagonally to the curb in a neat row.

As a fellow rider, it galled him to do so, but Richard reached for the first bike in the line and shoved it as hard as he could. It tipped and fell into its neighbor, dislodging that bike as well and pretty soon, all eight bikes lay on their sides in the gutter amid broken glass and leaking fluids. Richard turned to the diner windows and grinned a mouthful of sharp teeth.

The Demon Lords, predictably, came running out of the diner into the rain, shouting their anger on counterpoint to the growl of thunder. Richard lowered his head and popped his claws. "All right, who's first?"

A biker wielding a switchblade charged at him first. Richard ducked under a clumsy thrust and swept the biker's legs out from beneath him. As he fell, the biker lunged at Richard, catching him with the very tip of the switchblade. Richard's t-shirt split apart and blood welled out from a thin scratch, matting the tawny fur on his abdomen.

He roared like the King of the Jungle. The biker struggled to back away, but Richard grabbed hold of one of the man's flailing feet. He wrenched the biker's ankle, raking his claws through the man's filthy blue jeans, and then swung the man around like an Olympic hammer-thrower to hurl him against several of his companions.

The Demon Lords pulled out their knives and chains and went after Richard. He was outnumbered and outgunned, but so long as he kept the bikers busy outside, they might not hassle anyone else in the diner.

It was what superheroes were supposed to do.

He drove a fist into one biker's face, smashing his nose like a water balloon full of blood. Another biker lunged in with brass knuckles, but Richard turned to catch the blow on the meaty part of his shoulder instead of his jaw. His arm went numb almost instantly and he knew he was in trouble. A bicycle chain wrapped around his legs. His feet slipped on the wet cement and he crashed to the ground. Hard steel-toed boots drove into his sides, his legs, his head. He felt a rib go, and boot sole caught him between the eyes, lighting up his vision like a photographer's flash.

Still, he tried to fight back. Richard took a kick to the jaw in order to hamstring a biker, slicing through his Achilles tendon with his claws. The man went down screaming, which made most of the bikers pull back. The one who didn't had a bike chain, and he swung it down at Richard so hard that it whistled like a train. Richard rolled to one side and then the other to avoid the steel links, but with every motion, the ends of his broken ribs rubbed together and nearly made him faint.

"Stop it! You're killin' him!" screamed one of the waitresses from the diner doorway.

"Shut up, or you're next," yelled a biker.

"Wait," said a voice that hissed like anger in the rain.

Blows stopped hammering down upon Richard. His eyes wouldn't focus, and the world tilted around him, an amusement park ride out of control. Strong, knobby hands lifted him by his mane, adding throbbing agony to the other injury pain flashing through his body. Richard dimly felt his feet dangling as Demon Lord himself held Richard above his head.

"You think you're a tough guy?" asked the man. He punched Richard across the jaw, making him see stars. The biker wasn't just big, he was strong—inhumanly so. "You gonna be a hero?" *Punch.* "Save the day, get the girl?" *Punch.* "Let me tell you something, hero. There ain't no such thing in this world. There's only the strong and the weak." *Punch.* "You weak, man."

Somehow, despite his senses reeling from the repeated blows, Richard found the strength to rake his claws across the Demon Lord's face. The biker screamed and dropped Richard, who collapsed into a bleeding heap upon the cement.

"Call the police!" screamed the waitress. "He's going to kill him."

"She's right," hissed the Demon Lord. Blood ran down his ugly, misshapen face from four deep parallel scratches. One of his eyes was already swelling shut, but that didn't stop him from lunging down to pick up Richard and drive a knee hard into Richard's guts.

The broken rib grated. The pain of it galvanized Richard and he fought back tooth and nail, understanding that he was no longer fighting for the safety of the diner, but for his own life. He roared with all the power of a lion ruling the African veldt, found a reserve of strength, and attacked the Demon Lord.

The ugly biker punched at Richard again, just missing Richard's solar plexus. Richard responded by clamping his teeth down upon the biker's misshapen knuckles. The man howled as bright, hot blood flooded into Richard's mouth. He spat out a chunk of flesh and a lump that could have been a knuckle. "Come on, you ugly bastard," he said through swollen and split lips. "I got plenty more."

The Demon Lord staggered back, clutching his ruined hand against his chest. "You ugly son of a bitch just made the last mistake of your life." He fumbled inside his jacket and withdrew a small pistol.

Richard had never been at the wrong end of a gun before. Every nerve screamed for him to duck, to flee, but he squashed down that cowardice. "You leave this town. You're not welcome here. Leave, or I'll tear out your throat."

The Demon Lord raised his pistol and Richard knew his death was at hand. He didn't close his eyes, didn't back down. He would face his end like a man, not a coward.

A sudden sound of blows striking flesh in the rain made the Demon Lord pause in his execution. An odd look came across his face and a trickle of blood ran from the corner of his mouth to mix with the rain coursing down his skin. He opened his mouth to speak, but seemed to have no air to do so. He collapsed onto the pavement.

The elderly Asian man who'd been eating soup in the diner stood behind the Demon Lord, his fingers pushed together like spear points. He stepped over the Demon Lord, who was either unconscious or dead, and retrieved the biker's pistol.

The other bikers decided discretion was the better part of valor and fled on foot, leaving their bikes where they'd fallen. A siren cried in the distance, perhaps in response to the street fight.

The Asian man tossed the pistol into a storm drain and then looked down at Richard. "You are a brave warrior," he said. "And you are a fool. You have much to learn." He nodded at Richard and turned away.

Richard felt sick to his stomach with the taste of the Demon Lord's blood still fresh in his mouth. One of his eyes was swollen completely shut and his entire face felt like it had gone through a meat grinder. His broken rib burned in his side, and his kidneys throbbed from repeated blows. He couldn't imagine ever hurting worse. He wondered if anyone had called an ambulance for him when they'd called the police. He wondered if any doctor would even treat a freak like him.

A dozen yards away, the Asian man stopped and turned his head slightly back to speak, his voice barely carrying over the hiss of the rain. "Are you coming or not?"

Richard had nowhere to go, no prospects. The Asian man had, for whatever reason, saved his life. Richard didn't know a lot about how the world worked, but he knew enough that if his life was saved, it was no longer his; it belonged to his savior. Whatever the man had in mind for Richard, he would suffer through it, because a debt was a debt to be paid in full.

He struggled through the pain to get back to his feet and limp after the man. "Yes."

狮 和 五 致 死 蛇

ABOUT THE AUTHOR

 Ian Thomas Healy dabbles in many different genres. He's a ten-time participant and winner of National Novel Writing Month and is also the creator of the *Writing Better Action Through Cinematic Techn-iques* workshop, which helps writers to improve their action scenes.

When not writing, which is rare, he enjoys watching hockey, reading comic books (and serious books, too), and living in the great state of Colorado, which he shares with his wife, children, house-pets, and approximately five million other people.

Visit www.ianthealy.com for more information.

狮 和 五 致 死 蛇

ABOUT THE ARTIST

Jeff Hebert is the creator of the HeroMachine online character portrait creator. He lives in Durango, Colorado, where he pursues his lifetime dream of drawing superheroes all day while not wearing pants.